Anchored Hearts

Surrendering Hearts

#1

Julie Arduini

Visit Julie Arduini's Link Tree to learn more about her passion to encourage you to find freedom by surrendering the good, the bad, and---maybe one day---the chocolate.

http://linktr.ee/JulieArduini

ISBN: 978-1-7336876-4-5

Cover created by Surrendered Scribe Media.
Photos courtesy Shutterstock.com, Pixabay.com.
Published by Surrendered Scribe Media, Youngstown, Ohio, 44514

To Mom. I will never forget your loving support. You are missed.

Prologue

March 1997

Julia Turmeric stared at the cordless phone in her hand and expelled a slow whistle. After a decade in the news field there wasn't much that surprised her. Until the call from her childhood best friend, Lisa Bell Hart.

The buzz of the newsroom swarmed around Julia, but her focus remained on the disconnected call and Lisa's announcement. She was, after five years as an infertility patient, pregnant. She was expecting sextuplets, a first in America. A risk so high Lisa's medical team was advocating selective reduction.

A set of finger snaps brought her back to reality. "Jules! What's going on? I've been talking to you about Hussein's latest statement and I didn't even get an eye roll."

She turned her head to her cameraman and held up the phone. Her reply came out as fast as syrup near the bottom of the bottle. "It's my best friend from back home, Lisa Hart."

Walt, her favorite colleague, nodded. "Oh, right. The reporter you worked with at that little station Upstate, right?"

Julia bit her lip as she replaced the phone to the base. "Yeah. She's pregnant." It still feels foreign to say. After all the years Paul and Lisa struggled, this was amazing news. "With sextuplets." This was global news.

Walt coughed. "I remember you saying something about it, that she and the husband had been trying for a while. She okay?"

Julia sighed, still trying to process the news. "I knew when they were doing infertility treatments there was a chance of multiples, but this?" She ran a finger through her long, straight ebony hair. "The doctors asked them to reduce, but she's serious about her faith. Very pro-life."

He picked up a tripod. "She's keeping all of them?"

Julia nodded, still amazed at all Lisa had shared in that call. She tapped the camera. "And Lisa wants us to document their story." Microphones from rival networks begging for information danced through Julia's imagination, pushing aside the statistics she knew about high-risk multiple births.

December 1998

Julia unbuckled the network's car seat belt and stared at the ranch-style home in front of her, a deluge of childhood memories returning. *I can't believe I'm back in the Finger Lakes region.* "How are Lisa and Paul taking care of six babies in this little house?"

Walt took the keys out of the ignition and shrugged. "This is your old Big Flats neighborhood, right? You grew up with brothers and sisters." Walt, always so practical.

She pulled down the visor mirror and applied fresh lipstick. "Not six born at once." She snapped the visor back in place and blotted her mouth with a tissue. "If anyone can do this, it's Lisa. That girl could make the hardest person smile and tell their story to her for the camera. I still don't understand why she didn't keep our pact. In college we said we'd go national together."

"Love changes everything." Walt chuckled. "Ask my ex-wives. They were all in at first." He winked. "Then they got to know me."

Julia rolled her eyes and gestured toward the house with chipped paint and missing chunks of sidewalk leading to the front door. "Can you get some exterior shots? I'm going in."

She closed her eyes for a moment and took a deep breath before ringing the doorbell.

Gail Bell, Lisa's mom, opened the door, cradling a baby. The instant grandmother of six wore a wide smile. "If it isn't little JT from down the street. Come in."

Julia recalled the childhood name for Lisa's mom. "Hi, Mama G. Who do you have here?" Julia glanced at the newborn and then peeked past and observed the upheaval ahead past the kitchen. Car seats. Baby swings. Unopened gifts.

Gail's shaky laugh echoed in the foyer. "If he didn't have a tag, I wouldn't know. This is James Matthew Hart, number four of six."

Six babies. This is so surreal. Julia looked down the hall and saw a swing in motion. "My cameraman will be inside soon. We have a lot to do. Can I see Paul and Lisa?"

Mama G. nodded and strolled down the hall to the living room. The couch and TV were there, but everything else was baby related. More swings. Baby chairs. Cradles.

Julia sucked in a breath as she processed the scene. A man and woman were in front of her on the couch, each holding a baby. On the floor a woman with blonde hair sat near the swings, watching the remaining three fight sleep as they rocked back and forth.

Gail lowered her voice. "Lisa, Paul. Julia's here."

The two rose from the couch and faced Julia. Lisa navigated through the maze of equipment to reach her friend. Her eyes were bright, despite the circles underneath. "Julia! Thank you so much for doing this. It means everything to Paul and me that you're the one covering our journey."

Julia leaned in for a quick hug. Gone was the designer perfume Lisa always wore. Her best friend smelled of spoiled milk. "Are you kidding? Do you know how many stations around the world want to interview the parents of the Hart sextuplets? Not only did you two refuse selective reduction, but had the babies stay the longest in the womb than any other multiples in the country. You are all medical miracles."

Lisa glanced at Paul, who was at her side. "It's all God. He blessed and took care of us."

Paul chuckled. Wisps of light blond hair fell over his eyes. "And we pray He keeps providing. We need all the help we can get."

August 2001

Julia touched the ends of her newly-cut hair, the hairspray hold keeping her trendy bob in place. The New York City humidity seemed extra miserable, but the five-hour trek to Corning didn't seem to provide any relief. *What good is this short hair if sweat still drips from it onto my forehead?*

Walt shook his head as the Hart home came into view. "Look at all the tricycles."

"It's crazy. At least that means the kids are more mobile than the first time we met them." Julia gazed at the colonial home and smiled. "This place is bigger and more beautiful than Lisa said. It's amazing how the community pitched in and had this home built for them."

He nodded and pulled into the long, blacktop driveway. Three of the kids blew bubbles in the yard. "Viewers eat this up. They love this family. Lisa was smart to lock you in as a lifetime interviewer no matter what job you have, or what station."

Julie smiled. Lisa may have left the news business for home life with the kids, but she was savvy. Every year the media sent Paul and Lisa publicity requests to see the kids and interview them. Lisa found a lawyer willing to draft an exclusive agreement that gave Julia the only access to the Hart sextuplets.

"And now that I'm co-anchor of *Rise and Shine*, I think ratings will skyrocket. Moms watch the show, and they adore Lisa." Julia reached for her briefcase and looked out the window. "Speaking of, here she is."

Lisa sauntered over to the news van, her long hair piled on top of her head. "Julia. Walt. It can't be another year already."

The two exited the vehicle and greeted the *Faces and Places* magazine's Mom of the Year with a hug. "What's almost three years old like? Does it get worse than terrible two?" Walt opened the back of the van.

Lisa shook her head; her voice breathy as if she had run from the time she woke until now. Her long hair twisted on top of her head, secured by barrettes. No makeup that Julia could see. "All I can say is if your producer wants a transparent look at life with sextuplets, these kids have plenty of action to show you."

Julia heard a screech, followed by a cry. One of the boys held an empty bubble bottle while one of the girls had wet, soapy hair. Julia tapped her favorite cameraman. "You can start by taping that."

September 2003

Julia tripped over a backpack on her way to the spacious Hart kitchen, the sink full of dirty dishes, the dishwasher humming in the background. Jimmy and Kelly, babies four and five, were eating at the kitchen table, the area full not just with food, but crayons and coloring books. There was a pile of unopened mail. "Hey, guys. Can I ask you a couple questions?"

Jimmy looked to his sister, then to Julia. "Is it for TV?" He reached for a baby carrot.

She nodded.

He narrowed his eyes and took a bite. "Are you gonna ask about school?"

Julia smiled. "Yes, that's what everyone wants to know about."

James reached for a cucumber slice. "I can make it easy. We all hate it."

Julia bit her lip to kill the temptation to laugh.

Kelly nodded. "Hate it."

January 2004

Julia tucked a piece of hair behind her ear as she looked at her notes for her upcoming interview with the latest A-lister actress. The morning show and evening magazine duties gave her a lot of assignments with Hollywood's elite, but few gave Julia joy in prepping for the meeting.

She took a sip of her coffee and heard a knock on the door. Glancing at her office clock, she saw that it was late in the evening for visitors. "Who is it?"

"Julia." His voice cracked. "It's Walt."

Julia stood and jogged to the door. He was always home and with his family once his assignments were done. She opened it, ready to invite him in, when she saw his hands shake and his eyes full of tears. "What's wrong?"

"I told the brass I would be the one to tell you."

Her eyebrows furrowed as she tried to discern what he was saying.

"Julia, there's been a terrible accident back in your hometown."

She felt the pit form and enlarge, as she instantly thought of her parents and siblings. "Dad? Mom?"

Walt shook his head. "Lisa and three of the kids."

Julia felt her knees buckling beneath her. "Tell me they are okay."

She never, in all her years choosing Walt as her cameraman, saw him cry.

"Lisa's gone."

Anchored Hearts Cast of Characters

Jordyn Hart ---Sextuplet #1. Weekend news anchor at WFRN in Elmira, the same station where her mom and her mom's best friend, Julia Turmeric, started.

Ryan Hart ---Sextuplet #2. Jordyn's confidante. After high school he went into the Navy, another choice that separated him from the rest of his siblings.

Evan Hart ---Sextuplet #3. Always thinking of ways to keep "The Hart Sextuplets" in the public eye despite the other siblings resistance.

James Hart ---Sextuplet #4. Very protective of his sister, Kelly. Was in the car accident that killed their mom.

Kelly Hart ---Sextuplet #5. Was born with slight medical issues that meant she needed more care than the other siblings, and was the reason her mom traveled that day. Kelly was in the car.

Paige Hart ---Sextuplet #6. Reserved compared to the others. Was also in the car the day of the accident and suffered an injury she remains self-conscious about.

Paul Hart ---Father of the Hart Sextuplets. Widowed after the accident. Recently married Shelly, a neighbor who helped raise the kids.

Lisa Hart ---Mother of the Hart Sextuplets. Worked as a reporter at WFRN in Elmira until she married and had fertility issues. Famous for believing all six embryos should remain viable. The country grieved when she was killed in a DWI crash. Grew up with Julia, they were best friends.

Julia Turmeric---Grew up in the Elmira area and was Lisa's best friend. Both started careers at WFRN but after Lisa died, Julia focused on work and climbed the TV journalism ladder. She is the morning anchor for the national morning show *Rise and Shine*, and hosts her own magazine show, *Wednesday Nights with Julia*. Earlier in her career Lisa and Paul locked Julia into a contract as sole interviewer for the Hart Sextuplets.

Spencer Collins---Binghamton WFRN reporter and substitute weekend anchor. Very driven to secure a 6pm anchor slot to provide for his brother.

Carson Collins ---High school senior football standout.

Vince Tidwell---WFRN General Manager, based in Elmira.

Joe Munson---WFRN Program Director, based in Elmira.

CHAPTER ONE

Jordyn Hart traced the outline of her wrapped chocolate lying dormant in her pantsuit pocket as soon as the hot studio lights warmed her face. She pursed her lips and resisted the urge to fidget rather than attempt to discover the fate of her sweet treat. With the television camera focused on her and America's news sweetheart, Julia Turmeric, Jordyn swallowed and tilted her head as she offered a smile almost as warm as the lights. Once again, time for the annual live interview with her siblings.

Julia leaned back in her chair and shook her head with a laugh. "I can't believe I'm sitting here with you all for the twenty-fourth time." She lifted her black-rimmed glasses off the bridge of her nose. "I didn't even need these when I first introduced America to you."

Jordyn glanced down the row, each of her siblings in place by birth order. She was the first, but only six minutes separated Jordyn and Paige. Ryan, the second born and Jordyn's rock, sat as straight as if he was still in the military. She was pretty sure even those who trained him in the Navy smiled more than he was for the camera. But he showed up for the interview. That was something.

"Jordyn, let's start with you. You're a young woman nearing the quarter-century mark. What's life like for you?" The interviewer was much more than *Rise and Shine's* anchor with her own Wednesday evening show, *Wednesdays with Julia*. To her, she was their "Aunt" Julia.

"I'm as surprised as you are. Seems like yesterday you interviewed us from the house where we were bouncing on the trampoline and having water gun fights." Jordyn moved a piece of her hair behind her ear. "These days I'm anchoring the noon report here at WFRN, your first station. I love it, and it runs in my blood, as you know."

Julia's face softened. "Folks, as most of you remember, their mom Lisa worked with me at WFRN. Our dream was to move up together and eventually host a national show together. Jordyn's got the chops to take my place, honestly."

Evan turned in his chair. "Unless I go viral and beat Jordy to it."

No one groaned, but once cameras were off, chances were high for payback.

Julia faced the third in line. "Okay, Evan, you've always loved the spotlight in our other interviews. I'll skip Ryan for a moment and chat with you. What does your life look like?"

He cleared his throat and Jordyn shot a glare his way. *Evan better not think this interview is all about him.*

"Well, Julia, I'm at a crossroads, which for my age group I think is common. I'm single, trying to find my place. I work, but it's not a career, it's a job. I really believe this year for me is making things happen before I'm twenty-five."

Ugh. Why do people eat up Evan's empty talk? Jordyn silently prayed the camera wouldn't catch James rolling his eyes.

Julia leaned in.

Please don't lob him a softball question.

"Let's dive deeper by asking again. What does that look like, Evan?"

His movement made a slight sound against the vinyl chair cushion. "I want to work in media, but not the same road you or Jordy are on. I'm not sure what that looks like yet." He winked. "What I do know is I have a vision for what I want our twenty-fifth interview to look like."

Julia's eyes widened, but she otherwise maintained composure. "Well, America, you heard it here first. I guess I'll be hearing from Evan." She pivoted to Ryan. "I know he wishes I'd skip him altogether, but I'd hear it from viewers, especially the ladies, if I didn't ask for your update, Ryan. What's going on now that you're out of the Navy?"

Jordyn tried to gauge his mood but a peripheral view didn't offer any clues, just the way Ryan liked it.

"I can't believe I'm saying this, but I relate in a small way to where Evan's at. I'm trying to find my place in the IT world. I have a job in programming and bought a starter home in Watkins Glen. It's all recent, and I have my work cut out for me." He sighed. "Especially with the house."

Kelly piped up. "That none of us have seen."

Julia tilted her head. "She raises a great point. You're the second of the sextuplets, but have always done your own thing. Watkins Glen is a good forty minutes away. The rest of you are still at home, right?"

Paige nodded and adjusted her glasses. Jordyn wanted to wince, but maintained her on-camera friendly face. *How many times have I begged her to get contacts?*

James looked to Kelly. "We're away during the school year. Finishing up our degrees."

Ryan shrugged. "I guess I've always marched to my own beat."

"Nothing wrong with that. So, James. Refresh our memories. Why are you still in college when Jordy, Evan and Paige already graduated with their Bachelor's?"

James ran a hand through his dark hair. "When Ryan left for the Navy and the rest went to college, Kelly and I didn't feel ready. We took a year or so to work and figure out what we wanted to pursue academically. The state university system was kind enough to let us take advantage of the sextuplet high school graduation gift to attend one of those schools tuition free, so we're at Cortland."

Kelly smiled, most likely pleased with his response so she wouldn't have to speak.

"That leaves you, Paige. What's new since our last interview?"

Paige, on the other side of the line, was too far away for Jordyn to gesture that Paige move the hair out of her face. "I'm like Evan as well. I don't know what my career looks like. I work as a hostess in Corning. Nothing exciting. I guess Jordyn is the only one who knows what she wants in life and is going for it."

Jordyn tried to interpret her sister's comment. If Paige was jealous, it wasn't for Jordyn's lack of reminding all of them life was short, live full. As if Julia read her mind, the topic changed to the one they all dreaded.

"The hardest interview I've ever had was the year you lost your mom. You were six. Fast forward and since last year's update, your father re-married. Kelly, tell us a little about that."

Kelly's eyes widened for a moment. She took a deep breath and offered a flat smile. "Dad is our hero. He never said it, but even with all of us under his feet, he was lonely. Mom was his best friend. Her death robbed all of us, especially him."

Julia slowly nodded her head, as if giving Kelly permission to continue.

"Raising six of us took a lot of helping hands. A group of ladies from church volunteered with everything from changing diapers to laundry. One of them was Shelly Hoffman. After mom was gone, those ladies kept helping. Shelly was an angel. She was our neighbor and gave up her free time to help our family. After high school with the house a little quieter, Shelly and dad had time to talk. Their friendship grew and the rest is history."

Jordyn realized as the monitor flashed a wedding photo, she was grinding her teeth. Hard.

If Julia carried any issues about her best friend's widower re-marrying, she carried on like a professional. "Ryan, what's it like after all these years to see your father married?"

Ryan didn't flinch or hesitate. "Dad's happy. That's all I've wanted for him. The fact that he married someone who helped tie our shoes and put band-aids on our scraped knees through the years is a bonus."

"Jordyn? What's the biggest adjustment? As we look at previous footage, you were always taking care of everyone after your mom passed away."

She tried not to wince at the video showed her putting tuna casserole on the table at age twelve for the world to see. As well as vacuuming at eight. Helping Evan adjust his tux tie for prom. "I guess the biggest change has been Shelly's dog. She's a barky little thing that takes some getting used to."

The siblings chuckled and nodded.

Julia joined them, having been caught in Gigi's chaos during a Christmas break visit. "I'm a cat person myself, so I understand." She faced the camera. "Well, we're going to talk about memories with the Hart Sextuplets after this break. Stay tuned."

Once they heard the all-clear sign, Julia's team refreshed her make-up. Jordyn stood and smoothed out her pantsuit, her hand finding the bump of chocolate. She reached in and grabbed the foiled treat, thankful as melted as it was, the ooze stayed in the wrapping. As she walked to the nearest garbage can, her general manager, Vince Tidwell, waltzed up, his smile wide.

"I love these interviews, Jordyn. Ratings gold for Julia, and the locals stay tuned to WFRN to see their number one Hart ."

Jordyn tossed the candy and brushed her hands together to ward off any chocolate that might have landed. "Thanks, Vince. Is my dad here? I wanted to make sure he took his cholesterol meds."

Vince glanced around. "He was watching from the conference room. Speaking of, before you go out and celebrate tonight, stop in there. The WFRN team is here to cheer you on. Say hello, and then I have a quick announcement. I won't keep you. Promise." He offered a fatherly wink.

Jordyn heard the thirty second call so she nodded and made her way back to the stage. "Sure thing. Any hints?"

His grin increased. "We'll be talking promotion."

♡ ♡ ♡

Spencer Collins reached into the potato chip bowl for a third time as the conference room monitors faded to black, signaling the end of the live interview. The heavy wooden door opened and Vince, the station's GM, blew in like a microburst.

"Amazing show, right? I feel as though when Julia Turmeric graces this building, everything she touches turns to gold." Vince's smile could power all of New York's Southern Tier. "Anyway, thanks everyone for staying late. Jordyn's taking her mic pack off and will be in shortly. I won't keep you long. Help yourself to more snacks. There's plenty left."

Spencer poured an ice water and took a seat across from a couple Elmira-based reporters. He pulled out his phone and checked to make sure he didn't miss any texts from his younger brother, Carson. Seeing none, he reached for a couple chips and tried not to get grease on his suit pants.

When the door opened again, Jordyn Hart pushed through with a friendly grin and a glance round the room. Even though the studio lights weren't around, her hair carried a sheen as she stood near Vince. "Hi, everyone. I hope I didn't keep you all waiting. I wanted to find my dad after the show."

Vince poured her a glass of ice water and handed it to Elmira's only noon anchor. "Nonsense. Now that you're here, let's get down to business." He gestured for her to sit on the other side of the table, while he sat at the head.

Spencer sipped on his drink, stealing a glance at Jordyn. They'd crossed paths a couple times when he gave a live report from Binghamton, but this was their first time in the same room. Something about those big brown eyes and the lingering trail of rose and vanilla created an energy around her. He took a deep breath and intentionally shifted his seat so he'd instead focus on Vince and the big announcement.

The boss cupped his hands together and placed them on the table. "WFRN is the Southern Tier's leader in news. *Rise and Shine* is the most watched morning program in America. We're going to marry the two by creating a local morning show that will usher in Julia's national program." He walked over to the conference room laptop and touched a few buttons. An image appeared on the huge screen in front of them. "I present *Early Rise and Shine*, premiering sweeps week in November."

Spencer stretched his legs under the table as he took in the bright blue, orange, and yellow logo. Impressive. The move made sense. Why though, was he invited to attend?

Vince returned to his seat; his smile as electric as the logo. "The co-hosts will be Jordyn Hart and Spencer Collins."

At the mention of his name, Spencer snapped to a ram-rod posture and found his throat felt as if he'd swallowed sand instead of potato chips. The reporters across the table clapped, but the room seemed to close in. Vince's words sounded muffled as Spencer absorbed the news.

"We start tomorrow at eight. Although I know who I want for producer, there's still a third co-host spot to fill, as well as a meteorologist. If you're interested in hiring the third the co-host slot, e-mail me. Jordyn, I know you have family obligations tonight, but let's have a working lunch tomorrow." Vince shifted to Spencer. "You're going to be working out of Elmira from now on. If you can join us for the lunch, please do. I understand you have loose ends to tie up in Binghamton."

Spencer's tongue felt like the time he got stung by a bee and realized he was allergic. Everything felt swollen and words didn't seem able to come out. He had his dad to consider. Carson, his baby brother. The commute. Packing up his desk.

Jordyn's kind voice rose above Spencer's ailments. "I think this might be the first time I'm at a loss for words. You know how to surprise a girl, Vince. Thank you for thinking of me." She reached for her purse. "Spencer, I look forward to working with you. My family's waiting for me, but we'll talk soon."

Spencer swallowed hard. "Sounds good."

Vince glanced around the table. "Excellent. It's going to be extra busy around here, but I'm so excited for the opportunities *Early Rise and Shine* will give. Thanks, everyone, for staying around. Goodnight."

Jordyn gave a wave and hurried out, the sound of her heels walking at a fast clip after the door closed.

Spencer grabbed his phone and reached in his pocket for his keys. He balanced the two in order to drink the last of his water, and dispose of his plastic cup in the can near the exit. Before he crossed the threshold, he heard Vince call his name.

"Spencer, just a second." Vince gestured for him to return to the room.

"Sir?"

"What do you think? I had trouble reading your face. You must be an excellent card player."

"I don't play." He scratched at the nape of his neck. "I'm stunned. I never thought about a local morning show, let alone me being a part of it. I guess my vision was anchoring the six."

His boss nodded and took a sip of his water. "You've mentioned that, and I'm listening. The timing isn't right, though. This will build your following and give you more experience. Joe Munson and I have been talking and we're excited to see the chemistry between you and Jordyn. She's a dynamo, and your potential is amazing. It's going to be great, Spencer."

Spencer's phone vibrated and he took the opportunity to exit. "I'll do my best. Thank you, Vince. I'll see you in the morning."

Once he was able to find a corner in the hall, he checked his screen and noticed a text from Carson, his only sibling.

Head's up. I just got home and Dad's not here. I think he's at Santino's.

Spencer groaned. The man refused to carry a cell phone, so locating him was never fun. Santino's, the most popular restaurant and bar in Elmira, was usually his dad's destination.

Thanks. I'm still in town. I'll swing by and check it out.

He tried to think of a prayer, even a quick one, to send up as he once again went on a trek to rescue his father who was drowning his grief along with each glass of liquid tranquilizer. Words failed, just as all the prayers Spencer had uttered in the year since the casket lowered his mother into the ground.

CHAPTER TWO

Jordyn heard her name before the Santino's front door closed behind her. She looked to the right and saw Evan standing in the corner, waving. Two wooden tables shoved together to accommodate her siblings and Aunt Julia. Returning the wave, she pasted on a smile and made her way to the empty chair next to Ryan.

As always, Evan wasted no time asking questions. "Is it about our twenty-fifth interview? What's the big announcement?"

Ryan released the first groan.

Jordyn rolled her eyes. "No. Vince has a new morning show starting sweeps week, *Early Rise and Shine.*" She looked to Aunt Julia. "Obviously leading in to your program. I'm one of the co-hosts."

Evan slumped to his seat, unimpressed. Ryan offered a slap on the back. James and Kelly were further down the table and gave a thumb's up. Paige, on the other side, let out a rare squeal.

Julia, directly across, raised her glass of water. "Congratulations. That's a great step on the career ladder."

Jordyn shifted in her chair and reached for a piece of garlic bread. "It's not six-o'clock."

It was Ryan's turn to roll his eyes. "You can't copy every move mom made."

The comment landed square in her gut. He had a way of knowing her better than anyone and calling her on it. She took a bite of the bread and glanced around. "Where's Dad?"

James replied before Evan had the chance. "Shelly remembered Gigi hadn't been let out in a while. They went home. Dad said eat a dozen wings for him."

Another emotional hit. As long as she could remember, Santino's was part of their interview experience. Spill their heart out on national television. Go to celebrate. Eat wings. "Ugh, that dog." She was about to vent further when she heard the sound of glass crashing at the bar. An older man trying to leave his stool had a bunch of napkins in hand.

"Jordy, I ordered mild wings for you. I can't stay long. It's not fun driving those country roads after midnight. If it isn't a deer or fog, there's often a drunk wobbling home." Ryan chuckled as the man tried to clean his mess as the wait staff swarmed around him. "Like that guy."

"Thanks, Ry. I have an early meeting as well. I'm pretty beat. Do those interviews drain anyone else?"

Paige looked to the floor. "Only when we see a video of Mom."

Julia bit at her lip. "Never gets easier. You all handled it like champs. Head's up, though. Once you get through the publicity for turning twenty-five, not long after that will be the anniversary of the accident." She cleared her throat. "It's my job to tell the entire story."

Ryan's eyes narrowed and he tossed a chicken bone on his plate with a clang. "You're going to interview Mom's killer."

Julia leaned in. "She's the driver of the car that caused the accident."

Jordyn shrugged. "Sounds like the woman's a killer to me."

Julia sighed. "It's not happening right away. I'm giving you time to prepare. This isn't easy on me either." She glanced at her phone and grimaced. "My boss arranged a private flight for me so I can get back to the city and host tomorrow. I have to go."

The atmosphere felt like a kid popped a balloon. Kelly was the first to break the tension. "Thanks for having our backs, Aunt Julia. The interview was good. They always are."

The rest of the siblings nodded. No denying that.

Julia stood and placed her purse strap on her shoulder. "I love you goofballs. Tell your dad I said bye. Remember the network has the tab for tonight." She waved and maneuvered past the tables until her tall figure disappeared.

Ryan stifled a yawn. "Man, knowing the network pays makes me want to order more."

A waitress with braids arrived with a cake. "Julia Turmeric ordered this for you all. Happy Birthday." She placed the sheet cake on an adjoining table and a guy with a stack of plates, napkins, and forks followed, setting them next to the dessert. "By the way, I love your interviews. I've followed your lives since I was a kid. I always wanted to be part of a big family." With that, she giggled and left with her colleague.

Evan offered a fist pump. "Yes! Ry, you have to stay. This cake looks amazing."

Ryan scowled, although he did crane his neck to peek at the buttercream overload. "Only Jordy can call me that. I really have to go. I'm sure you can handle my piece."

Evan shrugged and walked over to the dessert table, slicing up pieces. "Your loss."

Jordyn's wings arrived and she really wanted to skip them, scarf down the cake, and head home. "At least stick around until I'm done. We never see you anymore."

James nodded. "True story."

Kelly's face appeared as she leaned past James. "It's as if you try to stay away."

Ryan cracked his knuckles and put his arms around Jordyn and Evan's chairs. "Alright. You're all like squawking chickens. You could visit me and help work on the house you know."

There was a smattering of snickers as Evan delivered plates with generous slices of chocolate cake and white frosting with ribbon curl edging. "Serve us this cake and we could build you a deck in an hour. This is going to be a sugar rush."

This time Ryan allowed a hint of a smile. "When the house is finished, it will be worth the work. It's kind of my life. I don't mean to avoid you."

Paige pushed her black frames up her nose. "I miss hanging out like this."

"Maybe we can start a Sunday dinner or something." Kelly's soft voice broke through the white noise around them.

Jordyn longed for such a scene, but it would look far different from her dreams. "It would mean listening to Dad and Shelly chastise us for not going to church."

No one replied. Instead, forks scraped against cake plates. Jordyn picked up her third wing and bit in. She wasn't ready for that lecture. After all, they were only following Dad's lead after many years of refusing to set foot in God's house. When she finished the last wing, she pushed the plate of bones aside and stood. "I have to get home. I'm glad we were able to get together, all of us. Love you."

A chorus of "love you" echoed around the table as she pushed her chair in and looked up to Ryan. With his tall frame, broad shoulders and military haircut, it was easy for him to lead her through the restaurant to the front doors.

As he held it open for her to walk past, Jordyn nearly ran into a man Ryan's height coming in. She regained her balance as she recognized his face. "Spencer Collins?"

♡ ♡ ♡

Spencer ran a shaky hand through his hair as he stopped. Jordyn stared, her mouth agape. Of all the people to run into.

"Hey, hi! I've barely run into you my three years at WFRN, and now, twice tonight."

Jordyn cocked her head as if she were taking mental notes. "Small world, right? This is where we always go after the annual interview."

Spencer looked out of the corner of his eyes and could see the bar. He had to get over there. "People do travel from all over for the wings."

This banter was worse than a chat during a middle school slow dance.

She glanced at the man holding the door, who gestured to follow him.

Spencer thought he looked like Ryan, her next oldest sibling.

"Good seeing you. Excited for our meeting tomorrow." Jordyn turned and walked past her brother.

Spencer offered a limp wave and beelined for the bar area. He spotted his dad at the end, teetering on the edge of a stool. Saturated napkins lined the counter in front of him, and he pointed a finger towards the bartender.

"Dad, what's going on?"

The thirty-something with a Santino's apron leaned forward. "He dropped his glass and it shattered on the floor and counter area. We cleaned it up, but he wanted to help."

"My hand slipped." His dad's tone was sad, like a child caught with his hand in the oatmeal-raisin cookie jar.

"He's upset because we wouldn't let him touch the glass. He's all paid up, but he's cut off. Enough alcohol for tonight."

Spencer nodded, feeling as tired as the bartender looked. "I appreciate it."

The man grunted and moved to the other side of the counter to take an order. Spencer sighed and stood beside his dad. The once gallant and strapping firefighter was a mere shell due to his grief.

"Time to go home. Let's head to my truck, okay?"

He waved Spencer off. "I have mine in the lot."

"You aren't driving anywhere. Carson and I will get it tomorrow. C'mon." Spencer reached for his dad's upper arm and helped him off the stool. Once they started walking, he secured his arm around his dad's waist.

"I don't deserve you boys." His voice wobbled and the sadness bounced off the restaurant walls.

Spencer ignored the chatter and tried to pick up speed so they could get to his truck. The sooner they could escape the gawking restaurant crowd, the better.

"Your mom would be so mad to see me like this." His dad stumbled at the exit, but regained balance. "I never drank before— you know."

Spencer winced at the mention of his mom's death. His stomach felt like concrete as he tightened his grip. "Dad, just walk. We can talk later."

There was a pause, and his dad turned to face Spencer. "You're mad."

"No, I'm not." Spencer fought to contain his frustration "We need to get home. It's late."

That satisfied him, and their awkward stroll continued. His trusty Ford was parked on the street, only a few cars away.

"I'm sorry, Spence. I don't want you late for work."

"It's okay. I don't go in until the morning."

His dad nodded, and they continued a few more feet in silence. When they reached the vehicle, Spencer fumbled to reach the keys in his pocket without losing his hold on his father. Keys in hand, he hit unlock on the fob.

"It smells funny in here."

"I'm sure it's my cologne. It's fine, let's go." Spencer released his grip and opened the passenger door.

His father shuffled toward the seat. "I could use a boost, son." The word boost ushered a chuckle.

Spencer sighed and obliged. Once he straightened, he noticed a car with squeaky brakes pull out of the lot. The noise was enough for his dad to turn his head toward the approaching vehicle and mutter about how loud that car was.

"I know, Dad. Let's get your seat belt on." Spencer kept one eye on the car as he heard the belt click into place. The car didn't accelerate, but loomed closer, enough for Spencer to see the driver.

Jordyn. As she applied the brakes for the red light, she turned and locked eyes with Spencer as his dad lifted his hands and drew his son into a drunken hug. When Spencer pried himself away, the light was green, and his colleague was gone.

CHAPTER THREE

Jordyn threw the cotton sheets to her feet at the first sound of her alarm. At six-thirty, birds were chirping and sunlight filled her room. She didn't feel the same enthusiasm as the cardinals and chickadees, but there was one thing to be thankful for as she headed to the shower. It wasn't November when *Early Rise and Shine* would demand her wake-up would be at three.

By the time she reached the kitchen, Paige was pouring milk into a bowl. Jordyn scooted past with a terse "Good Morning" and beelined for the coffeemaker. Once she got that started, she reached for the wheat bread and placed two slices in the toaster.

Paige took a seat at the kitchen island. "Long day ahead?"

Jordyn pushed the toaster button down and faced her youngest sister. "I start with the first meeting for *Early Rise and Shine.* I have a feeling that will take a while. You?"

She shrugged and put a spoonful of something sugary in her mouth. Once she swallowed, she replied. "I want to get a good workout in at the gym before work. I work noon to close, so it's busy. Should be good tips with the Rotary Club having their dinner tonight."

Jordyn nodded, remembering Paige's stories about working at the local hotel chain restaurant where the civic clubs meet. Members tended to arrive early and enjoy appetizers or a drink. More often than not, more than one drink. The thought gave her a flashback to the night before at Santino's. The dazed look on Spencer's face when she drove by. What was he doing? Who was he with? How drunk was the person?

"Jordy? Hello?" Paige's hand waved to grab her attention.

She checked on the toast and returned her focus to her sister. "Sorry. What did you say?"

"Shelly put up a white board to keep track of everyone, so she knows who will be home each night for dinner. She asked that you write your plans out." Paige pointed to the wall above the mini desk where they kept mail and office supplies.

Of course she did. Jordyn rolled her eyes and looked at the board. "We're twenty-four. If we aren't home, I think we'll figure dinner out."

"Well, we still live at home, so don't think you're too sophisticated for the board." Paige chuckled. "Oh, and she made a holder for all our keys. Labeled and everything."

Paige's tone gave off the impression she liked all of Shelly's handiwork.

The toast popped up and Jordyn reached for it, then pulled back when it burned her finger. "She's a regular Martha Stewart."

"You're cranky. You need to drink that coffee."

Jordyn ignored the commentary and visited the white board. She reached for a purple dry erase marker and scratched WFRN. After replacing the marker cap, she finished preparing her coffee and grabbed the toast. "Have a good day." Jordyn placed a piece of the dry bread in her mouth to avoid further chat. With coffee and toast in hand, she found her purse, car keys, and headed off to the driveway.

Her compact car received a lot of jokes over the years, but it was her pride and joy that got her where she needed to go. Sure, she needed to take it in for a brake job and oil change, but for a free car courtesy of the manufacturer as a high school graduation gift for each sextuplet, how could she complain? The trusty vehicle took the windy, steep driveway like a champ.

Driving past the orange and maroon mums Shelly had planted, Jordyn lamented the many changes since they moved to the East Corning home as kids. Another free gesture from the community, the home sparkled on moving day. The four-bedroom, three-bathroom Colonial had been built from scratch, filled with new appliances. Almost twenty years later, and the siding could use fresh paint. The swing set and treehouse hadn't been used in years, both donated from a local construction firm. The neglected and faded surroundings felt foreign. The only improvement to the landscape was the flowers. The most significant change—Shelly. With that realization, Jordyn found a country radio station to drown out her frustrations.

Twenty minutes later, Jordyn scanned her WFRN badge and entered the back entrance. Her best friend and producer, Natalie Greenway, met Jordyn before she could reach her cubicle.

Nat smiled and handed her an iced mocha. "Great interview last night. Figured you could use extra caffeine."

Jordyn took a sip and placed her purse under her desk. "You're the best. Did you hear the news?"

"About *Early Rise and Shine*? Yes, I was supposed to be there but no one was able to sit with my grandma, so I stayed with her." Natalie put her hands on her hip. "In fact, Joe tapped me to produce. I'm headed to the same meeting you are."

The news was as comforting as the amazing cold drink. Jordyn reached for her friend's arm. "I haven't had a lot of time to process the job change, but you being involved? Love it."

The two made their way to the conference room a few minutes before eight. Once they entered, Jordyn scanned the room for Spencer. Something about seeing him in that truck near Santino's unnerved her, even though she couldn't complete the story based on a quick glance.

Vince strolled in wearing a crisp gray pinstripe suit. For an Upstate New York station director, he dressed as if he was one of the Manhattan executives Aunt Julia had to answer to for the network. As polished as Vince was in the outfit and his salt and pepper slicked-back hair, he was a fair boss with good ideas.

I hope Early Rise and Shine is one of them.

News director Joe Munson crossed the threshold next, with Spencer behind him. Jordyn felt her stomach fill with butterflies at the sight of the six-foot reporter. She couldn't place one specific trait about him that made him stand out, but something about Spencer created a rapport with WFRN viewers and caused her to hope he took the empty seat next to her. The butterflies went into hyperdrive when Spencer pulled out the chair to her left, and he whispered hello in a husky voice.

I'm going to need more iced coffee.

Vince started the meeting with a stroll to the front of the room. Always the showman, he pressed the wall button that brought down the screen. "Ladies and gentlemen, you're my *Early Rise and Shine* team. Starting in November, Jordyn and Spencer will be the faces of this new enterprise, but all of you, and more people to come, will be just as important to the show." He turned toward the news director. "Joe? Can you bring up the presentation?"

Jordyn focused on the image ahead of her. A sleek new stage with LED TV's behind the long desk. Colorful, updated logo with WFRN *Early Rise and Shine.* Below that bold, fancy text was *with Jordyn Hart and Spencer Collins.* Impressive.

"Construction on the new stage starts Monday. We're knocking out a wall in the break area and changing that up a bit. There shouldn't be any disruption in your work. We'll use the same kitchen set that noon does, and the next slide shows the interview and weather stage."

This time Jordyn glanced over to Spencer to see if she could read his expression. His eyebrows arched as he sat back in the swivel chair and stared forward.

Vince cleared his throat. "Jordyn and Spencer, I went with name recognition for the names. Nothing personal, Spencer."

Spencer nodded. "No problem, sir."

Joe's baritone voice entered the mix. "An immediate change is with Spencer. We'll keep you as reporter, but based here in Elmira. You'll also prepare for the show. Get to know Jordyn."

A great idea. I can enjoy his woodsy scent and find out more about his trip to Santino's.

Spencer flashed a smile in her direction. "Sounds like fun. I need to figure out some logistics. I watch out for my kid brother, and he goes to school in Vestal. That's a forty-minute commute. Not something I'm up for so early, and in the winter."

Joe tapped his pencil a few times on the table. "We'll help you through the transition."

Jordyn raised her hand. "I'll work with you on it."

I'm sure my grin is as lopsided and goofy as a kid on Christmas morning. "I appreciate it."

With that behind them, Vince continued. "This week Joe and I are interviewing meteorologists. We're also adding a roving reporter of sorts to the team. That person will visit a business or event each day and report live. I'd like to hire from within, if possible. Jordyn, Spencer, we want you to be a part of those decisions. You should receive the interview schedule by day's end."

Wow. The leadership really put time into this.

Natalie nudged Jordyn's elbow. When she looked, her friend offered an excited thumb's up. The show had all the makings of a ratings hit, something to make viewers get up earlier to watch. Jordyn offered a subtle nod before returning her attention to their bosses.

"Now the fun part. We'd like ideas for programming. There are segments we'd like to see weekly. Natalie, Joe, and I discussed it a little, but let's chat."

Jordyn couldn't resist another peek. Spencer had a compact notebook open with his head down, scribbling. What was he writing? Ideas? A grocery list?

Another nudge. "What do you have, Jordyn?" Natalie took a sip of her drink.

A daily morning show from five to seven. She tried to think of conversations with Aunt Julia over the years. "How about a call-in with a doctor? We could field calls on the flu season, allergies, heart disease prevention. There's so much we could talk about."

Natalie opened her phone screen and started typing. "I love it. Each week could offer a different topic."

"And doctor." Spencer added.

Joe swiveled a quarter of a turn. "Spencer? What ideas do you have?"

"My mom loved Valentine's week on the talk shows. The weddings where the viewers would choose the dresses and tuxes? She went crazy for that stuff. Jordyn? Is that something that you think viewers would tune in for?"

Jordyn swallowed and tried to find her voice after picturing them working on a wedding together. "Absolutely, I do."

♡ ♡ ♡

Spencer shaded in the last triangle in the sun he doodled in the upper corner of his notebook. Ninety minutes and the meeting showed no signs of ending. Although his legs felt stiff and his backside numb, Jordyn was as animated as when the meeting began. Her brown eyes widened with every new suggestion and her hands gestured with increasing speed as she joined the conversation. Then again, she had an iced coffee she kept sipping.

"How about this one? Each week the team shares their favorite life hack, an event, a feel-good story." Jordyn tucked a sleek piece of black hair behind her ear.

Joe's response was as dry as sand. "Worked for Oprah. As long as we aren't giving away cars."

Spencer chuckled and looked over at his gorgeous colleague. "I'm not very creative. I'll need help." He admitted.

Jordyn's long eyelashes moved almost at the speed of her talk. How much caffeine did she drink? "I bet you have a lot of favorite things. For instance, Santino's." She dropped the restaurant suggestion like a bomb.

Spencer's chest tightened. Was she pouncing on his scene with his father? "You're right, Jordyn. If this moves forward, I'm sure I'll come up with a highlight each week." *Please let my expression be emotionless. And that she'll drop the Santino's angle.*

Before Jordyn could investigate further, Natalie faced her. "You need to be prepared that WFRN will be live at the fair all week."

As soon as the word "fair" came out of Natalie's mouth, Jordyn's expression darkened. A flicker in her eye, fast as it was, appeared to be a flash of fear more than iced coffee moving through her. "No. You know what a fiasco I am around animals."

Joe suddenly lit up. "It's going to be great. We have a lot of 4-H viewers. They need to see the station personalities with the fair animals."

"Especially you, Miss Hart Sextuplets." Natalie clicked her tongue.

Jordyn groaned and took a last gulp out of her drink. "You know I hate when you call me that." She faced Spencer, who completed his sun drawing and caught her gaze. "Tell me you're great with animals."

"You're not?" He arched his eyebrows. "You already handle dogs and cats on the noon report, right?"

Joe snickered. "Apparently you haven't seen those segments. You'd think we'd handed her a tiger instead of a kitten."

"You guys are terrible. I didn't have pets growing up beyond some fish. Then Shelly moves in with that yappy mutt. There haven't been a lot of positive experiences."

Spencer detected a catch in her voice. This was a real fear for her. All those years watching those interviews, seeing her onscreen as the subject of news and then the reporter, she came off as nearly perfect. The fair was the longest running one in the Finger Lakes region. Yeah, he'd wrangle a goat for her.

Vince looked at his phone screen and closed the laptop. "Great meeting. I have another to run to, but we've made great progress. Joe and Natalie will continue to meet and sort these ideas out. When they have a better idea of what programming will look like, they'll bring the rest of you back in." He turned his attention to the anchors. "Spencer and Jordyn, I'll see you at the interviews." He left before anyone could respond.

Everyone else stood and Jordyn disposed of her empty cup in the receptacle near the conference room door.

Spencer gathered his things and caught up with her. "Hey, when can we meet to go over my move and get to know each other better?"

Jordyn smiled and tapped a few times on her phone. "The sooner the better. You don't want to be driving back and forth."

He pictured Carson and his dad. There was no way he could leave them alone. "How's today look?"

She scrolled through a couple of screens and opened her mouth to speak, but Natalie popped next to Jordyn and tapped her on the shoulder.

"Um, Jordyn? Didn't you add it to your calendar?"

Jordyn turned, head tilted. "Add what?"

Natalie rolled her eyes. "Your lunch with Kent Misny."

Spencer ran through his mental Rolodex. The name was familiar. "Who?"

"You've probably seen him on the noon. Financial advisor. And Jordyn's boyfriend."

CHAPTER FOUR

Jordyn poked at her limp tossed salad and tried to pay attention to her company. Kent Misny was an informative guest on the noon report for the viewers in need of financial advice. But for titillating conversation over lunch? She really wanted to call Nat and scold her for declaring to Spencer this guy was Jordyn's boyfriend.

Kent wiped his mouth with his napkin and returned it to his lap. "Everything okay? You haven't eaten much."

She slid the fork around until it rested on the plate. "The salad doesn't taste great. It's almost like it sat out all morning. Besides, I have a lot on my mind. I probably should head back to the station."

He looked at his watch, one that seemed to tell time, give messages, and share the weather forecast. "You still have thirty minutes. Thinking about the financial segment? Those calls were good ones."

Jordyn fought the urge to roll her eyes. The entire noon report was a distraction. She wanted to start working on *Early Rise and Shine*. And find out about Spencer and what she saw outside of Santino's. Finally, set him straight about her and Kent. Because as far as Jordyn was concerned, the two were not boyfriend and girlfriend.

"Actually, the new show. I'm not sure how much longer Joe will have me anchor noon. Same for Natalie producing. Once I know who our replacements are, I'll let you know so you can meet with them and discuss continuing your feature with them."

Kent paused, his fork mid-air. There was a slight twitch in his right eye. "Wait. I might not be on air anymore? We won't be working together?"

Only if my prayers are answered. "I don't know. Everything is new."

He reached across the table and held her wrist, an awkward gesture that didn't feel romantic at all. Did he mean to clasp her hand? "You'll go to bat for me, right? We have a thirteen percent increase in new clients. The partners believe our relationship with WFRN is part of the success." Kent never shied away from bringing numbers into his chat.

Jordyn shook her hand free, pushed her plate away and reached for her purse. "You and your firm are well-acquainted with Vince and Joe. You could talk to them."

He smoothed out his maroon tie. "I might work at Baker, Misny, and Wheeler Financial, but I'm no Hart Sextuplets, darling of the media."

She felt a stab to the gut. That was not who she was. Not to people who mattered. "I need to get back to work. Take care." Jordyn rose and started for the register.

Kent stretched out to touch her once again, but she dodged his stiff attempt. "Jordyn, wait. Are you mad? Let me pay." He stood, but Jordyn shook her head.

"I'll take care of my check, thanks. Talk soon." With enough distance between them, she waved and bee-lined for the checkout. Why had she agreed to lunch anyway? Right. Because it had become tradition after his weekly feature. His boring, self-centered, lackluster appearance that was as dull as her salad.

Jordyn used the five-minute trek back to the station to shake off her time with Kent. Did she only appeal to people because she was part of a large family? Because her parents chose not to dispose of any of them when they learned about the six? She scuffed her heel on the sidewalk. *Would I be less offended if he noted my journalistic skills?*

She was still processing it when she returned to the news area and discovered Spencer already had a desk. Right next to hers. He was typing away on his laptop when she dropped her purse in her drawer, reached for a piece of chocolate, and closed the drawer hard enough to get his attention.

Spencer looked up and offered that adorable uneven grin.

Success. "Hey. You're getting settled in."

He looked around at his desk with no pictures or personal effects. "A place to sit, basically. How was—lunch?"

Jordyn noted his pause. "Nothing special." *Catch my bored tone, Collins.*

He typed a few clicks and stopped, locking eyes with hers. "The food or the company?"

She felt the salad seasoning course through her veins as she stumbled to find her focus. "Both." Before Spencer could return to typing, she rushed her words. "Natalie was teasing me about Kent. We are not dating." Jordyn swallowed hard and opened her laptop, but couldn't resist stealing a peek.

Spencer nodded, the top of his brown hair in need of a trim moved with the shake of his head. "Good to know." He froze and then looked to his monitor. "I mean, good to know about the food. I'll make sure not to go there."

Jordyn stifled a giggle and booted up her computer. *Nice save, Spencer.* "Are you available now to talk about the show and how to make your commute easier?"

He pushed his chair back and rose. "Let's do this. Conference room?"

"Sounds good." She reached into her drawer for one more piece of candy before grabbing her phone and running to catch up with her new co-host.

Within seconds she was matching his stride as they entered the meeting area together. Jordyn took a seat first, her back to the door. The chair next to her wheeled closer and suddenly the cushion expelled air as Spencer settled in, and his woodsy scent trailed behind.

"So. In twenty-four hours you transitioned from satellite reporter in Binghamton to co-anchor in Elmira. How do you feel?" Jordyn popped the sugary treat in her mouth.

He sighed. "Kind of a whirlwind. I wanted a promotion but figured maybe I'd anchor weekends. That would have made commuting easier because I would have been in Vestal during the week."

His breath, as crisp as a winter's morning, stirred Jordyn's senses. *He's sitting so close. And smells fresh. It's like a visit to the Adirondack Mountains.* Jordyn cleared her throat in an attempt to re-gain focus. "You said you have a brother?"

Small flecks of gold brightened against his royal blue eyes. "Carson. He's a senior in high school. Good football player, actually. I don't want him to transfer if I can help it."

Carson Collins. She'd heard the name when she subbed for the weekend anchor and listened to Cal Grimes cover sports. "How about your parents? Doesn't he live with them?"

Spencer looked to the ground and shook his head. "My mom passed away a couple years ago. Dad isn't able to look out for Carson right now. I've been his caregiver lately."

The memory of Spencer at Santino's came to mind. As did driving past him and an older man. Was that his dad? "I'm so sorry. I can see your dilemma." Jordyn opened her mouth to probe further, but closed it.

He shifted in the chair and glanced her way. "Do you think there's an apartment I can find halfway between Elmira and Vestal? Carson has his license so I think he can drive dad's truck to school and back. Then I can leave before dawn and know he's okay."

Jordyn unlocked her phone and scrolled through her contact list. "Let me look at something here." She found the address and nodded. "Found it. I have a thought. I'd have to call Aunt Julia, but I'm almost certain she'll agree to my idea. Hold on."

Spencer looked like he swallowed a hot pepper. "Are you talking about Julia Turmeric? As in national news anchor Julia? Where are you going with this, Hart?"

She waved him off in a friendly dismissal. "She's our rock. Aunt Julia's kept in touch and provided for all of us through the years, especially after our mother was killed."

"My mom loved her. She said Julia was the last true journalist out there. I guess in a way that's why I went into journalism. News was a big part of our evenings."

Jordyn started typing a text, but paused when she heard Spencer talk about his childhood. Precious memories she wished she'd had more of with her mom. Her throat suddenly dry, she looked over to Spencer and caught his gaze. "Julia has a home in the area for weekends and vacations, but she's too busy to use it most of the time. My brothers take turns caring for the property, otherwise it's empty."

Spencer tilted his head. "Sounds nice. I'm not sure I understand."

"I think you and Carson can live there."

. ♡ ♡ ♡

Spencer watched as Jordyn waited for her godmother and mentor to return her text. The girl exuded confidence and yet humility as she casually reached out to one of America's most influential voices. He almost pinched himself to prove the last twenty-four hours were real.

A notification beeped and Jordyn picked up her phone, and then smiled. "I knew it would be fine. She told me to call Ryan and set up a tour for you and your brother. The house is outside of East Waverly."

Spencer knew the location from reporting. Outside East Waverly meant deep in the hills. Midway between Vestal and Elmira. Private. He knew a retired NBA coach kept a home that way that the man used during deer hunting season. "Wow. That's a nice area."

She flashed a small smile. "It's no Manhattan. For Julia, it's a quiet respite. It's sad she can't visit more often."

Carson's gonna flip.

"When's a good time for the tour?"

Jordyn kept typing, paused, and another ding sounded. "Ryan said he's free tonight. Are you?"

Spencer opened the calendar on his phone. "Carson's out of practice at six. Would seven be too late?"

Her ebony-colored hair moved slightly as she shook her head. "Perfect."

Although the two continued show related chat through the afternoon back at their desks, Spencer kept his eye on the wall clock. He couldn't wait to go home, grab a shower and a bite to eat, and tell Carson they were going to tour Julia Turmeric's country home. And possibly live there.

Once the time displayed four, Spencer packed up his laptop and phone, pushing his chair in. *Stay casual. Don't let Jordyn see you're in a hurry to get ready.* "Catch you later."

Jordyn looked up from her monitor. "Right. Looking forward to it."

He headed to the employee exit and turned to wave, but she'd already returned to her work. For a few moments he paused to watch her lean close to the screen, hair behind her ears, fully focused on whatever was on her laptop. Could have been edits for a story, or even reading an email. Whatever Jordyn was doing, Spencer enjoyed a last glance before exiting.

An hour later, Spencer left the steamy bathroom wearing his maroon robe. He slowed as he entered the living room on the way to the bedroom. His father sat rod-straight on the worn plaid couch, staring ahead at the television. Spencer tilted his head for a better view to the end table. No beer cans. *Thank God.* "Dad, Carson and I aren't going to be home tonight. Should I make you grilled cheese?"

An arthritic, curled hand waved him off. "No, thanks. I'll make something. Will I see one of your reports tonight?"

Spencer's chest felt lighter as he noted the sober response. "I didn't have the chance to tell you. WFRN is starting a morning show in November. I'm the co-anchor, so they pulled me from Binghamton reporting."

His dad turned, a healthy pink hue dotted his cheeks. "That's a big deal."

"With Jordyn Hart ."

"Really?" Now his father was invested, completely turned toward Spencer. "She's the one with the brothers and sisters that anchors the noon report?"

Spencer nodded, recalling how adorable she looked when he left work. "That's her. I have to get going, but there are a lot of changes happening because of the new show. I won't be around as much."

Or at all if I take Carson and move away.

57

"No problem, son. Your mom would be calling everyone in her walking group about this. You're doing great work." The compliment hit Spencer square in the heart like a sledgehammer as he trudged to get ready for a meeting he conveniently neglected to share.

When Carson arrived home with football gear covered in dirt and perspiration, he beelined for the kitchen. "Who wants to make me some scrambled eggs while I shower?"

Spencer pointed to the athletic equipment and gestured its destination, nowhere near the kitchen. "Take the shower. We have an appointment. I'll get you drive-thru."

Carson raised his eyebrows but didn't ask any questions. He took care of the gear and moved toward the bathroom. "What do I wear?"

"Church clothes." Spencer looked around as soon as the words spilled out.

Their dad's head jerked away from the television screen; his face now pale. Lines of grief creased his forehead.

Carson stopped so fast his tennis shoes squeaked against the wooden floor. "We don't go to church—"

"Anymore." Their father's tone spoke volumes against his brief answer. God was not a part of the Collins family. Not anymore.

Spencer sighed and pinched the bridge of his nose. "Wear something presentable. No shorts. No t-shirts. No holes in anything." All the air seemed to leave their shared space as he felt more parent than sibling.

"Will do." Carson pushed open the bathroom door as he offered a mock salute.

Thankfully a double hamburger and fries solved his kid brother's frustration because Carson wolfed down the food as Spencer drove west toward East Waverly. With each mile the younger Hart grew more engaged with their evening adventure.

"We're seriously going to Julia Turmeric's house. For a tour. To see if we'd like to live there. Dude, you're blowing my mind." Carson placed his hands above both ears and opened his palms, using mind blown sound effects to enhance his point.

Spencer offered a grin. "Feeling the same, bro."

As the miles progressed, he turned off the highway and navigated rural roads that led uphill with more trees than homes. After five miles through twists and sharp turns, the GPS announced the destination was on the left.

"I see a driveway with miniature lampposts on both sides." Carson craned his neck. "Wait, those lights line the entire drive."

Spencer took in a slow breath. Was he nervous about seeing a celebrity home or meeting Jordyn? "No wonder we never heard about Julia having a home around here. It's hidden."

The two remained silent as they followed the blacktop driveway for a quarter of a mile. The lampposts lead them to a log cabin A frame with attached garage and a separate barn.

"Can I snap this?"

Spencer turned off the ignition. "Social media?"

Carson nodded.

"Absolutely not. Our goal is to avoid upsetting America's favorite anchor." And Jordyn. And Dad.

"No one's going to believe me. But I won't take pictures."

"Good. Let's see if Jordyn's here." Spencer opened up the door and noted a truck parked off to the side of the barn. Probably Ryan's.

As if on cue, the man that held the door open at Santino's emerged from the barn and marched toward them. His hair was closely cut, almost military style. Although he wore jeans and a crisp turquoise shirt, Spencer observed caked dirt on the guy's boots.

He decided to make the first move by stepping forward with his hand extended. "Ryan Hart? I'm Spencer Collins. This is my brother, Carson."

Ryan's grip was strong, and Spencer felt calluses. "You were at Santino's."

"Yes. I thought that was you. I admit I have trouble keeping the Hart brothers straight."

Spencer heard tires on the blacktop, but Ryan kept his attention on them. "All you need to know is I'm the oldest brother, and the smartest." His tanned face was emotionless for a long pause. Just when Spencer was certain his knees would buckle from intimidation, Ryan broke into a grin. "I'm just kidding. James is pretty smart. Seriously, though? I'm the strongest."

Jordyn's small SUV came into view and she waved and pulled in behind Spencer's truck. He gestured for Carson to give her space as she joined their little circle. Her ponytail swung as she jogged over and gave Ryan a hug.

Once she broke the embrace, she stepped back and greeted the Collins brothers with her megawatt smile. "Thanks for coming out. I think you're going to love it here."

Spencer breathed in her honeysuckle scent. What was it about this family that made his knees wobble? "The driveway's impressive, so I'm excited to see the rest." He faced Carson. "Jordyn, this is my brother, Carson. Carson, Jordyn Hart ."

"I'm a huge fan, Miss Hart." His brown waves bobbed as he offered his hand and shook hers.

"That's so kind. Thank you." She winked and nudged Spencer's arm. "Did you put him up to this?"

Spencer raised his hands in surrender. "Definitely not. Ready to dazzle us with your presentation skills?"

The circle broke up as Ryan took the lead by heading to the garage door. "Let's go. I have a forty-five-minute drive ahead of me."

The garage had a stone and epoxy floor that Spencer figured they could eat on. The white walls were pristine with a few tools hung. "Is this a new house?"

Jordyn jumped ahead and opened the door that led from the garage to the kitchen. "No, Julia bought it about a decade ago. I told you she rarely visits."

The kitchen appeared just as unused. Granite tops with wood cupboards that might be cherry. Spencer wished he knew home features and repair like his dad. A pang of regret struck him in the gut. *Please let Dad be sober when we return.*

Carson ran his hand across the island. "Man, the whole football team could sit here."

Ryan chuckled. "Wait until you see the dining room."

Every step gave Spencer an opportunity to take in Jordyn's fragrance and banter with Ryan. She bounced up the spiral wooden staircase and stopped in the middle of the carpeted hall.

"This is the softest rug. You have to feel it." She placed her hands on Ryan's shoulder as she slipped off her tennis shoes. "Seriously. It's the best."

Carson looked to Spencer and shrugged.

Ryan rolled his eyes. "Jordy, put your shoes back on. No one wants to smell that."

A hint of sadness flashed across those mocha-colored eyes. She picked up the shoes and moved ahead to the master bedroom.

After a pause to touch the white flooring, Spencer walked around the spacious area with a canopy bed and generous sized bathroom with a garden tub and separate shower. When he reached the closet, Jordyn was next to him, turning on the light.

He leaned in and brushed her side with his. "I didn't take my shoes off, but I bent down with my hand. It really is a soft carpet."

Her grin could have powered the house and all the lampposts down the drive. "Thanks, Spencer. What do you think so far?"

"As a reporter I know I should always be ready to speak, but words fail me. If I were Julia, I'd be here every weekend."

Her soft laugh was as melodic as harp strings. "Her place in the city is pretty amazing. Her neighbor is one of the Kennedys." She turned off the light but didn't move. "Truth is, I love this place more."

They concluded the tour on the deck with acres of woods in front of them.

Carson noted the rabbit munching on grass. "I don't see this too much in Vestal. Too many cars."

"I've seen a lot of wildlife here. Deer, turkeys, even a bear once." Ryan moved toward Spencer. "What do you think? It's a lot closer to WFRN than Vestal is. Julia has a company come to mow and plow. I handle little repairs, which is hardly ever. Given all the work piling at my new place, I'm tempted to move in here myself." Ryan cracked.

Jordyn left the deck and visited the landscaping dotted with hardy yellow mums.

"I love it. It's amazing. But I'm not sure I could swing the rent."

Ryan kicked at a pebble. "Julia texted me before you arrived. She said you're doing her a favor. If you can cover the utilities, don't worry."

Carson started to cough so hard Spencer glanced over to make sure he wasn't choking. Once he recovered, he asked, "Julia Turmeric said we can stay rent free?"

"She sees potential in you, Spencer." Ryan took his keys out of his pocket. "I'll lock up. Think about it and let Jordy know. If you take it and need help moving, I'm sure my siblings and I can help." They shook hands and Ryan met his sister by the flowers to say goodbye.

Spencer stood on the barn-red painted deck, unable to move. After so much grief, the last twenty-four hours were full of so much goodness he couldn't process it. He leaned on the railing and looked toward the roses where Jordyn stood, bringing a bush full of red blooms close to her as she bent down. He noticed how her dark hair shone against the last rays of the sun for the day.

"Dude. Can't you hear me?" Carson joined him at the railing.

"Sorry. What did you say?"

The teen followed Spencer's gaze and cracked a smile. "No wonder you didn't answer."

Spencer narrowed his eyes. "I have no idea what you're talking about."

Carson scoffed as he left the railing. "You like Jordyn Hart." His teen demeanor was as energized as Jordyn's smile. "As in you like her, like her."

Anchored Hearts

CHAPTER FIVE

For once Jordyn hoped she had beat Natalie to work for some pre-meeting chit-chat, but her friend's car was already in the WFRN lot. Did she have a secret cot and just sleep here? The girl was always at the station. Jordyn walked past her desk and peeked into the conference room where Natalie sat with Joe.

"Am I interrupting? Nat, I brought you an iced mocha." Jordyn lifted the cup.

Joe gestured for her to enter. "Just what she needs. Caffeine." He rolled his eyes.

Natalie ignored the remark and reached for the drink. "We're getting our notes ready for the interviews. Meteorology in the morning, the afternoon is about the reporters."

Jordyn took a seat across from them. "I saw an email come through, but I haven't had a chance to read it."

Because I was showing Spencer around.

"You've got a few minutes. The email has attachments of each candidate and their resume. We may ask a couple to sit with you and Spencer for some banter and fake reporting to check the chemistry."

Jordyn nodded, wishing she'd taken a seat on the other side so she could watch the door. "Sounds good." She glanced at her boss. "Although you never tested Spencer and me together."

Joe kept his focus on his notes. "Didn't need to. We knew you two oozed charisma that will charm viewers."

And maybe each other?

Spencer sauntered in a couple minutes before nine wearing khakis and a light blue dress shirt and navy tie that accented those eyes Jordyn enjoyed stealing peeks into. He greeted everyone by name and sat by Jordyn, leaning in toward her. "If we get a break before your newscast, I'd like to talk about the house."

He smelled of mint and Jordyn imagined it was the same chill that skiing the Alps would give. "Sure, no problem. I enjoyed meeting your brother. Nice kid."

He grinned as he opened up his phone. "Thanks. He's been through a lot, but doesn't let it get to him. Maybe that's why he's so good at football."

"The discipline?" Jordyn sipped her iced drink.

"I was thinking more about how he probably deals with his feelings on the field instead of talking about them."

The conference room intercom went off before Jordyn could reply. Sophia, the receptionist, announced that the first interviewee was in the lobby.

Joe took out a folder and spread the contents across the table. "Show him in, please." He looked to Jordyn and Spencer. "Just out of college. Interned at the Buffalo affiliate."

Jordyn clicked on the email attachment with the nine o'clock slot. Craig White. Recent grad from the State University of Buffalo. Resides in Cheektawaga. She remembered a childhood birthday where the siblings were gifted tickets to watch the Buffalo Bills game. At times the snow was so blinding she had trouble seeing the field.

The door opened, and a lanky, six-foot-maybe-three man in an ill-fitting suit entered and walked straight toward Joe, hand outstretched. "Thanks for the interview, Mr. Munson. I'm Craig White." He shook Joe's hand, then Natalie's. He turned toward Jordyn and his jaw dropped. "Hey. You're the Hart Sextuplets. My mom said you worked at this station. She loves your family and those interviews."

Jordyn stood to offer her hand for a firm shake, and then returned to her seat, praying that would be the end of the Hart Sextuplets talk. "Pleasure to meet you, Craig."

"I mean that Evan, he cracks me up. We think each year that Ryan's going to jump up and just pummel him."

We all wonder about that. "Evan is a character, that's for sure." She looked to Natalie in hopes she'd jump in and start the interview.

"My mom cries every time Julia Turmeric shows the clips of your family story. She can't believe God would take a mother away from six kids and a loving husband."

Jordyn shifted in her chair, wishing there was a button that could drop her to another floor. Another building. She bit her lip and lifted her phone, pretending to be reading her notes.

Spencer stood. "Hi, Craig. Spencer Collins. I'm co-anchoring *Early Rise and Shine* with Jordyn."

The recent grad switched gears and apparently forgot about the Hart Sextuplets as he greeted Spencer and took a seat. Twenty minutes of questions later about his degree, technology level and graphic editing process and how he feels about early morning shifts, Jordyn was more than ready for the next candidate. They were a smaller market, but Craig belonged somewhere even smaller. And far away from her.

By ten, they had interviewed three people. No one jumped to the forefront with great communication skills or solid experience. As they waited for the next person, Joe took the break to pour himself a cup of coffee. "I have a good feeling about the next one."

Natalie tapped her pencil against the table. "Jordyn, he's from SUNY Albany."

Jordyn perked up at the sound of her alma mater. "Really? Same year?" She grabbed her phone and started to scroll.

"No, two years ahead. Rich Wakefield. He's been in South Carolina and Michigan since graduating. He's got some footage on YouTube. Good stuff. Riveting live hurricane coverage."

Spencer chuckled. "Maybe we can ask him if he'll hold farm animals for you?"

Natalie's burst of laughter was all Jordyn needed. She giggled along until Joe returned with a man not quite six feet, tanned complexion, and a crisp suit that looked custom made. When he introduced himself, the rich baritone voice was instantly one Jordyn knew belonged on television.

"Rich Wakefield. Congratulations on the morning show." He shook hands and took a seat at the head, between Joe and Jordyn.

"Thanks for making the trip. Let's get started with that topic—mornings. How do you feel about early mornings? We do have some unpredictable winters when the public relies on the meteorologist to be their guide before they do anything." Joe asked.

He made a point to look everyone in the eye. This voice belonged on a jazz recording. "I grew up not far from Albany. Those snowstorms made me want to pursue the field. I want to be the one that informs the community and helps them make their plans."

Joe nodded but otherwise remained expressionless. "Where do you see yourself in five years?"

Same question Jordyn remembered from her own interview. Was Joe testing Rich to see if he planned to move on soon after establishing the morning show?

"I've already moved around since graduating. I wanted to get my certification with the American Meteorological Society, and I did. With that in hand, my goal is to use those credentials and grow with the team." He turned toward Jordyn and Spencer. "Bottom line, I don't have plans to leave."

Spencer caught Jordyn's gaze and raised his eyebrows.

After a few more questions, Joe placed his hands on top of the files. "If you have the time, I'd like to see you read with Jordyn and Spencer. *The Early Rise and Shine* stage isn't ready yet, but we can use the six o'clock desk."

Rich played with a button on his suit jacket. "Of course." He stood. "Lead the way."

Five minutes later, they sat together at the anchor desk. Spencer on the left, Jordyn in the center, Rich on the right. Natalie brought up the teleprompter, using a script from the night before. The three read through effortlessly, even executing segues without problems. It was melodic and Jordyn felt a chill travel up her spine. They were a good team.

"Okay, thanks. Mr. Wakefield I will be in touch by week's end. Jordyn, I know you have to prep for noon. We'll reconvene at one to talk about our fourth member."

The trio stood, and Spencer took the initiative to join Rich and shake his hand. "Well done."

"Thanks. Here's hoping we can do this permanently." He turned to Jordyn. "You look familiar. What other stations have you anchored?"

She pursed her lips as she discerned his expression. Was he serious? "This has been my only station. I was on the network the other night with Julia Turmeric. Maybe you saw me there?" Jordyn flicked a stray hair out of her face.

The candidate shook his head. "Nope, I haven't watched national news recently." He appeared to ponder a bit more, but then the crease in his forehead smoothed and he smiled. "Oh well. It's good to meet you anyway. Take care." Rich waved and nodded as soon as he saw Sophia ready to escort him to the front door.

Spencer stuffed his hands in his pockets. "What did you think?"

"Confident. Qualified. And so cool."

He looked over at Jordyn, head tilted. "Come again?"

"Rich Wakefield has no idea who I am or that I'm part of that dreaded Hart Sextuplets label. Joe has to hire him."

. ♡ ♡ ♡

Spencer took long strides to catch Rich before he left. Thankfully Sophia kept him in the reception area, talking. He heard something about who sat where in the newsroom when he stepped in. "Excuse me. Rich, I wanted to let you know that was an impressive interview."

Sophia used the interruption to dash back behind her desk while Rich fished for his car keys in his suit pant pocket.

"Thanks, man. This is an exciting opportunity. I'd love to land it."

"I'm rooting for you. I know Jordyn had to like the fact you didn't know her as one of the Hart Sextuplets."

Rich chuckled and leaned in. "Honestly? I know exactly who she is. Everyone in Upstate New York does. Her family has been showcased on our television screens for years."

Spencer arched an eyebrow and took a step back. "I'm confused. Why did you act like you didn't remember her?"

"I did my homework. I know she hates being called one of the sextuplets. It's important to get on her good side. She not only is a big part of WFRN, but the girl's godmother is also Julia Turmeric." Rich made a "ca-ching" sound and gesture as if he hit the jackpot. "I have to get back to Albany. Good to meet you. Hopefully I'll see you soon."

Rich left Spencer standing in the lobby with his jaw dropped. *Did I just encourage a complete jerk to get this job?*

He shook off the shock and headed to his desk. Jordyn would be prepping for the noon broadcast, and he figured it was a good time to check out the other WFRN reporters' resumes. Before he settled in his seat, his cell vibrated. Dad.

"Do you know where my truck keys are?" No hello.

Spencer glanced at his watch. If his dad had been sober the night before, there was a good chance withdrawals were kicking in. "Carson has them."

"Why does he have them? He's in school. I need them now." His voice sounded raspy and desperate.

Spencer looked around and realized the newsroom had a bit of traffic. No one seemed to be listening but if the call was going to go like other times with his father, the volume would increase. From both of them. He headed toward the employee exit. "Carson needs a vehicle for school and practice. Remember, I have to go in earlier these days. Come November, I'll be leaving for work in the middle of the night. This will be the best plan."

"What about me? Smitty's waiting for me at Santino's." Smitty. Great. Dad's favorite drinking buddy. They'd retired from the fire department together.

By now Spencer was outside and headed to his truck for privacy. Although the late August sun wasn't as hot, beads of sweat still dotted his forehead. "That's not a good idea. Can you wait until I get home? We have to talk, anyway."

The silence dragged on long enough Spencer checked the screen to make sure the call didn't drop. Finally, a sigh. "I should have my own truck. You're treating me like a child."

"That isn't my intention, Dad. I have to go. Are you going to be okay?"

"Sure. Will you bring me a meatball sub?" There was a flicker of his old dad in the way he asked for dinner. Maybe he'd sleep through the withdrawals and make progress.

"You got it. See you later." The call ended and Spencer laid his head back on the headrest. Although his dad had been the beloved fire fighter, it was the night after the funeral when the drinking became constant. Ever since, Spencer felt as if he was the one putting out fires.

Spencer returned to his desk in need of caffeine. He poured a cup of coffee and watched Jordyn on the monitor as she ran the mic pack through her jacket. He lingered at the drink station, hearing her giggle over something Natalie said. *Maybe Carson is right.* What's not to like about Jordyn?

Once her broadcast ended, Jordyn opened her chocolate drawer and unwrapped a piece of candy.

"Good show. I take it you enjoy sweets?" Spencer teased from his desk.

She sat down and sighed. "You sound like Ryan. I'll get a salad once we finish these interviews." She picked up a manila folder. "Did you read any of the information Joe printed out?"

Do I tell her about Rich before we move ahead to the reporters?

"A little bit. Say, what did you think about Rich?"

Her eyes brightened at the sound of the weatherman's name. "So good. Polished. Seems like he'd make a great member of the team." Jordyn looked at her watch. "We better get in the conference room. Time to work on the last round of interviews."

Spencer nodded and picked up his phone and folder. It didn't seem like a good time to warn her about Wakefield. Maybe he wouldn't get the job. "I'll be right there."

Casey Butler was the first to sit at the long table and share her desire to join the *Early Rise and Shine* team. Spencer knew her from Binghamton. She was good, but had a habit of interrupting the anchors during live segments. Something she did to Joe during the interview.

Myles Simpson walked in with great posture and a warm smile, shaking Spencer's hand first. "Nice to meet you. I was the spring intern here from Elmira College. Jordyn and Joe taught me a lot."

Jordyn crossed her legs. "We sent poor Myles on a lot of coffee runs during that hostage situation on Fifth Street."

Joe nodded. "That was a long day. Myles, this position involves travel across Steuben, Chemung, Schuyler, and even Broome Counties. You'd be expected to reach out and sign up businesses that are opening, reopening, have a special promotion, something worth you spending the broadcast being on location live. What are your thoughts?"

"I spent a lot of time on the phone during my time here. I made great connections with several businesses, and I'd like to think I could establish even more if given the chance." His voice was even, and he looked Joe in the eye.

Natalie shifted in her chair. "What about the travel?"

Myles nibbled on his bottom lip. "I'm working on it. During the internship I was a student on campus. I used the bus for any transportation. Now that I graduated, I'm trying to find a good car in my price range."

Spencer looked at his folder and made a mark. Not having reliable transportation was a huge concern. He didn't envy Joe making these decisions.

The last interview was with Courtney Tate, Elmira reporter. Another candidate Jordyn and Joe were well acquainted with. She laughed with Jordyn as they remembered live disasters like Black Friday shoppers arguing with Courtney about the president or the zoo trip where the penguins refused to leave their sanctuary to show off the expanded pool.

"You sound quick on your feet. That's important for this position." Spencer noted.

Courtney brushed a bit of her auburn-colored hair behind her shoulder. "I'd like to think that's my greatest strength. And as we've already pointed out, I have established rapport with Jordyn."

Joe looked up from his notes. "The hours are very early. Are you okay with that?"

"I thrive on a few hours of sleep."

Jordyn took a turn. "This isn't hard-hitting news but community work you'd be doing. Do you think you'd grow tired of it? We want the *Early Rise and Shine* team to be a family for our viewers. It won't work if you get bored and leave."

Courtney took her time locking her mint-green eyes with everyone in the room. "I love a challenge. I'm good at what I do. Take a chance on me. You won't be sorry."

Spencer studied Courtney as she spoke. She certainly appeared confident. As Joe wrapped the interview up, she stood and met Spencer's gaze one more time. "I really look forward to hearing from you." And as Courtney stood, she gave a quick wink his way.

Jordyn met Courtney at the door and walked out with her, oblivious to the gesture. Spencer didn't know what to do. Maybe she's just friendly? If it was flirty, what a mess the show would be in to have both Rich and Courtney on board.

Joe joined him at the end of the table. "Thanks for joining in, Hart. I learned a lot watching you interact with everyone."

"Oh really? Any frontrunners?"

The boss moved toward the exit and shut off the lights. "Nothing official. I sure was impressed by Rich Wakefield and Courtney, though. What a powerhouse team, am I right? You, Jordyn, Rich and Courtney."

Spencer's throat dried as he considered the deceitful meteorologist and the too-confident reporter. "It would be something, that's for sure."

CHAPTER SIX

Jordyn pushed open the door to the new studio and avoided the sawdust and tools still cluttering the floor. There was still some touch-up work to complete, but after six weeks, the *Early Rise and Shine* set looked ready for Jordyn to take her seat. She tip-toed the best she could on heels for her safety against the construction and made her way to the ergonomic chairs. Behind her were rows of LED screens that could display thirty different scenes, or one huge one. Definitely a far cry from the WFRN pictures when her mom worked there.

The door opened and footsteps headed her way. Spencer. Jordyn smiled and patted the seat next to her. "Try it out."

He turned around as if making sure no one else was around. "You know Vince wants to visit here for a big reveal."

"He agreed that we need the set for promo work before he has a chance to see for himself. C'mon, it's coming together. The set's nearly done. The chairs are comfortable. Joe hired everyone. It's exciting, don't you think?"

Spencer offered a sheepish grin as he sauntered over. He pulled his chair out and sat, then pulled up to the desk. "This is sleek." He ran his hand over the smooth top, wide enough for their iPads and phones. Below him was another screen built into the desk.

"The technology is crazy. My dad knows all this stuff. Ryan too."

Spencer turned around. "We have almost as many screens as the national news."

Jordyn smiled. Not quite the truth. Still, the pressure to deliver the ratings began to crowd her excitement. Enough that she stood and left the platform.

"You okay? You're kind of pale." Spencer squinted, then rose and was at her side. His stare at the close proximity was as unnerving as the stress of the new job. "Did you eat some bad chocolate?"

His ever-minty breath brushed her cheeks.

"There's no such thing as bad chocolate." She looked over to the desk, wishing she were closer so she could lean on it. In the month or so they'd worked together, Spencer only grew kinder and more compassionate. "It hit me that we're in a room with a high price tag. It's up to us to make this show work."

Spencer stepped back. "I've been up a few nights with those same thoughts."

Jordyn swallowed, her throat feeling as though she ate dust for lunch. "We're going to be a hit, right?"

His turquoise-colored eyes shone as he nodded. "Absolutely. We better meet Natalie. I heard her tell Joe we have three outfit changes for these promo shots."

"And that Joe wants to film us around town." Jordyn pictured the October wind wreaking havoc on her hair.

"Busy day. Let's go." He extended his hand as a gesture for her to go first. With each step she took, she willed herself to stand tall and confident in her heels. Then again, tripping and having Spencer catch her didn't seem so terrible.

Natalie greeted the pair by handing them each a hanger wrapped in plastic. "Joe's late. Last-minute phone call. He wants to start with you two at the desk. Courtney and Rich will be here in twenty minutes."

Jordyn knew when Nat didn't greet her, it was crunch time. She headed to the small women's dressing room and locked it. With the plastic covering off, the outfit was a black pantsuit with a royal blue blouse. Chances were the LED screen colors would accentuate their wardrobe. She changed quickly, trying not to create static cling with her fine hair against her fast movements.

She left the dressing room and returned to the new set. Sam Pellicano, one of her favorite camera operators, was already in place. She glanced at the sound booth and noticed a few people ready to work. Lights flickered, and the screens came on with the WFRN logo, complete with the bright blue background.

Spencer entered in a dark suit, white shirt, and red tie. Not a wavy hair out of place. He strolled over and nudged her lightly on the arm. "We look sharp."

"Are you ready for your face to be on the back of our transit system?"

He chuckled. "With my long face I'll probably be part of the bus exhaust."

Jordyn giggled and tapped his arm in return.

They both took seats and waited for Joe or Natalie with direction. It was Joe who marched in, frustration lining his face. "Sorry I'm late. Let's capture intro video first, then still photos. Rich and Courtney will join shortly, then we'll go on location to finish up."

The crew nodded throughout the set. The teleprompter came to life.

"We have three scripts ready. Fifteen-second, thirty, and sixty. Fifteen first." Joe barked. While the teleprompter scrolled to the right place, the news director looked to Jordyn. "I was on the phone with your friend Kent. He's worried now that since you're no longer reporting at noon that he won't have a weekly spot anymore."

Jordyn maintained her smile so Sam wouldn't chastise her as he prepped the shot. "What did you say?"

"I told him the two of you have good enough rapport on air that he can keep the noon and also chat live with you on *Early Rise and Shine*."

Before she could respond with her own argument against the plan, their cue started and Sam was filming. Her grin frozen, her voice sounded an octave higher as she recited, "Hi, I'm Jordyn Hart and this is Spencer Collins. We're the anchors of *Early Rise and Shine* starting November third…"

. ♡ ♡ ♡

Spencer took a cleansing breath as he watched Joe move calmly from one topic to another. More like he threw Jordyn a curveball regarding the finance guy and his boring weekly features, then moved on to starting their promos.

They completed the last of the scripts for just the two of them and had another wardrobe change. Jordyn looked to the floor as she scuffed off the set.

He gave a slight jog to catch up with her. "Having fun yet?"

She looked up, those brown saucers showing no trace of irritation. "I wish my focus was better. Joe took me by surprise back there."

"Maybe Kent can give money advice and handle the pet adoption segment at the same time."

Jordyn's grin grew as she rolled her eyes. "You're too funny, Collins." She sobered as she stopped in front of her dressing room door. "How's the house?"

He paused next to her. "Perfect. I love how my driving time is cut in half. Carson's doing well getting to school on time. He thinks he's something else staying at Julia's place, but hasn't told anyone."

She opened the door. "Great. So glad it's working out. See you outside."

Spencer nodded and made the strides down to his dressing area. Thankfully she didn't ask about his dad. The dilemma whether to bring him to the house or let him stay alone gave Spencer a good week's worth of ulcers. With his father tucked away in the woods without a vehicle, Spencer thought he'd feel more at peace. If the last few years taught them anything, it was to never take anything for granted when it came to family. He never thought they would be without their mother. Or that his strapping, fire-fighter hero of a dad would drink his retirement away bent over a barstool.

When he re-emerged on stage, Rich and Courtney were standing at the ends of the platform. Jordyn followed Joe's instructions on where to place her hands as she remained in place beside Rich.

Courtney gestured for Spencer to join them. "You're next to me."

Spencer took a few paces before settling between the women. "Joe, is this how we'll be each morning?"

Jordyn gave Spencer a sweeping gaze that he couldn't quite discern. Was she curious about his question or jealous he was also near Courtney?

"Except Courtney will be on location each day."

Did Jordyn just grin?

"Hopefully she brings all the perks back." Rich straightened his tie and looked to Sam, who was snapping pictures with the digital camera. "You know, the bagels, the pizza, ice cream sundaes."

Spencer's stomach growled as he considered the restaurant openings and new menu promotions. "I'm going to need new pants before Thanksgiving."

The group finished the set shots and Joe sent them to change for Elmira promos.

Natalie handed off wardrobe changes. "Courtney and Rich, you take these two and meet in the lot. I'll take you two to Elmira College." She handed Spencer and Jordyn their last set of clothes. "Joe's taking you guys downtown to the shopping district."

Spencer lifted the plastic off the hanger to find a dark brown sweater and tan khaki pants. It was the kind of outfit he'd wear on a date. Was that what they were going for?

He found Joe in the driver's seat of one of the WFRN cars, waving him over. Spencer turned back to the door, wondering if he should wait for Jordyn. She pushed the exit open and stepped out in an outfit nearly identical to his, except her sweater was black.

"Are we going far? This is itchy." Jordyn's nose scrunched as she scratched at the back of her neck.

Joe started the car while Spencer and Jordyn gave an awkward dance trying to decide who would sit up front and who would be in the back. After three odd maneuvers, Jordyn took the front seat and put on the seat belt.

Spencer felt the rough material brush against his back. "Jordyn's right. This is itchy."

"You two sound like children. It won't be long. Make sure you don't complain about the clothes in public. We have a marketing deal with that big store in the mall where my wife maxes out our credit card." Joe sounded like he needed a nap.

Jordyn nodded and pulled the visor down, then turned on the light next to the little mirror. She played with a few strands of hair and dug in her purse, and within seconds applied a red shade of lipstick. "Are we all getting clothes from there?"

"Yes." Joe turned his head and smiled. "In fact, there's Rich and Courtney wearing the new Elmira College sweatshirts. That's some bright purple and gold."

"Dad looked into that place for us when we were seniors in high school. Private school. Times six. I think he cried tears of relief when the state college director reached out and offered us all free tuition and board."

Spencer thought about the monthly payment he was still making on his school loans. Private school was never in the cards for him, either.

The trio started their journey through Elmira talking about the show. Spencer recognized the shopping district and wondered where Joe planned to have them film the last promotion. The Historical Society made sense. Elmira was known for Mark Twain living there, a Revolutionary War camp, and astronaut Eileen Collins. The area also boasted the first store Tommy Hilfiger opened, as Elmira was his hometown. Maybe Joe wanted them at the place where his things were still available.

Five minutes later, Joe pulled into a familiar parking lot.

Jordyn chuckled. "Santino's?"

Joe turned off the engine, twisted around to the seat next to Spencer's, and pulled up two folders. "Two scripts for Santino's. It's a staple in the community. Jordyn, you go there every year after the sibling interview. It makes sense."

Jordyn didn't reply, but opened her folder and read the short text. Spencer started to glance at his, but noticed the truck parked next to them. It sure looked like Smitty's, his dad's drinking partner.

If he picked up his dad and they were intoxicated, this promotion would be Spencer's swan song.

"You two ready?" Joe opened his door and stepped into the gravel lot.

Spencer felt every muscle tense as he joined them and walked to the front of the restaurant. If silent prayers had power, he just sent a 911-level request in hopes that his father would not be inside the restaurant.

CHAPTER SEVEN

Jordyn glanced around the restaurant to see a few families dining and a handful of people at the bar.

Joe waved her and Spencer ahead. "We have the back room reserved, and they have a curtain that can block us off from others. Give me a few minutes to set up."

"I'm going to get a glass of ice water. Want anything, Spencer?" Jordyn tried not to stare at the muscles under his sweater.

Spencer looked around the restaurant before landing his gaze on her. "No, I'd be the one to spill it all over my clothes. I'll help Joe." He sounded distant, as if his body was in the building, but his mind was somewhere far off. Was he thinking about Courtney?

Oh, Jordyn. Stop. She's a friendly reporter. Nothing more, nothing less. "Okay, I'll be there in a few." She waved and made her way to the bar.

A stocky man with salt and pepper hair sat, stirring his drink. Jordyn stood to his right, noticing the bartender was an acquaintance of her brother, James. She smiled at both gentlemen. "Hey, Nick. Can I get a glass of ice water?"

The man with a scruffy beard and flannel shirt nodded. "Anything for my favorite anchor. My boss says you guys are shooting promos here. Something about a morning show?"

The older gentleman shifted in his seat and nodded as he looked at her. "Hart girl," he slurred, and gulped his drink.

Jordyn tried to focus on Nick and not the intoxicated curmudgeon. "It's true. WFRN has a new show, *Early Rise and Shine*. I'm really excited."

Nick placed her ice water on the wooden bar. "Good for you. I don't envy those hours, but you'll be great. Tell James to give me a call when he's in town."

Jordyn picked up the tall glass and smiled. She turned to make her way to the back, but nearly ran into a man heading to the bar. He looked familiar, but she couldn't quite place him. Older, like the guy nursing his mixed drink.

The man swayed for a second, then regained his balance. "Jordyn Hart?" His volume was a bit louder than it needed to be for the smaller afternoon crowd.

"Yes, that's me. Hello." She noted Joe already had the curtain closed, so no one back there would know she was stuck trying to reach them.

The man's bright, glassy blue eyes twinkled as he grinned. "My son works with you! I'm Ray Collins."

A brick dropped into Jordyn's stomach. The guy was familiar because she'd run into him before under similar circumstances. And he was also the man she'd seen with Spencer in the truck that night. "Mr. Collins, good to see you."

His breath reeked like someone imbibed past their first beer of the day. "Is Spencer here? Are you working on something?"

She opened her mouth, but no words came out. Although not fall-down drunk, Mr. Hart could easily disrupt the promos. Infuriate Joe. Upset Spencer. Finally, something that wasn't a lie tumbled from her mouth. "I'm sorry that I can't stay and talk, but I do have to meet with my news director. Take care."

Jordyn took advantage of the man's slower response time and started for the back. She snuck behind the curtain to find Spencer adjusting the light, whistling, as if he didn't have a care in the world.

He looked over and spotted her. "There you are. Where did you get the water? Chemung River?" His smile was another knee-buckler.

"Something like that. Are we ready?"

Jordyn worked through the video and still pictures, her attention on the curtain. She wasn't sure what scared her more, informing Spencer his drunken dad was at the bar, or the possibility of Mr. Collins busting through before she had that chance.

An hour later, Joe put the digital camera on a nearby table. "And that's a wrap. Good job, you two. If you don't mind helping me take the equipment apart, we can get back to the station and call it a day."

Spencer nodded and walked to the light.

Time to tell him. Jordyn marched over and placed her hand on his arm. "Hey, Spencer. Do you have a minute?"

He looked at her hand, and she jerked it away. "Everything okay?"

If only there was another curtain we could disappear behind. Jordyn whispered, "I ran into your dad. Here at Santino's."

Spencer's cheeks went from a rosy pink to a linen white in about two seconds.

"He asked about you, but I didn't confirm you were here. I don't know if I did the right thing. I know when I'm working, I don't love family run-ins." She swallowed hard, hoping he'd blink. Speak. Anything.

"Um, okay. Thanks. Is he still here?"

Jordyn shrugged. "If you want to check, I can take care of this. Go ahead."

He gave a curt nod and sprinted toward the curtain, not even looking back.

Joe stopped looking through the camera stills and scrunched his eyebrows together. "Everything okay?"

She stared at the flap of black cloth, stirring from the swift current Spencer created with his abrupt departure. "I'm not sure."

. ♡ ♡ ♡

Spencer raked his hand through his hair and sighed as he approached the bar. Smitty started blinking once they spotted each other.

Before Smitty could nudge his dad as a warning, Spencer posted himself between the two senior citizens. "Dad, what are you doing here?"

The elder Collins shifted in his chair, not to look at Spencer, but peek at the dark curtain. "You've been here the whole time?"

Spencer counted the empty glasses on the bar. Six.

Smitty patted Spencer on the back. "Your dad wanted to watch you work."

Okay, so they're both coherent. "This isn't about me. Drinking the afternoon away isn't healthy." He faced Smitty. "You shouldn't be driving."

His dad chuckled. "You'd rather I stay in that woodsy prison and rot."

"I'm trying to keep you safe." He closed his eyes for a moment. "I have to finish up in there. No more drinking. And I'll order a ride for both of you."

"Am I allowed to go back there?" His dad sounded wounded.

"Actually, we're just packing up." Spencer bit on his bottom lip. "If you don't touch anything, you can come back."

The two slid off the stools and shuffled behind Spencer. He held open the curtain and let them walk through. "Joe, this is my dad, Ray, and his friend, Smitty."

The men waved in rhythm while Jordyn nearly dropped the tripod.

Joe offered a small smile. "Good to meet you, gentlemen. Spencer, I'm taking the cameras out to the car."

Spencer nodded, unsure what to do with the two men who definitely didn't need to go back to the bar.

Before he could say anything, Jordyn walked up with those wide eyes and a glow on her face. "Would you two like to see the script we were working with? I have it over on this table." She gestured them forward, and like obedient children, they followed her.

Spencer took the opportunity to finish packing. Every time he returned to the back room, Jordyn was talking. His dad stood, nodding every so often.

"I get up at five. Can't shake the old shifts. I'm going to watch your show." Smitty kept his gaze on her.

Her voice raised an octave as she tapped Smitty on the arm. "That's great. You're going to love it. The set is amazing."

"What's it like to work with Spencer? He was an uptight kid." His dad leaned forward as if he were sharing a secret.

Jordyn's giggle didn't help Spencer's mood. This wasn't how he'd pictured the afternoon. He ignored the chatter about his serious demeanor and headed back to the car with the last of the equipment. While outside, he called an Uber for Smitty and his dad.

Joe shut the trunk and walked up to Spencer. "Everything okay in the back room?"

What part? My dad there, intoxicated, saying who knows what? Jordyn egging him on? "It's—less than ideal." Spencer blew out some hot air as he looked to the restaurant.

"My brother is a recovering alcoholic." Joe dug a card out of his wallet and handed it to Spencer. "I know for our family, when he was out drinking in the early afternoon, that was never a good thing. If you need to talk, call me. This also has rehab info on the back."

Joe left it at that, no questions no judging, just the observation and the card. He turned and started back to Santino's.

"Thanks, Joe." Spencer called out as he picked up his pace to catch up. Joe already had the door open and was stepping inside.

A minute later, Spencer found the group in the back, with Joe opening up the dark curtain.

"I'm all packed up. I'll head to the car. Don't be long." Joe turned to the men. "Take care, Ray, Smitty." And he was off to the parking lot.

Spencer stalked over to the merry band of intoxicated men and Jordyn. "Guys, an Uber is going to be here in five minutes. I'm texting everything to your phone, Dad."

The trio sobered and Jordyn stepped back. "Gentlemen, it was great talking to you."

Smitty waved. "Catch you on the TV. Thanks for showing us the script."

Jordyn ran a hand through her hair and then gave her head a shake as she took out her sunglasses. "The pleasure was mine." She looked at Spencer. "I'll meet you at the car."

Spencer nodded, besotted by the adorable way she looked after playing with her hair, yet disappointed he had to deal with his dad. "C'mon, Dad. I'll make sure you get in the right car."

He led the way outside, no one speaking. When the correct vehicle approached, Spencer felt his jaw unclench. One less thing to worry about. The men climbed in the back and put on their seat belts like obedient toddlers afraid of discipline.

"Your dad needs out every once in a while, Spence. He lost everything when your mama passed." Smitty sobered long enough to deliver cold truth.

Spencer took in a slow breath before exhaling. "I agree. To a card game. A walk in the park. A trip to the library. Not a bar. Goodbye, Smitty. Dad." He closed the back door and tapped the roof, and the car slowly pulled from the curb.

Joe had the car running in the parking lot with the interior already heated by the time Spencer joined them in the lot. The news director gave no emotion regarding the wait. He pulled to the end of the gravel area. "You guys look amazing in the still shots. I'm sure the video work is just as good."

Both Jordyn and Spencer were in the backseat, and mumbled thanks.

"Any word on how Natalie did with Courtney and Rich?" Jordyn asked.

Joe signaled a right turn. "She texted a couple minutes ago. They finished about the same time we did. Nat said the two are naturals together."

The two continued their promo banter during the short drive back to the station. The three quietly returned the equipment. Spencer felt like he was being watched as he worked, but wasn't ready to talk. Not until he could approach Jordyn alone.

Once the car was empty, Joe confessed he wanted to edit the footage before going home. Jordyn fished out her keys and started for the employee exit when Spencer reached for her arm.

"Hey, do you have a minute? I want to talk about Santino's."

Jordyn pointed outside. "Is the lot okay? It's probably more private than the newsroom."

Spencer nodded and held the door open for her. "I know you wanted me to be able to focus earlier, but I wish you would have told me about my dad being at the bar. The delay meant he was able to drink even more, which is the last thing I wanted."

Jordyn looked up with those amazing brown eyes, even wider than usual. "I was trying to help."

"I know. It's just, things are kind of complicated with my dad and I like being hands-on and informed." Although his tone was calm, Jordyn's demeanor didn't look like she was receiving his words as nicely.

100

She put her hands on her hips. "I understand a complicated family. Trust me. But it never gets in the way of my work. I wanted the same for you."

Spencer kicked at a stray pebble. "Jordyn, I'm not mad at you. I'm giving you direction in case this happens again." He let out a sigh. "Which I hope it doesn't."

Those chocolate-colored eyes now transformed to a dark thundercloud. She narrowed her gaze and kept her hands on her hips. "Well, I am mad. Frustrated is probably more accurate. I even stepped away from my work to entertain them. I was showing them the script to help." Jordyn's arms dropped to her sides as she lowered her voice. "I'm sorry. I meant no harm. Everything was for you."

He stepped forward, wanting to reach out to her, but her forehead had a crease he'd never seen before. The honeysuckle aroma surrounding her was as intoxicating as the situation back at Santino's, but he kept his hands to his side. "I didn't ask you to. I could have handled it."

She scoffed and kicked at the ground, bringing her even closer.

"My dad wasn't always like this. I'm trying to figure it out. If you want us to move…"

Jordyn held up her hand, then moved it to his chest. On top of his itchy sweater. "Spencer, I don't want you to move. I understand your concerns about your father, but he was fine. I was trying to help. That's all I've ever done. Julia's house. Not telling you about Smitty and your dad. Spending time with them while you packed up. I'm not a bad person. Like you, I enjoy handling issues. And people." Her lashes lowered and Spencer couldn't tell if she was about to cry or slap him.

Spencer moved his hand over hers. He swallowed as she looked up and brushed the corner of her eye with her free hand.

"Spencer." Her voice was deep and sultry, making Spencer unable to recall what they were even talking about.

He reached for the other hand and started to lean toward her, the air charged between them. Jordyn's mouth slightly parted. If it was to talk or something else, Spencer didn't process it. Caught up in compassion and confusion, he moved closer. Before Spencer could place his lips on hers, a car door slammed.

Jordyn flew back as if a car bomb just detonated. "It's Nat. Natalie's here." She put even more distance between them.

Spencer stood still, the sweater feeling a hundred pounds with the heat they just generated. He looked over and saw Natalie, Rich and Courtney leave the other WFRN vehicle. Jordyn was already heading toward them, leaving him in a trail of confusion and the tantalizing honeysuckle that was everything about Jordyn.

CHAPTER EIGHT

Jordyn stepped into the kitchen, her hands still shaking from her near kiss with Spencer. Natalie must have noticed her awkward rush to greet her in the lot, but Nat had raised her eyebrows. Jordyn considered texting Spencer, but what would she write? *Sorry we fought? See you tomorrow? How's your dad? Nice almost kiss?*

"Hey, Jordy. How was work?" Her dad came into the kitchen with his laptop bag and a cheery whistle. He walked over and gave her a peck on the cheek before checking his mail.

"We did promos today. You should see the set. It's almost done. Really state-of-the-art stuff." Jordyn twirled a strand of her hair as she fought images of Spencer moving so close she could feel light stubble.

"I'd love to. I think I'm having lunch with Shelly tomorrow in Elmira. Maybe we can swing by."

The mere mention of Shelly's name felt like a semi-truck drove across Jordyn's shoulders. After so many years with just her dad, she missed their one-on-one time. "Sure. Just text me so I can meet you in the lobby."

Evan slid into the kitchen, flew across the polished floor, and crashed into the wastebasket. "Look who's here. How's the morning show, Jordy?"

She spun around in hopes of swatting him with her mail, but missed. "Coming along. What brings you here? Get fired already?"

Their dad cleared his throat and Jordyn mouthed she was sorry.

"Not yet. I have a side gig anyway." He stopped by the fridge. "Can I be a guest on the show? I'm working on something for our twenty-fifth interview."

Ugh. His plans never ended. What could Evan possibly be dreaming up for them? "I'd have to hear your thoughts before I talk to Natalie."

Evan crossed his arms against his chest. "Don't you trust me?"

Jordyn opened her bank statement and glanced at her sibling. "Not even a little bit. You know I can't have you on a live interview if I don't know what you plan to say."

The two stared at each other for a long moment before Evan sighed and opened the fridge. He pulled out a container and placed it on the island counter. "I'm still talking with a connection Aunt Julia gave me. When I know more, I'll tell you. Promise."

Jordyn walked over for a peek in the container with enough lasagna for both of them. "That's all I ask. Can I have some of that?"

He rolled his eyes but nodded. "Get two plates."

After dinner, Jordyn joined her dad, Evan, and Paige in the living room. The WFRN six o'clock news was on, and as soon as Courtney appeared on the screen to report on the upcoming city council meeting, Jordyn leaned in.

So did Evan. "She's cute."

"You work with her, right? Isn't she part of the morning team?"

"Yes, Dad. She will go out each morning to a business. A roving reporter, I guess." As Courtney's auburn waves tossed in the breeze, her words were clear and crisp. She was good.

"How about your co-anchor? The one from Binghamton?"

Jordyn felt her heartbeat race at her dad's mention of Spencer. She had to play it cool or Evan would pounce like a cat on a ball of yarn. "He's a pro. All four of us make a great team. Now we have to convince the audiences out there." She instinctively touched her chin, remembering the sizzle between her and Spencer when he placed his hand there.

"WFRN isn't afraid of promotion. Your face will be plastered across Route eighty-six on all the billboards." Her dad smiled before returning his attention to the television.

Jordyn's phone vibrated and she noticed a text from Natalie.

I finally have time to talk. What was going on in that parking lot?

Jordyn stood with phone in hand. "I need to deal with this. I'll be in my room. Dad, don't forget your medicine."

She rushed toward the stairs, but heard Evan in a mock whisper, "Okay, Mom."

With her bedroom door shut, she unlocked her phone and dialed Natalie.

Natalie's sing-song voice flowed through the speaker. "An actual call and not a text? This is going to be juicy."

Jordyn sat on her bed and played with a loose comforter thread. "Nat, we're working professionals. This isn't high school." Then why was her heart beating as if she was?

"You're in your twenties and still live at home. Give me this moment. Something happened with Spencer. What?"

Jordyn rolled her eyes. Another remark about still being at her childhood home. "Okay. I think we were going to kiss."

She waited a few seconds before Natalie's screech came through. "What? Joe and I knew you two had great chemistry, but that's an implosion."

"We didn't kiss. We argued. His dad was at Santino's, and he had been drinking. I got the impression it's a problem. I thought I was helping, but Spencer wasn't pleased."

Natalie scoffed. "So he tried to kiss you?"

Jordyn tried to piece the scene together, but the only image that came to the forefront was him caressing her wrist, holding her hand, and leaning in. "Maybe because I put my arms around his neck. Ugh, how do I look at him? We start the show in a few weeks."

There was a sigh, and then a pause. "You already answered that. You're a professional. Do you like him?"

Jordyn picked up her pillow and hit herself with it. "Nat, I can't."

"Sure, Joe will have a fit, but there are a lot of news colleagues who date and even marry. He seems like a really sweet guy."

"That's not it. I mean, Joe's reaction makes it even easier, but I can't. I made a vow that I'd never involve myself with anyone who is surrounded by alcohol. I'll never forget dad's face when he told us a drunk driver killed mom. I won't lose a piece of my heart twice."

. ♡ ♡ ♡

Spencer watched a squirrel scurry in front of him as he drove up the curved driveway to his new home. If only life could be as carefree as the furry animal scampering off to the woods. Instead, Spencer needed to find food, check on Carson, and confront his father. Again. All while trying not to re-play his almost-kiss with Jordyn. Although, that would be his choice for how to spend his evening.

He took off his loafers and decided his first order of business needed to be his dad. Spencer sauntered past the kitchen and went to the living area where the combination of alcohol and television game shows had apparently lulled his father to sleep on the leather couch.

Okay, that conversation is on pause. Spencer pulled out his phone and opened up the app that showed Carson's location. Almost home. Time to find dinner.

Ten minutes later, Carson was in the kitchen looking over Spencer's shoulder, watching water boil. The younger Hart dropped his gym bag to the side and poured a tall glass of milk. "Dad okay?"

Spencer dumped spaghetti into the pot and faced his brother. "He's asleep in the living room. Smitty took him to Santino's today."

Carson shook his head, too many emotions passing his face for someone so young. "I hoped having the truck would keep dad out of trouble. How did you find out?"

"I was filming promotions with Jordyn at the restaurant. It was a mess." Spencer stirred the pasta, still seeing Jordyn talking with the older men, the way she insisted she was trying to help. "Jordyn saw them first and decided not to tell me. They ended up watching us pack up before I called a ride for them."

"You and Jordyn okay?" Carson set the milk down and moved to the counter to butter a couple slices of bread.

"Dude, I'm making spaghetti. We'll eat in a few minutes."

"Don't worry. I've got room for carbs." He took a bite, then swallowed. "How about you answer my question?"

Carson was like a dog with a bone. *I guess the dedication was good for football. For me? Not so much.*

"Sure. We're professionals." Except for the part where they held hands, wrapped their arms around each other, and were ready to kiss.

"Uh-huh. There's no way you stayed silent when Jordyn made a decision without your knowledge. You're way too uptight for that."

Ugh. That word again. "I mean, we talked about it." Spencer poured his concentration into checking the pasta tenderness.

"I bet you did." Carson chuckled in between bites. He peeked past the kitchen. "What are you going to do about Dad?"

Spencer sighed. "I want to talk to him. He can't be driving around with Smitty. He also can't be drinking here. We're guests."

"You know, a guy on the team told me about his youth group. He shared that he had a real problem with vaping, got really sick from it. Eric said his youth pastor helped him, and he believes his faith in Christ is what keeps him clean."

As soon as Spencer heard the word "Christ," he grimaced. "Where was Jesus with mom?"

Carson looked to the floor. "I don't know. But I do go to bed every night thankful Mom never blamed God for her cancer. She knew where she was going for eternity. I've got to believe if Mom faced such a hideous disease and stayed faithful, maybe this Jesus thing could be an answer for Dad."

Thankfully the pasta was done. Spencer had no desire to keep the conversation going. Carson didn't see their mom on morphine, losing control of her limbs in spastic waves. Only Spencer heard the guttural sob from his dad the moment his wife passed.

"Dad sat in the same pews we did all those years. Look where he is now."

Their dad roused from his slumber an hour after the brothers finished their dinner. Carson was upstairs working on homework while Spencer cleaned the kitchen. He heard his dad shuffle to the fridge.

"I wrapped a plate of spaghetti for you in there." Spencer's tone was as flat as fizzless pop.

His dad scratched his head and took the plate out. "Thanks, son." He took the wrap off and headed to the microwave. "That Jordyn is one beautiful girl, inside and out."

Spencer scrubbed the countertop. "Yes, she is."

"Did the promos turn out okay?"

"Joe said the still photos were great. He's probably still editing the video footage." The microwave beeped, and Spencer took the notification to face his dad. "We have to talk about your drinking."

His dad took the plate and trekked to the dining room instead of the kitchen island.

Spencer followed, sitting down across from him. "What you're doing is more than a couple of drinks after mowing the lawn. You were drunk today. I could see it in your eyes."

"Drunks slur. I spoke fine at Santino's and you know it." He kept his head down, slurping the spaghetti.

"Alcoholics feel they must have a drink to function." Spencer tried to come off as matter-of-fact, but he knew he sounded superior. And that was always a trigger for his dad's anger.

"Spencer, I'm still the head of the house here. You're not going to talk down to me and tell me how to live my life. Just because you packed me up like the rest of your junk and moved me to this hideaway doesn't mean you're in charge." He stabbed at the pasta.

"Dad. That's not fair. I didn't want to leave you alone. I couldn't leave you alone."

"I've been alone since the second your Mama died."

The air filled with grief and pain. How could Spencer get anywhere when all roads led back to his mom's death?

Two hours later, Spencer laid in bed with a thousand thoughts buzzing through his mind. Was he wrong about his dad? Had he cut Carson off too soon once the faith talk started? Would Jordyn treat him differently when they met at work? He grabbed his pillow, put it over his mouth, and screamed. When he went to return the pillow under his head, the corner hit the edge of his night table and knocked something off.

Spencer turned on the small lamp and found his mom's Bible on the floor. As angry as he'd been after her death, he never moved her Bible after unpacking. Keeping it in a dusty box seemed disrespectful toward her. He reached down and grabbed it, noting the book was open to the book of Proverbs. Although a faded yellow, there was a passage still highlighted.

Trust in the LORD *with all your heart; do not depend on your own understanding. Seek his will in all you do, and he will show you which path to take.*

Spencer stared at the last words. His path was anything but straight. Wasn't that God's doing by taking his mom? With that thought, the *do not depend* jumped out. Could his understanding be wrong? Screaming into the pillow no longer seemed like a solution. He turned the page and scoured for more of her highlighted passages. He read Proverbs and back into the Psalms until he fell into a peaceful sleep.

Anchored Hearts

CHAPTER NINE

Darkness surrounding her, Jordyn swatted at her phone in an effort to switch off her alarm. She pushed out a long sigh. *Well, you signed up for this. Welcome to your first of many two o'clock wake-up calls.* She crawled out of bed and traipsed to the bathroom, careful not to disturb Paige. The lukewarm shower woke Jordyn up and allowed time to collect her thoughts.

Natalie confirmed the first *Early Rise and Shine* schedule before Jordyn had gone to bed. Banter between the team. A video package of each member and their background, starting with her. After commercial, Spencer and Jordyn would deliver the news, followed by Rich's first look at the weather. Another commercial, and then Courtney would give a tour of the set. Each half-hour would feature a greeting from a prominent citizen from the area congratulating WFRN on the new morning show. The five o'clock slot would be the Elmira mayor. The third set of commercials, and then a re-hash of the first half-hour, with tweaking. The only thing Jordyn didn't see on the schedule was how to interact with Spencer. Since their argument and near-kiss a couple of weeks ago, they were kind and cordial. And all kinds of awkward.

By three-fifteen, Jordyn was already at her desk sipping coffee and looking over the newswire from overnight. Spencer walked through the newsroom wearing a pair of black-rimmed glasses and carrying a travel mug. His charcoal suit and red tie looked so gallant on him Jordyn nearly choked on her drink.

"So, our first morning." Jordyn searched his eyes, hoping to find a peace that could carry her through the next few hours.

"Nervous?" His voice sounded even huskier, probably the early morning and lack of talking.

Jordyn sighed and nibbled on a hangnail. "Terrified."

Spencer cracked a smile, and it changed the atmosphere from tired and flat to alive and encouraging. "Totally understandable. It's going to be great." He reached into a desk drawer and pulled out a well-worn book. "A couple weeks ago I came across my mom's Bible. I've been reading it. Wasn't anything I planned on doing, quite the opposite actually."

Jordyn raised her eyebrows. Where was this going?

"Anyway, not only do I feel close to my mom when I'm reading it, but all the anxiety I've been fighting about the show and other things has disappeared too." His eyes locked with hers.

"Your mom sounds like my parents." Jordyn nibbled at her bottom lip before continuing, her volume fading. "After the accident, we stopped going to church. Dad's Bible collected dust. And I haven't prayed since Shelly sat me down and shared that mom was on the way to the hospital with James, Kelly, and Paige."

Spencer let out a low whistle. "That's a lot to deal with as a child. At least I was in college with my mom." He looked at the clock on the wall. "Anyway, we should go in the studio. My point in all this deep talk is that I know it's going to be okay. We're going to be great."

Jordyn breathed in slowly, amazed at how relaxed she felt. "You know it."

When the digital clock showed it was four fifty-nine and forty-five seconds, Jordyn cleared her throat and brushed her hair behind her shoulder. *Please don't let there be dandruff on my navy blazer.* She looked down the long news desk and saw Courtney in her tomato-red floor length dress gaze straight ahead at the camera, completely focused. Rich cracked his knuckles and straightened as he stood at the end.

"And here we go." Spencer chuckled. "Let's have a great show."

Seth, the Production Assistant, counted down while Sam pointed to the camera. They were live.

Jordyn smiled and followed Sam's direction. "Good Morning, Southern Tier. I'm Jordyn Hart and this is *Early Rise and Shine.*" Once the first words were out, she felt her shoulders relax.

"I'm Spencer Collins and we're the anchors who will wake you up each weekday from five to seven." He looked to Rich, who had a megawatt smile ready to light up Elmira.

"You can count on me, Rich Wakefield, to deliver your first look at the weather so you can plan your day."

Courtney rounded out the introductions. "I'm Courtney Tate, and I plan to show you everything our area has to offer. You're invited to join us—"

Rich continued. "Monday through Friday."

"At each of our live locations." Spencer added.

"And right from the comfort of your home." Jordyn said.

"Early Rise and Shine." The team announced in unison.

Beyond the camera Jordyn noted Natalie, Joe, Seth, and Lauryn, the floor manager, offered their thumb's up. Smiles. High-fives.

Spencer turned to Jordyn. "The anchor desk isn't too new for you, right, Jordyn? Viewers know you best from the noon report. What do you think about all this?" He extended his arms to show off the set.

She glanced around, the screens, news desk, and interview area all so new she could still smell the paint. "You're right, Spencer. I spent eight months as the noon anchor. This is exciting." Jordyn shifted in her chair. "You're a WFRN veteran. Tell us a little about what you did before this opportunity."

Jordyn noticed Spencer connected with the camera as if he could see every viewer watching. "I grew up in the area, but my

WFRN career started at the Binghamton station. If I look familiar, I was probably the reporter delivering the Broome County news." He chuckled, "Which for outside live shots, I think it rained or snowed nearly every time." Spencer made the transition easy for Rich to share how he came to the area and WFRN.

Courtney shifted her attention from the camera to her colleagues. "I guess that leaves me. Like Spencer, I've been a reporter, but I was based here. That will help me as I visit area businesses in Chemung, Steuben, Schuyler, and Broome Counties. I know the area well." She paused. "However, we don't know each other. We realize you, the viewer, are getting acquainted with us too. Each of us took a little time in front of the camera to share a little bit about ourselves. What do you think? Should we play it?"

"Absolutely." Spencer answered on behalf of the team.

With the video packages playing, the four leaned back in their chairs.

"What a rush!" Rich pumped his fist in the air.

Courtney rolled her shoulders and neck. "That's not what I was going to say. I'm so nervous my stomach has been doing flip-flops."

Natalie's voice boomed across the stage. "Great start everyone. Don't lose the momentum."

Jordyn watched the monitor where Courtney's package ended and Rich's began.

"Aw, that was great, Court. You're a literacy volunteer," Spencer noted.

"With a cat named Russell," Rich added.

When it was Spencer's turn, his video showed him in Vestal at the football field where Carson played. "I'm Spencer Collins. I'm an Elmira Free Academy graduate, and earned my degree from Syracuse. I'm a son and a brother. This is the baby of the family, Carson. He's a senior and I'm glad I'm not a sports reporter because I can't be objective." He nudged the high schooler and then grew serious. "Truth be told, I don't think I can be objective about *Early Rise and Shine*, either. I'm really excited to share the desk with Rich and Courtney. And Jordyn? I think she's the best in the business. I've been a fan for a long time." He held up an old newspaper clipping that the camera zoomed in on. It was the Hart Sextuplets on their thirteenth birthday. There was Jordyn with braces, glasses, and a good inch taller at the time than Ryan.

Jordyn turned her focus from the monitor to her co-anchor. "I didn't know you followed our story."

He shrugged. "My nose for news started young. But it's true, Jordyn. I think you're a great journalist. We're going to have an amazing ride."

. ♡ ♡ ♡

Spencer wished he could rewind the last minute and say anything that would take the bewildered look away from Jordyn. Did his compliment scare her? Was he coming off as fake? Whatever she was thinking, her video package started and she pursed her lips and watched.

He couldn't help but observe as Jordyn's life played out before her. When her voiceover reflected on the nation embracing the family tighter as they grieved the loss of her mother, Jordyn sat rigid, devoid of emotion. Something told Spencer this wasn't even the hundredth time she's had to share the heartbreaking story with the country. What did seem new while Spencer watched was the amused expression Jordyn carried as the Hart Sextuplets played volleyball during a vacation. James and Kelly collided. Jordyn ate a face full of dirt in pursuit of a dig. Ryan seemed to be the natural athlete of the six.

And it was Ryan WFRN approached for a congratulations message. He was in a living room area with cream walls and no pictures. The couch was a dark brown and looked like it had seen better days. "Jordy, you started as the family tattler, but look at you. You might not be as great as coffee, but you're also what every morning needs. Congrats, Sis."

Courtney leaned toward Jordyn. "Aw, that's so sweet."

Suddenly, two more figures appeared on the couch. Jordyn's eyes narrowed as the couple held hands and faced the camera. "Jordyn's been my helper and right hand for a long time."

"Oh, Dad." It was almost a whisper, but Spencer heard her talk to the screen.

Mr. Hart squeezed his wife's hand.

Shelly Hart smiled as she looked at him, then the camera. "Jordyn, I've known you for a very long time. You've worked hard for this. Congratulations. We love you."

The video faded to black and the show went to commercial. Spencer stretched his legs and nudged Jordyn. "So that was nice. You have a lot of people who love you."

She reached under the desk and pulled out a granola bar. "Lucky me."

"What? Your family seems very close. What's wrong with that? You'll notice my dad wasn't part of any welcome message."

Jordyn stuffed that snack down like a pro.

Was she hungry? Nerves? Avoiding an answer?

She dusted off her lap, checked her teeth with a compact mirror, re-applied her lipstick, and adjusted herself in the chair. "My family is close."

Natalie announced thirty seconds in their earpieces.

Spencer straightened in the chair and fixed his tie. "I don't understand."

Jordyn faced the camera, so her answer looked like she was telling the audience her personal thoughts. "Shelly isn't family."

Once the show wrapped, Vince walked onto the set, clapping his hands. Joe and Natalie were behind him.

"Congratulations on a fantastic show. Let's meet in the conference room at ten. I'd like to go over what worked, what we can tweak, what's happening tomorrow. Then, let's go out to lunch to celebrate. My treat." Vince ran a hand through his silver mass of hair. "See you at ten."

Spencer walked by the live monitors, Julia Tumeric's face on all the set screens. *First show over. Thank you, God.*

Vince was already seated in the conference room when Spencer filtered in with a fresh cup of coffee. Natalie was behind him, and she made a beeline for the empty seat next to Jordyn. Spencer took a glance around and pulled a chair out next to Joe.

Natalie sounded as if she had finished a handful of energy drinks. "Our Facebook page is blowing up. You guys killed it today."

Rich and Courtney shared a high-five.

Spencer unlocked his phone and opened the social media app.

Joe scrolled through his phone. "Collins, you are something of a heart-throb on here. The ladies love you."

Jordyn looked away as soon as Spencer locked eyes with her.

He shrugged. "I'm sure it's the sweet grandmothers. They tend to fall in love with me."

Vince chuckled, but quickly returned the focus back to the show. "I'd like to go through each segment and share our thoughts. Joe, cue us up."

Spencer glanced at a few of the Facebook posts and closed his phone. Judging by the app, it did look like a lot of people tuned in. Now for the critique.

The re-watch took as long as the show itself. Vince was into detail. Not just what the viewers saw, but the tech things off screen that affected the show. He noted a couple of times Rich used his hands to the point of distraction. There were a couple volume issues. On the plus side, he loved the segues they used. The banter was natural. "Bottom line? The four of you look like you've been a team for a long time. That was my goal for this first show."

"Second shows and beyond are a challenge. The high of the first show starts to fade. Don't let it happen. Keep bringing your best." Joe challenged.

"And on that note, let's go to lunch." Vince stood.

Since their work day was done, Spencer decided to take his vehicle and head home after. He looked for Jordyn, wondering if her plan was the same and if not, would she want to ride with him. They hadn't been alone since the promotions. The argument. The almost kiss.

She was already out of the conference room, so Spencer headed to their desks, hoping to catch her there. He was a few steps away from her area when he saw a huge vase full of roses taking up most of her desk.

"Wow. From your dad?" Spencer leaned in and took a whiff. There had to be about two dozen of the red flowers in the wide vase.

She shook her head. "No. Kent Misny."

Spencer pulled back with a wince.

Anchored Hearts

CHAPTER TEN

Jordyn's eyes widened as Spencer backed away from the bouquet as if it held bees. His smile disappeared and he dug in his pocket and produced a set of keys. Was he upset about Kent sending flowers?

"Did you want something, Spencer?" She tucked a strand of her hair behind her ear, trying to appear casual.

He held up a faded WFRN lanyard containing the keys. "Did you want to drive to lunch together?"

Jordyn froze at his invitation. The last time they were in a car together, they nearly kissed. "Thanks, but I think I'm going with Natalie." She crossed her arms.

Natalie leaned back in her chair without looking at the two. "Sorry, Jordyn. My seats are full of clothes my grandma wants me to drop off to charity. I plan to drive myself."

Oh, great.

Spencer didn't wait for further excuses. "C'mon, I'm hungry."

Jordyn silently followed him to his truck, her heart pounding harder with each step. Her brain knew she had to apply the brakes to every good thing she was seeing in Spencer. Her heart wasn't getting the message. If only she could convince Spencer he didn't have a chance because of Kent's grand gesture. If only she could convince herself.

Once they buckled in, Spencer turned to her, his kind smile focused on her. "I'm just going to come right out and say it."

Jordyn lungs tightened and all oxygen left the vehicle. She wanted to reach for the door handle and escape, but every part of her felt weighted with sandbags. "Okay. Go ahead."

He winked. "We were amazing today, right? I think the show could compete against bigger cities and we could beat them in quality and ratings."

She breathed in the deep air that suddenly returned. "Absolutely. I mean, we crushed it. All of us."

He nodded and started to drive. "I knew you'd understand. Bragging isn't something I want to be known for, but we've worked hard the last few months. It showed."

"Vince and Joe are right, though. We can't get complacent. If anything, we have to work harder."

Spencer agreed and continued to drive in silence for a while.

Jordyn, her breathing back to normal, pulled out her phone and checked messages. Kent wanted to make sure she got the flowers.

Gotta make sure I keep my anchor girl happy so I keep my slot!

128

She rolled her eyes. Of course all those roses were about him.

Spencer broke the quiet. "Reading all your congratulatory texts?"

Jordyn let out a sarcastic chuckle. "Not quite." She sent a quick message back to Kent.

Thanks for the gesture. They smell great.

"So, Kent really went all out with those flowers." Spencer's words were tentative, like the time she crossed a wooden bridge with a couple missing planks.

"Looks that way." *Let's keep this generic. No need for Spencer to know Kent wasn't romantic.*

He glanced over, and that small look sparked like a million volts of electricity between them. Spencer had this energy about him she'd never experienced before. He had a power to distract her focus and render her senseless. If only they weren't in a moving vehicle. Would she jump out? Or move closer to experience a kiss?

"He doesn't know you well. Roses aren't the way to your heart." Spencer returned his gaze to the road, but his tone was confident.

"Kent's known me longer than you have." *Reign in the sparks, Jordyn. Reign it in.*

"True, but he doesn't pay attention." Spencer pulled into a vacant parking space on the street and turned off the ignition. He unbuckled his seat belt and shifted toward her.

Jordyn swallowed in hopes of not expelling a nervous cough. "And you do?"

Girl, you're opening a door you might not be able to close.

Spencer took the keys out of the ignition and held them. "Your favorite scent is honeysuckle. It's the perfume you use."

She shook her head. "Kent might know that. Honeysuckles are hard to turn into a pretty bouquet. It's more of a bush."

His grin widened. "True. But he could have bought mums."

Jordyn narrowed her gaze. Where was he going with this? "Why would he do that?"

He sobered and kept his focus on her with such resolve she thought the car might implode from heat. "The real question is why didn't he? Kent should have bought yellow mums. You enjoy them. He got the most generic flower a guy could get that has no personal connection."

She nibbled on her lip, determined not to show her hand. Or heart. "Why should I receive mums?"

"You made a beeline for them when we toured Julia's house, bypassing all conversation to head for those yellow mums. And when I'm out on that deck, that's where my gaze always goes. I always think about you and how you enjoyed those flowers."

Jordyn blinked. As dry as her throat was, her eyes suddenly had moisture. No one had pointed out something so intimate about her apart from family. No one had been so accurate. "That's…quite an observation." She found the strength to unbuckle her seat belt and open the door. "I see Vince's car. We better go in before the celebration turns into a haranguing."

By the time the pair entered the Italian chain restaurant, everyone was seated. Jordyn looked around the two tables placed together for a spot. Two vacant chairs remained on an end.

Rich picked up a buttered bread stick from the basket. "Sorry, you're last to arrive. I'm hungry. All those nerves vanished once the show ended and I couldn't wait to eat."

Spencer pulled the chair out for Jordyn and then sat next to her.

She opened her menu and smiled. "I'm the same way. I couldn't even eat my dry toast this morning."

Courtney raised an eyebrow. "Why would you ever want to eat that?"

Jordyn looked up and realized the team was watching her. "Habit, I guess. When we were kids, I was afraid my brothers and sisters were going to miss the bus, so I made toast for them first." She shrugged. "By the time I finished spreading grape jelly and peanut butter on five pieces of bread, I grabbed mine and ran down the driveway."

"It's just me and my brother, Jordyn. I find these big family stories fascinating." Joe confessed.

She rolled her eyes and nudged Spencer. "Apparently you aren't the only one. That picture you have of me from my teen years, Collins, is hideous."

Spencer chuckled. "I wasn't treating the picture like you were some celebrity. Mom and I loved watching the news about you all. Like Joe said, the big family element was curious. I remember Julia showing viewers how volunteers helped your parents with laundry. Your grandmother explained the schedule for feeding everyone. Although the picture was of you, I kept track of the Hart story."

Natalie grinned so wide that when she held up the menu, Jordyn knew it was to hide the laugh ready to escape. *I shouldn't have told her Spencer and I almost kissed.*

"I need to confess something about the Hart Sextuplets." Rich cleared his throat. "At my interview I wasn't completely honest about you, Jordyn."

She took in a deep breath, prepared for the worst.

"I said I wasn't aware of who you were. Truth was, I read so much about you to prep for the interview that I knew you hated the sextuplet attention. I've followed your life story as long as Spencer has."

.♡ ♡ ♡

Spencer glanced over at Jordyn as he drove her back to the studio. "You okay?"

She stared straight ahead, but nodded. "Thinking about what Rich said. I guess I should be mad, but since he was hired, he hasn't used me or my siblings for anything job related. He's great at what he does."

"I think it was mature of him to admit it. He didn't have to. And you're right, he's a natural."

Jordyn offered a mmm-hmm and switched topics. "I'm looking forward to the 'getting to know us' segment tomorrow. Rich was mysterious about his secret talent. Any ideas?"

Spencer shrugged, remembering his own footage from a couple weeks ago. Once that airs, I'll never live it down with the team. "Joe wanted to keep it a surprise."

She sighed. "I'm not very good with that. Does that mean you won't tell me what your segment is about?"

"Nope. You'll have to watch like the rest of the Southern Tier."

He pulled into the lot and instantly felt his pulse quicken. *Does she think of our near kiss as much as I do?* "What do you have going on for the rest of the day?"

Jordyn pulled out her keys. "I hope to catch up with Paige. I haven't seen her in a while. Whatever we do, we won't take long. I could go to bed now."

Spencer nodded. "That alarm was cruel this morning."

He put the gear in park and faced her, car running, seat belt on.

She giggled and reached for the door handle. "The first of many alarms."

As the door opened, Spencer scrambled for anything that would keep her close. "Say, if you ever want to hang with someone who doesn't care about your celebrity, you can call me."

She dropped her hand to her side, eyes wide. "That's kind, thank you. It's not the issue that it was when we were kids."

"Still. I'm a phone call away."

Jordyn reached for her purse and pushed the door wide, unbuckling the seat belt and climbing out in one fluid moment. "Thanks again. For everything. But, I can't call you Spencer. Not like that."

Her words were fast and forced before she ducked back inside the vehicle to deliver the final blow. "Not ever."

Spencer could still hear Jordyn's door slam as he made dinner later in the evening. The look on her face—not angry, but resolute. Yet, she seemed sad. Almost like she was rejecting him under duress. As he stirred the spaghetti sauce, he considered her answer. It wasn't like he was asking her on a date, at least not officially, even if he had been fishing to gauge her interest. Well, now he had it.

Lord, really could use some guidance here.

Prayer was still new and as far as Spencer found it, awkward, but it felt right the more Spencer tried. Satisfied he'd done everything possible for now with the Jordyn issue, he checked the garlic bread in the oven and moved to the fridge to pull out a bag of prepared salad. When Spencer turned to the counter, he discovered his dad standing on the other side. Spencer opened the plastic bag and quickly surveyed his dad's appearance. The good news was the older man reached for a piece of lettuce and nibbled on it. He was upright and not swaying. On the other hand, his jaw was set and emotions in check.

"I want my truck back."

And there it is. Spencer sighed and rubbed the back of his neck. "Dad, we've been over this. Carson needs it for school. We only have two vehicles."

"I called the local fire department. It's volunteer. They need more hands. I can be a big help." His father's hands were steady as he enjoyed another piece of lettuce.

"How would that work? You don't know when a call might come in. Is it possible for you to take Carson to school, pick him up, and yet be available for a fire call? What about the days the alarm doesn't sound? That means you have a vehicle and time to waste. That's a dangerous combination." *I sound like the parent patronizing a child. But it has to be said.*

"The truck's in my name."

Spencer recognized the tone. His dad was drawing a line in the sand.

"So you pull rank and leave Carson without a vehicle his senior year? He also has football practice and a job. Dad, he needs a vehicle." *More than you do.*

"Maybe it's time to look into getting a third one."

The oven timer went off, and Spencer walked over and took out the bread. He then went to the cupboard and reached for three plates. "I don't know. Having another car doesn't resolve my concerns about your free time and what you would do with a vehicle."

"You don't trust me." His dad's steely gray eyes made it clear it wasn't a question.

Spencer closed his eyes for a moment. His only goals for the evening had been dinner and bed. Fighting with his father wasn't something he planned on or had the energy for. He spun toward the counter. "Okay. You want the truth? I don't trust you. The last times I've seen you in a vehicle, you were intoxicated. Imagine you with a car after a few beers with Smitty." He locked eyes with his father, refusing to back down. "At the very least, Carson gets left at school. The worst? You get in an accident and get hurt. Or kill someone else. Someone has to think about that scenario."

The elder Collins banged his fist on the counter with enough force that the salad bowl moved a couple inches. "Enough! You think the worst. You always have, Spencer. Give me some credit. If you thought more positive and didn't have your hands gripped so hard on everything, maybe—" He stopped, his breath ragged.

Spencer swallowed. "Maybe what?"

"Your mother would still be alive."

Anchored Hearts

CHAPTER ELEVEN

Jordyn stood in front of the family white board and glanced one more time at Paige's schedule. She was supposed to be done with her hostess job at the hotel at six. It was after seven, and the youngest Hart still wasn't home. Or answering texts.

Jordyn walked into the living room and found her dad and Shelly on the couch. Gigi chewed on a squeaker toy at her dad's feet. The two adults looked up as Jordyn sat on a chair opposite them.

Her dad put down the remote. "Everything okay?"

She shrugged. "I don't know. I wanted to hang out with Paige tonight before I go to bed. She isn't home."

He looked to Shelly. "Did Paige say anything to you this morning?"

"Not about working late. She said a conference was coming to town and expected to be busy."

Jordyn nibbled on her bottom lip. It was more information than she had. "I haven't seen her in forever. Come to think of it, I've hardly spent time with anyone but the WFRN team lately."

Her dad chuckled and handed the remote over to his bride. "You've been pretty busy, but we finished watching *Early Rise and Shine* a few minutes ago on DVR. The hard work paid off. Amazing show."

Shelly nodded. "Jordyn, you all looked like you could have been sitting with Julia representing the network in Manhattan."

Gigi hit the squeaker and gnawed at the toy harder for accelerated sound.

"Thanks. Speaking of Julia, she left a voicemail congratulating us." Jordyn remembered the flowers. "Oh. Kent Misny also sent me a bouquet of roses."

More chuckles from her dad. "He's a man on a mission."

"His agenda is making sure he has a slot on WFRN. Not me." Jordyn pushed away images of Spencer.

Shelly seemed able to read her mind. "You and Spencer Collins are perfect together. It's like you've anchored together for years." She winked. "He's easy on the eyes, too."

Jordyn glanced at her dad. If he was offended by the observation, there wasn't any indication. He put his hand on her knee and squeezed.

"Shelly's right. You two have amazing chemistry. Then again, so do Rich and Courtney. God's got a big plan for all of you. This show is going to be a game-changer for the area."

She winced at the God mention. Another by-product of marriage to Shelly. Her dad was back in church for the first time since her mom's funeral. "That's what we're counting on. I'd love to see viewers waking up with hope for their day and where they live."

The squeaking toy noise seemed to bounce off the walls. No one seemed distracted or annoyed by it, while Jordyn was ready to throw the toy down the garbage disposal. Stifling a yawn, it was time to head upstairs.

"I'm going to call it as far as trying to hang with Paige. If you see her, tell her I miss her."

"Will do. Love you, Jordy." Her dad's rich voice comforted her as she started to the stairs.

"Have a good night. Don't let the bedbugs bite." Shelly smiled as she delivered the familiar line she'd sang to them back when she was one of the volunteers serving after the accident. A saying she hadn't heard in years.

Jordyn paused, her hand on the iron railing. "Right. Don't let the bedbugs bite."

She completed the climb upstairs and went into her room. From her window she could see headlights pulling up the driveway. Paige? After a couple steps, Jordyn reached the windowsill and detected Paige's little SUV parking next to her car. Just as Jordyn was ready to close her blind and prepare for bed, she saw Paige trip and land on the sidewalk. That poor girl forced to wear heels for hours on end. As Paige regained her stance and kept walking, Jordyn turned from the window and made her way to the bathroom. Maybe tomorrow she could finally catch up with her sister.

. ♡ ♡ ♡

Spencer shifted in his rolling chair as he stared at the monitor. Natalie asked the morning team for their "I Love It" ideas so she could debut the segment for Friday. Joe advised them to think of things that would make viewers lives easier, local events to promote, or feel-good stories. With his dad driving the truck to the fire station for a meeting, Spencer could think of little else. Definitely not a love it idea.

He could sense Jordyn's presence before she sat across from him with that honeysuckle smelling perfume.

Looking up, she smiled and placed her purse down. "Hey, Spencer. Another good show today. Sophia told me we're starting to get fan mail." Jordyn waved a handful of envelopes with her other hand.

He leaned forward with a stretched-out hand. "You mean the *Early Rise and Shine* team?"

She shook her head. "Sophia said this batch is for us. I know social media has been heavy for the four of us, but she said older viewers send emails and letters. Looks like the mature audience has spoken."

Spencer accepted the envelopes she handed him and opened one. "Maybe this will help me come up with ideas for the "Love It" segment. Right now all I have is a blank screen."

Jordyn worked on her mail, pulling a piece of stationary out. "What's so hard? Think of your brother's football team or the pizza where he works. Didn't you say the cashier at the gas station dances as she finishes transactions? Boom. There's your list." She scanned the paper as he typed out her thoughts.

"Excellent. I had a brain freeze, couldn't think of anything. I guess my mind's on my dad—" Spencer glanced over when he noticed Jordyn wasn't offering any feedback.

Her hand shook as she held the paper, her cheeks moist as she wiped at the corner of her eyes.

Spencer rose out of his chair and handed her a tissue. "What's going on?"

Jordyn bit at her lip and shook her head.

Just what did that person write?

"Can I read it?" He waited while she sniffled and dabbed her cheeks. She thrust it in his hands and he brought it closer.

Jordan Heart,

Everyone is sick of hearing your sob story. Anyone who has lived in the Finger Lakes area knows your mom was a great reporter who died too soon. You're not all that. Find a different line of work and quit using her death to promote yourself.

Signed,

Over It

Spencer dropped the paper in the trash can. "Never pay attention to a letter the writer didn't have the courage to sign."

Jordyn sighed. "What if it's true?"

"Did you read the comments on social media? Remember the ratings from Julia's interview? You received that letter because the person felt comfortable enough to write it. Viewers are invested in you and your family. They feel they have grown up with you or raised you. And with that, people think they can offer unsolicited opinions." Spencer wasn't sure how he was able to string the words together as he fought the fire in his gut. Why did bullies pull stunts like that?

She looked up, a small smile forming. "They didn't even spell my name right."

Her chuckle offered proof the tears were about to subside.

Spencer held her gaze instead of reading his mail. "Do you enjoy what you do?"

Jordyn looked around the office with television screens on the wall. Phones ringing. Colleagues typing on their laptops. "Yes. I love working here." There was a clump of mascara on the edge of her eye.

"Then forget the haters." He took a fresh tissue and held it up. "You have a little something on your eyelash." His voice caught as he raised the thin paper.

Jordyn swallowed as she blinked and dabbed near the spot. "Oh. Probably makeup from my crying."

He nodded as he attempted to point to the clumped area.

She swiped everywhere except where the black goo resided. "Can you just get it? I don't feel like running to the bathroom for this."

Spencer grasped the tissue and bent down, lightly reaching for the mascara with a quick pinch. He lingered in the shared space for a long pause, the room heating up like a blow torch to ice. He cleared his throat. "Got it."

Jordyn nodded, her focus on him and not the paper he was ready to toss in the garbage. She exhaled, and he could feel his neck warm.

If we could be anywhere but in the middle of a news room. Spencer backed up and returned to his desk. "I found another idea to add to the I love list for Natalie."

She cocked her head. "What's that?"

Spencer lifted up the box. "Quality tissues."

Her chortle filled the room as she wiped at her eye again. "Something tells me Natalie's looking for more."

He nodded as he resumed staring at his screen. *Me too, Natalie. Me too.* Spencer shook away the longing and started typing.

It was almost time to leave when his text notification went off.

Home from fire department. All is well.

Spencer's shoulders relaxed as he closed the phone. He wasn't sure when the roles shifted, but he felt like a parent waiting for his teen to return with the family car. *Lord, is this how it's going to be every time dad has the car?*

CHAPTER TWELVE

Jordyn stifled a yawn as Joe closed the conference room door.

He returned to the head of the table in two strides and smiled. "Good news. Vince hired an outside firm to survey our viewers and the results are in."

Spencer placed his forearms on the table and leaned in. "What did you discover?"

Joe's grin widened. "The people watching consider you all part of their morning routine. They love when we showcase who you are away from the show." He looked down at a piece of paper, his index finger moving down. "Multiple responses indicated they consider the *Early Rise and Shine* team part of their family."

Wow. I thought the process would take months, not weeks. "That's great. Vince must be happy."

Natalie bit her lip. Was she trying to suppress a laugh?

Joe shook his head. "Yes, but he's already thinking of what else we can do to bring more viewers in, and have them as emotionally attached as the ones who replied to the survey." He opened a folder. "And we have a theme we're running all next week. 'At Home with...' Vince wants a segment each day next week featuring each of you at home. Talk about how long you've lived in the area. Share Thanksgiving traditions. Produce something from the home that means a lot to you."

Spencer coughed and reached for his water bottle.

Courtney shifted in her chair. "Are we filming where we live now, or where we grew up? I live alone in an apartment. My family's hosting Thanksgiving in Horseheads, though." A local family.

"Natalie will assign a crew to your family home. See if you can bake a pie with your mom or something."

Before she could respond, Spencer jumped in. "We're staying at Julia's house. Will viewers figure that out?"

Jordyn considered previous shows where Julia opened up about her private life, which was rare. The only time a crew filmed locally was right at WFRN and an exterior shot of Julia's childhood home. "It's okay, Spencer. Viewers have heard whispers that she owns a place in the area, but only a handful of people actually know where. Even less have even been there. I think you could film in the living room with the fireplace on and everyone would be in awe of the view."

Joe looked to Jordyn. "Any issues?"

She thought about Evan working the camera to plug whatever latest idea he had. Ryan probably refusing to show up. Shelly being interviewed as the family matriarch. Jordyn's stomach curdled at the image. "I'll figure it out."

Rich looked up from his phone, his piercing blue eyes focused on our boss. "I live in a tiny apartment that barely fits me and my stuff. I'm going to Saratoga Springs Thanksgiving weekend."

Jordyn couldn't place the tune Joe started to hum as he looked at his notes. He nodded and chuckled. "Got it. Rich, before you leave, we'll tape you bringing a pie to the Hart house. It will give viewers the perspective of an individual stepping into the chaos that is Jordyn's family."

Rich offered a thumb's up. "Works for me."

"Thanks for the love, Joe."

Spencer rose his hand. "What if I joined that visit for my segment? Two bachelors showing up and seeing the big family up close?"

What's his angle here?

"No, let's go with Rich. What I like about your story Spencer is it's a men's world. Plus, your brother is known to some viewers for his football accolades. I don't want to rob you of the family experience." Joe smiled and looked at his phone. "Okay, Natalie will follow up with the details. I have another meeting, so I'll see you all later."

Courtney was first to move her seat next to Natalie so Jordyn decided to stand and stretch her legs. Rich and Spencer were in the corner, so once Jordyn felt less stiff, she headed over.

"Spencer, why the interest in my house? Julia's place is a lot less lived in than where I reside."

He cleared his throat and avoided direct eye contact. "Honestly, us Collins men and our holiday preparations are boring. I'm afraid I'll put the viewers to sleep. No chance of that if I was going to your place."

Jordyn folded her arms against her chest. "I'd take a quiet experience any day." She turned toward Rich. "Don't bring a pie. We'll have a lot of them. Bring something random that will keep viewers talking."

Rich's eyes widened. "Like ice cream?"

Jordyn noticed out of the corner of her eye that Spencer was using his phone, most likely not engaged in the conversation. As soon as he finished typing, he put the cell down and stepped forward. "Any ideas, Collins?"

"Uh, pumpkin? You were talking pie ideas?"

With that, Jordyn took his reply as her cue to return to her desk. She rolled her eyes and started for the news room when she noticed Spencer's phone light up. It wasn't the most mature thing to do, but she slowed her pace to steal a glance at the incoming text.

Yeah, I'll help keep Dad sober for the taping

CHAPTER THIRTEEN

Spencer placed the turkey breast in the oven and set the timer. Thanks to his mom's notes, he had a pumpkin pie cooling before noon. Natalie promised a camera crew would show before two o'clock to capture meal setup.

Carson sauntered into the kitchen and stretched until his arms nearly hit the dusty ceiling fan. "Wow. Smells good. Never put this much effort in before." He glanced around the kitchen.

"We didn't have WFRN coming in. It's important that *Early Rise and Shine* viewers see us as a normal family." Spencer leaned back and tilted his head toward the bedrooms. Not a good sign Dad wasn't up yet.

"I'll keep an eye out." Carson's voice and tone sounded more like an adult than the kid brother Spencer pictured him as. The high school senior was over six feet, and thanks to strength training and conditioning, he was a solid mass of muscle. No more chubby layers or baby face.

Spencer swatted his hands toward his brother. "No. That's not your job." He cleared his throat. "It's mine. Besides, Natalie wants to make sure we talk football. Viewers love high school sports around here. The fact that you guys made the playoffs and you were the Southern Tier's athlete of the week makes you a great conversation topic."

Carson opened the fridge and unscrewed the cap off a milk jug labeled with his name and drank from it. Another sign mom was gone. At least Spencer bought a half-gallon just for Carson so no one else got the backwash. Carson returned the milk to the fridge and wiped his mouth on his sleeve as he leaned against the counter. "Maybe some college girls will notice."

They chuckled and Spencer rolled his eyes. "There will be plenty of time for that. You need to finalize college plans and graduate high school."

"I know. No need to nag." Carson let out a long sigh. "Coach is helping me narrow the options. I'm a little behind on applications but recruiters said no worries. What about you, big brother? How are things with Jordyn?"

Before Spencer could reply, he heard movement in the hallway and looked toward the bedrooms. Dad emerged, shuffling, but clean-shaven and wearing a smile. Instead of his frayed robe, he'd dressed in a nice pair of corduroys and a sweater Mom bought him a few Christmases ago. Even his hair was combed and slicked back.

The brothers exchanged looks, eyes wide.

"Sorry I'm late getting up and about. Hip's giving me more trouble than usual." His words weren't slurred.

"You're dressed up. Did Spencer make you?"

Dad's laugh was as hearty as roast beef on a Sunday. "No, Carson. I thought it would be a good idea to look nice for Spencer's work friends. It's Thanksgiving and seemed like the right thing to do." With that, he maneuvered to the coffee maker and started his morning caffeine ritual.

Just as Natalie said, camera operator Sam Pellicano texted he was at the door. Spencer sprinted to greet him as the oven timer sounded.

Carson's voice carried from the kitchen. "I've got the turkey."

Spencer rolled the sleeves up on his cable sweater and opened the front door.

Sam offered a two-fingered salute. "Happy Thanksgiving."

"Sorry you have to work. Hopefully we'll make this quick so you can enjoy a nice dinner." Spencer gestured him in, and Sam took the gear off his shoulder and placed it on the floor.

"I still have to film Jordyn. My fiancée is making her first turkey, so I'm not sure how it's going to go. She's watching YouTube for hints."

The two chuckled before they transitioned into work mode.

"Okay, just do whatever you need to do. I'll capture some footage. Natalie said you have scripted stuff to share. We'll do that last."

Spencer nodded. "I think you remember Carson from Vestal football. He just took the turkey breast out. The potatoes are almost done, and then I'll mash them." He turned to his dad. "How are the dinner rolls coming?"

The camera light turned on and so did the elder Collins grin. "A-okay, son. Two-minutes-and-they-will-be-done."

Sam bit his lip as the older man enunciated every word.

"Dad. Talk normally. Ignore the camera." Spencer ran a hand through his hair.

Carson faced the two, holding up a bowl of blueberries. "My job's done. The fruit is ready."

Dad looked to the camera, then the table. "You were always such a picky eater, Carson. That one Thanksgiving when your mother spent hours making the meal for her parents and us—you started to cry because all you wanted was blueberries." His laugh was faint, but Spencer knew the camera would pick up the audio.

Carson opened his mouth, probably to protest, but he picked up a blueberry. "She stopped everything to find a store that sold them."

Spencer nodded. "We never missed a year serving them."

The timer sounded again and the three turned their attention to the rolls. Dad reached into the potholder drawer and slowly put one on as the buzzer repeated. Finally he was able to pull out the cookie sheet full of bread, browned on top.

Spencer noticed something he hoped Sam didn't capture.

His dad's hands were shaking.

. ♡ ♡ ♡

Jordyn leaned over the stovetop to inspect the green beans. They didn't look anything like her mom's recipe. "Who added the almond slivers?"

Shelly turned toward Jordyn, apple in hand. "I did. It's a classic recipe." Her tone even, she returned to the countertop where she diced the apple.

James sauntered in humming a tune. "Smells good in here. Kelly and I wondered what time the camera person will arrive. We have a bet on whether dinner will be ready in time." He looked around at the stack of pans in the sink, the potatoes boiling, and the pumpkin pies cooling on the rack.

"Are you going to help?" Jordyn faced her younger brother, hands on her hips.

His tune stopped. "If you need me. Figured you'd want us to stay away."

Shelly's dicing slowed, but she remained in position.

Jordyn sighed and narrowed her gaze. "Fine. But that means not coming in here with ridiculous chat. Sam's due here at four-thirty." She gestured him to leave. "Tell the peanut gallery."

Once James retreated, she returned her focus to the beans. "We can't have the almonds in the beans."

Shelly kept slicing fruit. "Why is that?" a slight edge only the discerning would catch.

"Paige and Evan don't like them." Jordyn expelled a long sigh filled with hot air. "Besides, that's not our recipe. Every year we have beans without almonds. Celery and cream cheese. It's tradition."

When Shelly turned, she waved the vegetable peeler. "Jordyn, last year I was careful to follow every recipe and tradition that you grew up with. It's time you accept I'm not the neighborhood helper anymore. I'm part of this family." Her words came out as choppy as Seneca Lake waters.

"What does that mean?"

"I'm allowed to have a voice and to make choices. On holidays like this, it's fair that I incorporate my ideas and traditions as well." She put the peeler down and folded her arms. "And you are the only one giving me trouble every single step of the way."

Jordyn was about to debate when her father walked in, straight toward Shelly. "How are some of my favorite girls doing?" He planted a kiss on his wife's forehead.

Shelly reached for an orange and continued her work. "I think it's slowly coming together."

Her pointed remark hit Jordyn straight in the gut. She pushed the bean dish to the back of the stovetop, speechless. Once her dad left the area, she stalked to the refrigerator in search of the celery and cream cheese. The side dish all the kids groaned about until after Mom was killed. Jordyn pulled out the vegetable drawer and found broccoli, carrots, and an onion in its last days. No leafy, crunchy vegetable that made her remember her mother. "Unbelievable."

There were still twenty minutes left on the turkey so Jordyn marched to the mudroom and grabbed her red hooded jacket. She zipped it up over her black sweater and pushed on the garage door button. As soon as it opened, she walked out and started down the driveway.

With each pounding step on the blacktop, she silently lamented the situation. Shelly wasn't wrong, yet her grafting herself into the Hart family felt like a betrayal. And Jordyn's father, always her champion, now sided with his wife. Also, not a terrible thing, but still.

Jordyn was so immersed in processing it all she didn't hear Ryan enter the drive until he was nearly beside her.

He rolled down the window and leaned on the base of it, eyebrows raised. "Trouble?"

She stopped, angry tears forming. "If Shelly takes over everything, Mom's memory is gone."

Ryan put the car in park and nodded. "I get it. It's hard. Do you want to drive around a bit and decompress?"

Jordyn looked at her watch. "There's not a lot of time. The turkey is nearly done and Sam will be here soon and—"

Her brother's laugh cut through the air. "Jordy, there are several people in that house who know how to take a turkey out of the oven and answer a door. It doesn't have to be you." He gestured toward the passenger side. "Get in."

. ♡ ♡ ♡

Spencer swallowed the last of his mashed potatoes as if he had just consumed concrete. The longer the meal went on, the more he noticed Dad's withdrawal symptoms. They still had to tape Rich's visit before Sam moved on to Jordyn's Thanksgiving.

Thankfully the doorbell spared Spencer from imagining further scenarios where Dad broke down and succumbed to a drink or had some kind of physical reaction to the lack of alcohol. Spencer sprinted to the front door before anyone could move.

Rich held up multiple bags of chips, different flavors. "Hey, I'm single. This is what we bring." His chuckle relieved the tension in Spencer's shoulders. The meteorologist continued. "Thanks for letting me switch up the schedule so I could come here instead of the Hart House of Chaos."

Spencer directed everyone to leave the dishes for later and gather in the living room to watch football with Rich. Carson didn't need to be told twice as he landed on a beanbag chair near the widescreen television. Their father moved slower, but made his way to his worn recliner.

With the camera on his shoulder, Sam turned the device on.

"Spence, what's your favorite team?" Rich opened a bag of wavy cheddar.

"Bills. This is their year."

Carson's mocking chuckle boomed over the TV commentators. "I bet you say that every year."

Rich finished eating a handful and turned toward the high schooler. "Okay, Mister-Athlete-of-the-Week, who do you root for?"

Carson reached over for a bag of sour cream chips and tore into it. "Patriots."

The colleagues leaned back and howled. Rich rolled his eyes. "Traitor. No true New York State resident aligns with any New England team." He ate another chip. "Ever."

While the two bantered, Spencer looked over at his dad, hands gripping the armrests. "Everything okay, Dad?"

The older man shuffled forward to the edge of the seat. "Think I need to walk that dinner off."

Carson shot a look toward Spencer.

Don't let this be a ruse to find a drink. "Oh, there's time. Stay here and watch the game with us."

"Naw, that score's a blowout. I'll putter around the backyard." With that, he stood and shuffled toward the patio door.

Once it closed, Spencer rose from his seat. "Sam, I think that's enough footage. My dad's hips give him a fit with the changing temps. I should check on him."

When Sam turned off the camera, Rich stood. "I have my family Thanksgiving to get to as well."

The five minutes it took for Sam and Rich to leave felt like another vein was ready to pop on Spencer's forehead.

Carson opened the curtain and watched the vehicles head down the long drive. "Okay, they're gone. Do you think he went to find a beer he hid?"

Spencer breathed in deep and let the air out slowly. "I'm going to find out."

. ♡ ♡ ♡

When Ryan parked the car behind Evan's and led Jordyn inside, the roasted turkey sat in the foil pan, cooling. The side dishes were done, and Sam texted he was five minutes out.

"Thanks for letting me vent." Jordyn knew her unsentimental brother would resist a hug, but she was thankful that once again he listened to her and let her spew until she got her frustration out of her system.

He patted her on the back. "Just remember Shelly's trying. You should, too."

She nodded but didn't respond. Her phone notification showed a text from Sam, saying he was in the driveway. Time to show the WFRN viewers how the Hart sextuplets celebrated Thanksgiving.

Sam began filming when their dad started carving the turkey. The elder Hart rolled up his sweater sleeves and balanced the platter, the turkey, and the knife with skill. As he sliced into it, steam rose and a waft of Thanksgiving goodness floated through the dining room.

"You know, one of these years one of you should take over the honors. Won't be long and you'll be married with families of your own." He glanced around the table to hear a chorus of groans.

Ryan snickered, recalling the familiar phrase they used as kids. "Not it."

Even Jordyn grinned.

Shelly put her napkin on her lap. "You all deserve a future full of happiness. Kelly, I remember catching you more than once when you were younger putting a pretend veil on your head."

"Until Evan threw his sweaty gym towel on me." Kelly rolled her eyes toward him.

He shrugged and reached for a roll, but Ryan slapped his hand.

"Dude. Dad's not done carving."

Jordyn glanced at Sam, who showed no expression. What everyone would think of this chaotic group.

Their father put down the knife. "The turkey is ready."

Evan started to put the bread in his mouth.

"Before we go crazy, Shelly, would you pray?"

The sextuplets looked at each other before bowing their heads. The prayer routine seemed buried with their mom, along with church and other faith matters. Once Dad saw Shelly for more than a neighbor, he returned to all the religious habits Jordyn long forgot or cared about.

As soon as Shelly uttered "Amen," James picked up the bowl of mashed potatoes and plopped some on his plate. The turkey platter passed from hand to hand. No one spoke for a few minutes as they poured gravy, consumed bread, and reached for seconds.

When everyone slowed down, Shelly reached for Dad's hand and held it. "If it's okay, I'd like to hear what each of you are thankful for."

Paige nearly choked on her water.

"It's a wonderful idea, sweetheart. We are so busy running around doing our own thing, we forget about others and what's going on in their lives. I'd love to hear everyone's thoughts."

Jordyn dabbed her napkin on the edge of her mouth. "You go first, Dad."

Shelly smiled and squeezed his hand. "Absolutely. What are you thankful for, honey?"

Twelve sextuplet eyes lasered in on their dad as he moved his plate and sat back. "So many things. For one, Shelly and how her love and patience brought me back to God. If it weren't for her, I would have lived in silent bitterness until my last breath."

Jordyn dropped her napkin on her near empty plate. Dad? Bitter?

He continued, "Of course, all six of you. You're discovering your own identities, making a difference in the world—"

"Dad, I'm twenty-four and still in college." Kelly looked to James, who was still working on the mashed potatoes.

"Sweetie, you and your brother were smart enough to know after high school you weren't ready. You worked until you knew what you wanted to do. Now you're both pursuing an education, and I'm very thankful for that."

Shelly released her hand and grinned. "Beautiful. I'll go next. I'm thankful for my faith. The Lord has sustained me through more than I can put to words." Her words floundered toward the end, but she continued. "Of course, being married in my mature years and gaining you all as bonus family. I'm blessed."

Jordyn felt the gazes on her, but she wanted to revisit Shelly's remark about her life rather than conjure up why she was thankful. "Uh, I love my work and the WFRN viewers."

Evan spoke through a fake cough. "And Spencer Collins."

Ryan snorted so hard he started gagging.

Before Jordyn could slap Evan, Dad stepped in with a stern, "Evan. Enough." He turned to Sam. "I'm sure that comment will be edited out, correct?"

She didn't dare look at her colleague. She didn't know Sam well, but if he told Spencer, it would be like a high school gym locker.

"We're good, Mr. Hart." Sam cleared his throat. "You should keep sharing, though. I'll wrap it up after that."

Jordyn regained composure and pointed at Ryan. "We might as well do this in birth order. Ryan?"

He glanced around the table and drummed his fingers on the table for a few moments. "Can I pass?" After a few seconds of silence, the Navy veteran sighed. "I'm grateful, but sharing isn't my style."

Shelly's smile diminished, but her tone remained upbeat. "It's okay. I understand."

Evan rose and moved his chair back. "No problem, I'm ready."

Jordyn heard someone mutter, "No surprise there." She felt her stomach tighten as Evan grinned like he had won the lottery.

He shimmied his hands together and faced Jordyn. "I'm thankful because I've been talking to Aunt Julia, and she helped me make some connections. So, for next year's twenty-fifth interview, we're going big. Way more than a live interview."

Paige took off her glasses and cleaned them with her long-sleeved shirt. "What did you do now?"

"We're going to have a reality show."

CHAPTER FOURTEEN

Spencer sighed when he didn't find Dad in the immediate backyard, or even among the pine where he liked to walk. Rubbing his arms to ward off the chill, Spencer kept walking the Turmeric property, heading down a hill that led to a pond.

There Dad sat, on a bench, face in his hands.

What's going on? Was he drunk? Hurt? Spencer picked up his pace. "Dad? You okay?"

The older Collins straightened and quickly brushed his worn jacket sleeve against the corner of his eyes. "Spencer, what are you doing here?"

He paused to catch his breath. Time to return to the gym. "Looking for you. Is anything wrong?"

The bench creaked as his dad slid over to make room. "I like talking to your mom when I'm outside. Makes me feel closer to her." His voice caught and he tried to recover. "I miss her so much, son. There are moments the pain overwhelms me."

Spencer reached out and placed his hand on his dad's knee. "I can't begin to imagine. You two had a great marriage."

There was a slow nod. "The best."

When Dad shifted his position on the bench, Spencer moved his hand. "How can I help?" He silently noted that his dad's leg twitched to a fast beat.

There wasn't a reply right away. The elder man gazed at his shaking hands, and then pushed them down on his moving leg. "I thought drinking would numb the grief."

Now Spencer was silent for a moment. "Mom always said only Jesus can heal our pain."

A sharp, mocking laugh flew into the air. "But He couldn't heal her."

Lord, how do I walk through this emotional landmine? "I felt the same for a long time." Spencer jammed his hands in his pockets for warmth. "Did you know I found her Bible? I've been reading it. If all I read were her notes, they would be helpful. But, I'm reading the actual verses, too. They're coming back to me. It's healing."

This time Dad's chuckle sounded sincere. "She sure loved that book. Her faith was solid, right to the end."

Spencer breathed in slowly before daring to speak. "Dad, I'm worried about the drinking." He braced himself for a tongue lashing. "I want to help, if I can."

A speck of life returned to his dad's eyes. "Appreciate your concern. It's becoming a problem, I know."

Great. Now to ask Joe Munson what rehab center he sent his brother to. "There's so many facilities that can help. I promise to take care of Carson while you're away—"

Dad threw his hands up faster than a referee at a football game. "Whoa, Spencer. You're moving way too fast. I didn't say a hospital for drunks is what I need."

Spencer swallowed hard. This could turn ugly any moment. "It's called a rehabilitation center. The staff is trained to help with the withdrawal symptoms and teach you how to live sober."

"I know how to do that." He chuckled as if Spencer had asked if rain was wet. "I don't reach for alcohol. Easy."

"Dad, it's not that simple. The withdrawal symptoms are brutal. The staff can also treat you medically. They will perform a full checkup and make sure your liver is functioning at optimum level. It's really the best place to go for alcoholism recovery."

This time the laugh was mocking as Dad stood and marched toward the house. After a few paces he stopped and turned toward Spencer. "I'll do this my way. I'm not an alcoholic."

Spencer stayed on the bench for a few moments, too tired to pray or think. Instead, he sighed. And willed himself to rise and begin a slow trek back inside.

. ♡ ♡ ♡

Jordyn steamed hotter than the mashed potatoes as she digested her brother's dinner announcement. Why did Aunt Julia give Evan so much favor? "What do you mean, a reality show?"

Evan beamed, as if ignorant of the fact his siblings stopped eating and were focused on his every word. "I told Aunt Julia how we wanted to do something big for our twenty-fifth. We threw around some ideas and when I mentioned a reality show, she connected me with an agent."

Ryan picked up his fork, but instead of using it to continue to eat, he pointed it repeatedly in Evan's direction. "We did not want to do something big. You can barely convince us to do the interview each year."

James and Kelly nodded in unison.

Dad cleared his throat. "Let's hear Evan out. I'm sure there's a reasonable explanation as to why he'd get an agent before talking to everyone."

"I'm not so sure." Jordyn scoffed, pushing her plate back. Suddenly her stomach felt full and shaky.

Evan held his hands up in mock surrender. "You'll love this. I promise."

Twenty minutes later, as Paige put the last plate in the dishwasher and Shelly cut the pumpkin pie, Ryan expelled a slow breath. He turned to Jordyn, then to Evan.

"So, do you believe me? Are you in?" Evan's voice cracked as he waited on Ryan's reaction.

Jordyn replied before Ryan had a chance. "You really planned this to honor Mom? This isn't about showcasing yourself?"

Evan nodded. "Promise."

"I think you're short on a lot of details. There's no way I'm signing anything until I know exactly what this show is about."

Evan nearly flew out of his chair as he rose. "Awesome. I have a lot to iron out. It will be a quality project. You won't be sorry for agreeing."

James rolled his eyes. "None of us have agreed."

Evan passed his younger brother by three minutes a piece of pie. "Yet."

Jordyn declined dessert and stalked off to the living room. She chose one of the recliners to avoid sharing space with the dog that was nestled on the couch. The Bills, the Hart family's favorite NFL team, were the night football game on television, but that was still a couple hours away. "I need out."

Dad entered the room, patting his belly. "Where are you going, Jordy? I thought we could stream the parade."

"I need some air. I'll be back for the game."

He tilted his head, studying her. "Weren't you outside before dinner?"

Jordyn kept her gaze on the mud room and didn't answer. She wasn't sure how to respond, anyway. How much getaway time did a Hart require? Being around Shelly and Evan, apparently a lot.

She found herself on Route 86 heading east, passing the Elmira exit and WFRN. After forty minutes of driving, accompanied by her Christmas playlist, a familiar driveway appeared. Her SUV navigated the curvy driveway lined with lights. "Okay, Collins. I hope you don't mind me crashing your Thanksgiving." Jordyn muttered as she parked and climbed out.

. ♡ ♡ ♡

Spencer choked on his coffee when Carson announced Jordyn had appeared in the driveway. He grabbed his phone and checked notifications to see if he missed a work text. Nothing. "Can you get the door? I'll be right there."

Carson snickered, but at least he obeyed as Spencer jogged to the closest mirror and checked his hair. His outside stroll to find Dad earlier was a windy one, but nothing looked out of place.

When he reached the front door, Jordyn stood there in a green puffy coat, hands jammed in pockets. As soon as their gazes connected, Spencer felt the temperature rise. "Jordyn? Everything okay?"

She stepped forward. "I'm sorry. I needed out of the house and started driving. This is where I ended up." Her laugh was soft, almost apologetic.

Spencer looked around and realized Carson had already left the room. He inched closer, not sure if she wanted to take her coat off, or return outside. "Can I get you anything?"

With a shake of her head, Jordyn's glossy ebony hair moved with ease. "No, thanks." She glanced to the door. "Would you like to walk with me?"

His heartbeat accelerated as he nodded and dashed to the door to open it. She started with a brisk pace that Spencer matched. He quickly realized as she entered the wooded area and down the hill that his colleague knew exactly where to find the pond and bench.

"I'm sorry for interrupting your Thanksgiving." Jordyn didn't slow or sound breathy as they dodged twigs and rocks.

"No apology needed. We finished dinner and I was right here with my Dad not that long ago."

Jordyn nodded. "Everything okay?"

That's a good question. "Time will tell." They arrived at the bench and he gestured for her to sit first. "How about you? What's going on?"

Jordyn sat, her back against the wooden slats as she stared ahead at the pond. "Evan."

Ah, the mischievous brother. "Did he prank you?"

She sighed, her breath escaping like a breath of smoke against the cold air. "I wish." She turned toward Spencer. Her long eyelashes moving double time as snowflakes landed on them.

He edged closer, digging into his pocket to produce a pair of gloves for her. "You drove all this way. Feel free to vent."

Jordyn accepted the gloves and put them on. "Evan announced that he's been working with Aunt Julia to plan something big for the Hart sextuplets twenty-fifth birthday. They landed on the ridiculous idea of a reality show. He even has an agent thanks to her. What was she thinking?" Her words clipped together in a rush; those chocolate-colored eyes locked into his gaze.

"That doesn't sound like her. She's been very careful to protect each of you. A reality show sounds—"

"Tacky?" Jordyn huffed. "I know. That's what I can't get over. Evan says it's all about honoring mom and her memory."

An icy breeze swirled around them. "Do you believe him?"

Jordyn started to answer but closed her mouth. She shrugged and looked down, silence filling the air.

Spencer noticed her back moving in a rhythm, like when one is having a good cry. "Hey." He took his hand and slowly lifted her chin. When she met his gaze with a moisture-stained face, Spencer used the same hand to brush softly at her cheek.

Jordyn took her gloved hand and pressed on his chest, leaning in. She moved until both hands were wrapped around his neck and he felt a stroke against the back of his hair as her mouth rested softly on his.

Steadying himself against the harsh wood, he didn't care if his movements gave him splinters or if the snow picked up and piled on them. She might have found him first in their kiss, but in seconds, he wrapped his arms around her waist and drew her in. The embrace deepened as he was certain she could feel his heartbeat through his coat and sweater.

Jordyn returned the emotion with matched intensity until she whispered his name and returned her hand to his chest. She broke off first, out of breath.

"I'm sorry. I lost control. That wasn't what I had planned when I came here." Jordyn slid down the bench and the distance felt like miles.

Spencer reached for her hand that had rested on his chest and held it. "Jordyn, it's okay. It was mutual affection, and I'm not sad it happened." His voice deepened. "At all."

"I, I'm not like that. I don't do spontaneous things like that. It was the emotions. I won't do it again. Promise." She sounded like a frightened little girl as she jerked her hand away and bolted off the bench.

He rose and attempted to stand closer, but she backed away. "Jordyn. It's obvious there's something between us. We can be professional and explore this, don't you think? I've never been so mesmerized by a woman as I am you."

She shook her head. "No. This was a mistake." Her tone was business-like and distant.

"Don't shut me out. You drove here. You asked for the walk." He sighed. "You kissed me first."

Jordyn wrapped her arms against her chest, but he wasn't sure if it was out of defiance or warmth. "I know. Like I said, a mistake." She glanced toward the house. "I have to go."

"Please. I need to understand. Is it the show you're worried about? We'd never jeopardize our work."

She bit her lip and started to walk away from him.

The tenderness of her earlier touch faded with each step. Spencer jogged to catch up. "I'm begging you. Give us a chance."

Jordyn stopped and confronted him, her face once again wet and her voice cracking from tears. "I can't. I made a vow."

Spencer longed to wrap her in his arms to take away her pain but her stance made it clear she was off limits. "That you won't date a colleague? We can work through it."

A sob escaped. "I'm sorry." She spoke in a near whisper. "I made a promise to myself the day my mother died I'd never be friends or more with someone who has an alcoholic in the family." She shivered and another cry let loose. "Spencer, it's not work. It's your dad."

Anchored Hearts

CHAPTER FIFTEEN

Jordyn spent the drive home tapping the steering wheel, reliving the most beautiful moment and yet another tragic one she could recall. Anyone else would dive head first into the hope and romance Spencer offered. Yet as Jordyn fought a headache as she pulled into her parking spot, emptiness filled her. Alcohol robbed her of everything as a child. It wasn't going to happen again. No matter how it hurt.

Ryan's truck was gone, but it appeared like James, Kelly, and Paige were still home. Jordyn walked through the garage and into the mud room hoping Paige would be up for some girl talk. Instead, she found her youngest sibling in the kitchen, heading toward the garage exit.

"You're leaving? The restaurant is closed for Thanksgiving, isn't it?"

Paige nodded without looking Jordyn in the eye. "I have this party to go to with friends from work." She pulled her keys out of her purse.

Jordyn raised her eyebrows. "Isn't it kind of late?"

"You're only a few minutes older than me, Jordy, not decades. You sound like Dad." Paige scoffed and gave a terse "See ya" and then slammed the mud room door.

Nice. First Evan, now Paige. What was happening to this family?

Jordyn sauntered into the living room, afraid of what or who she'd discover. Gigi was in the same spot on the couch when Jordyn had left, but now the canine was flanked by Shelly on the right and Dad on the left.

"Jordy, the game started. Want to join us?" Dad offered, gesturing to the vacant spot on the couch.

She rarely missed a Bills game but her headache throbbed. "I'm going to pass, thanks. Early morning tomorrow." As soon as Jordyn replied, she shuddered. With *Early Rise and Shine* back live, that meant she'd have to face Spencer.

"Everything okay?" Shelly's tone sounded full of concern.

Jordyn waved them off. "Fine. Tired is all. Good night." She climbed the stairs as if it were a mountain challenge, her legs weary thanks to her drives and drama.

Once she nestled into bed, replays of her harsh protest and Spencer's pained reaction flooded her mind. He had every right not to talk to her again because nothing about her vow was his fault. Jordyn double checked her phone alarm and pulled the eye mask down. If only it could hide all her grief and fears.

The next morning Jordyn pulled out her favorite red dress. It was a great choice to promote the Christmas season, and the bold color gave her confidence. Sitting next to Spencer, she'd need it.

Shelly was the only person downstairs when Jordyn entered the kitchen to make coffee. Her step mother stood in her robe sipping out of a WFRN mug, standing at the breakfast island.

"What are you doing up so early? These are morning show anchor hours." Jordyn placed the K cup in the machine and pressed "Brew" without looking Shelly's way.

"I haven't gone to bed yet."

Jordyn raised her eyebrows but didn't think much of it. Maybe it was a menopause thing. Grandma Hart spent most of her visits complaining of that.

Shelly sighed and put the mug down. "Paige isn't home yet."

What a bomb drop. Jordyn moved to the windowsill to look out at the drive. The exterior garage lights were still on, a Hart courtesy at night for the member not yet home. "Where is she?"

"I don't know. I texted and called but she didn't reply."

Jordyn's heart started to race. What if there was another accident? She started for the stairs. "I'm going to wake Dad."

Shelly shook her head. "I wish you wouldn't."

The coffee maker percolated at the same rate as Jordyn worried. "Shelly, she could be in a ditch somewhere. What if she's hurt?"

Shelly opened her mouth to speak, but they both spotted incoming headlights at the same time.

Jordyn felt her stomach juices settle as soon as the car door shut and footsteps headed toward the house. "That girl has some explaining to do." She checked her watch. "Unfortunately, I have to take that coffee to go and leave for work."

"Have a great show, Jordy."

Jordyn transferred her hot beverage into a travel cup and mumbled a thanks. She headed toward the mud room to collect her purse and coat, and passed Paige. "We were about to put out missing person posters."

Paige scoffed as she hung her keys on the hook. "Last I checked, I'm over eighteen." She narrowed her gaze, one Jordyn observed was without wearing glasses. "And you aren't my mother."

Jordyn buttoned up her dress coat and reached for her keys. "We'll talk later." She walked away before Paige could respond.

Once again Natalie greeted Jordyn inside the employee entrance with more questions than a detective during an interrogation. "Girl. I watched the Thanksgiving footage. What was

Evan thinking? A reality show? How about Julia? What's her angle? You have to tell me everything."

The two walked toward the newsroom, Jordyn's mind flooded her with questions. *What is happening with Paige? How is Spencer going to act after she rejected him? Will Evan really move forward with his crazy plan?* "Nat, there's so much to the Hart Thanksgiving it could be a two-part special. How about yours?"

Natalie handed her a printout of the national news updates. "Not so fast. You have something to tell me. What else happened?"

Jordyn felt like she was back with Spencer on the bench. Their heated embrace in the cold night was what romance novels were made of. Her reaction, however, would cause a reader to toss the book in the garbage. "Let's do lunch. There's a lot to unpack."

Natalie's eyes brightened, then dimmed. "We can't. Don't you remember? Joe wants you to do a live at noon with Kent Misny."

The mere mention of that boring businessman gave Jordyn's shoulder a slump worse than the economy Kent was always talking about. "Ugh. He is the last thing I need to deal with today." She looked up from the headlines to discover one of her own: Spencer heading her way.

. ♡ ♡ ♡

Spencer slowed his pace as soon as he saw Jordyn in the red dress that reminded him of a cardinal his mom had loved so much.

He prayed the entire drive in to have the right reaction to her rejection. Admiring her in that dress robbed him of focus. And the ability to string words together to form a complete sentence in her presence.

"Good Morning, Spencer." Jordyn forced him to stop. "Ready for all things Christmas on the show?" Her gaze landed dead center with his, and he couldn't discern if she was silently pleading him not to speak of last night, or daring him to.

"Absolutely. Thanksgiving is in the rearview mirror." Spencer broke the stare and offered a weak smile. "See you in a few. I need coffee before I do anything." He took a step toward the kitchenette.

"Natalie, I'll see you later. I need caffeine as well." Jordyn scurried ahead and opened the door to the beverage area. "Spencer, can we talk about last night?"

He brushed past her, images of them on the bench commandeering his thoughts. Spencer handed her a WFRN mug and reached for another. "I don't think there's anything left to say."

She inched closer to the coffee pot. "What I said wasn't personal."

Spencer rolled his eyes as he filled his mug, refusing to look her way. Taking in her flowery aroma was another matter. "Jordyn, it felt personal. I really don't want to rehash it, but I'll say this much— you rejected me. Then you explain that my father's grief is the reason why."

Jordyn took a step back. "That isn't true. It's his drinking problem and my grief. I never want to hurt the way I did when a drunk driver robbed us of our mother."

"Your world is very black and white. You can't control circumstances, Jordyn. Sure, shut me out because of the demons my father is fighting. But don't kid yourself. Alcohol will still seep into your life. It's too prevalent in this world not to." Although Spencer's feet felt like concrete blocks, he willed himself out of her presence. At least until they were live, on air, smiling for all of the Southern Tier to witness.

. ♡ ♡ ♡

Jordyn steadied her coffee cup as she poured. She didn't know what she expected from Spencer, but his words stung. She swiped at her cheek and marched to her desk, ready to create dynamic segues for the show. Anything to take her mind off Spencer Collins and the amazing kiss they shared.

Once the show wrapped, Natalie helped Jordyn take off the microphone and took her by the crook of the arm. "I hate to do this to you, but let's prep for your noon interview. After the noon broadcast, Joe has a team coming to dress the set for Christmas."

"What's to prep? Kent's done this before, and he has no problem doing all the talking."

Natalie smirked as she opened the door to the conference room. "True enough. His firm bought quite a bit of ad time so Vince wants to make sure Kent gets top-notch treatment. He was made VP, so you need to discuss that."

Jordyn sat down and opened the folder already placed on the table. "I was really hoping with *Early Rise and Shine* that my interview days with him were over."

"So you could focus on Spencer?" Nat pulled out the chair next to Jordyn and leaned back with a smile.

"Not funny." Jordyn pushed the folder back and faced her best friend. "He's really upset with me."

"You couldn't tell. The sparks between you two on the show make me want to look for a fan. Or a hose." Natalie snickered. "Seriously, what's going on? Even our social media blows up each morning with viewers wondering when you two will get together."

Jordyn bit her lip. "We kissed last night."

Natalie sprung forward in her chair. "You've been holding back. We need to get work done, but give me the short version."

"I drove out to Aunt Julia's after Evan's announcement. It wasn't anything I planned, but Spencer was there and we talked. He kissed me. Shared how he feels."

"And?" Natalie's voice rose in volume and tone.

Jordyn looked to the door and let out a "shush."

"And?" This time Natalie whispered.

"I let him down. He didn't take it well, thought it was personal because I mentioned my vow about alcohol. His father has a drinking problem and it's too close to home." Jordyn took in a deep breath and held it for a moment before expelling. "He'll probably ask Joe and Vince for a transfer out of the show."

"That's not going to happen. Jordyn, you're guarding your heart so hard you risk never letting anyone in. I understand why you have your vow, but Spencer's a great guy. You're both great communicators, dynamic leaders, and loyal to family."

Jordyn reached for the folder and re-started reading the notes. "I'm not heartless."

Natalie put her hand on Jordyn's arm. "No. You aren't. But the rumors are out there. Reporters you refused to date. Kent's had plenty to say given he can't accept he's a huge bore. Now Spencer. It's not a bad idea to consider opening yourself up to a relationship."

There was zero chance Jordyn was going to show Natalie how difficult this conversation was to hear. Her temptation was to run to her desk, grab all the chocolate out of her drawer, and eat in a corner away from everyone. She looked up and smiled. "Thanks, Nat. I appreciate it. And I will work on it. Promise."

Three hours later, Jordyn sat opposite Kent Misny in the leather chairs, a glass tabletop between them. She ignored the red light on the camera and lobbed her first verbal softball his way. "So, Kent, since the last time you visited WFRN, you have an announcement. Care to let the viewers in?"

Kent took the bite and reeled in. "Absolutely. Since my father retired, I'm Vice-President at Baker, Misny, and Wheeler."

Jordyn forced a wide smile. "Congratulations! What does this title entail?"

He paused, looked to the camera, winked, and faced Jordyn. "There are new job duties of course. Lots of perks. But most of all, it gives me confidence. I feel I can ask hard questions and be respected." He cleared his throat. "With that, Jordyn, we need to celebrate the success of *Early Rise and Shine*, plus my advancement. What do you say to a steak dinner?"

Jordyn looked past the camera, her pulse increasing. Where was Natalie? The pressure of live television felt like a ticking bomb as she wiped her moist palm on her lap. She kept her smile and remembered everything her best friend had said. "I think that's a fantastic idea."

CHAPTER SIXTEEN

Spencer pulled down on the beige cashmere turtleneck and checked his reflection. The sweater was a last Christmas present from his mom, but it felt tight around the collar. He yanked it off and reached for a ribbed navy sweater. *I have to be comfortable and warm for the tree lighting. Nothing like live television and an itchy turtleneck.*

A fast, triple rap on his bedroom door interrupted his try-on.

"Spence, open up." Carson.

Spencer trekked across the hardwood floor and opened the door to find his little brother sporting a Syracuse University hoodie. "Can I catch a ride with you? We're going to the same place so I figured I'd save gas." Carson grinned. "And maybe I'll run into that cute reporter, Courtney."

"Forget it, little bro. She's too old for you." He picked a piece of lint off the sweater and grabbed his wallet from the nightstand. "Besides, Court's covering the parade in Corning and their tree lighting. What about Dad? Is he coming?"

Carson shook his head. "He said it's too cold for an event that's over in ten seconds."

That meant Dad would be home alone. Would he use the truck to find booze? Did he have a hiding spot in the house Spencer hadn't discovered? After three weeks without a drink, would tonight mark the end of his sobriety? "I'll ask. He seems interested in the *Early Rise and Shine* process."

Carson chuckled. "More like he enjoys chatting with Jordyn."

The mere mention of her name dried up Spencer's throat and made his eye twitch. Since the Thanksgiving rejection, he was polite but kept his distance once the camera turned off. "She's going to be busy." He crossed the threshold into the hallway and headed to the living room.

Dad sat with the television on, some court room show playing at a volume loud enough for the neighbors to deliver a verdict. He was in his black robe lounging in the recliner, a sure sign he was home for the night.

"Are you feeling okay, Dad?" Spencer stood in front of the television for a closer look at his father. Were there tremors? Shaking of any kind? Sweating? Were the withdrawals finally over? "I thought you'd like attending the Elmira tree lighting with us."

The patriarch looked up and batted his hand in a gesture that usually meant "nonsense." "What? Freeze my kiester for a fancy flip of a switch? I can catch the highlights at eleven."

Spencer observed Dad's speech was even, eyes clear. No shakes. Yet, the bricks laying a foundation in his stomach gave no peace. "Okay. Although the lighting doesn't take long, there's some fanfare that goes along with it. I don't know when we'll be home."

Carson nudged his brother's arm. "We'd best get going. Parking is going to be a nightmare."

Spencer nodded and moved away from the television. "See you later, Dad. I have my phone with me if you need anything."

Dad grunted, laser-focused on the judge banging her gavel.

Satisfied all was well for the moment, Spencer found his heaviest coat and left for the garage.

As the brothers headed west on Route 86, Carson was the first to break the silence in the truck. "Do you think Dad's drinking at all?"

Spencer glanced at Carson and back to the road. "It doesn't appear that he is, but the statistics of someone quitting cold turkey without a relapse aren't in our favor."

The younger Collins nodded. "I'm afraid I'm going to say the wrong thing and he'll start drinking again."

The confession nearly drove Spencer off the road. He could relate—probably why he was chewing antacids like candy. "Carson, if he falls back and drinks, that's his choice. We can't control that."

"So, you aren't worried?"

Ugh. Cornered. "I think about it, sure. Concerned is probably a better word, though."

Carson didn't speak for a few miles. When he did, his confession spoke for them both once again. "Since Mom passed, it sure has been hard."

Once they arrived at Twain Township Park, Spencer checked his phone to see if Jordyn or Sam had an update on where he should meet them. Knowing the gazebo was near where this year's Christmas tree was positioned, Spencer started toward the favorite place for weddings.

"Some of the guys from the team are at the hot chocolate stand. I'll see you later." Carson waved. "Tell Jordyn I said hello." He grinned.

Spencer rolled his eyes and continued his brisk walk. It didn't take long before he spotted Jordyn in a long, forest green coat. Her laugh floated through the air and seemed to warm the park area. *Definitely going to be a long night.*

. ♡ ♡ ♡

Jordyn gasped as soon as she saw Spencer approaching. Ignoring him with his black puffer coat accenting that broad chest and watching him smile as viewers greeted him along the way was as impossible as walking past chocolate. Everything about Spencer was professional, kind, handsome, and flat-out amazing. But she'd kept that vow for good reason. Even if she dared retract it, Spencer had given them enough space to fit a 747 through it.

Sam waved, marching up the sidewalk toward the gazebo, faster than Spencer, camera equipment in hand.

"Hey, ready to light up Elmira?" Spencer was at her side, an intoxicating woodsy aroma dazzled her as much as his smile.

Knees, be still. "I'm afraid with these big gloves on I'll hit the switch before we're given the cue." She lifted her fur insulated hands and giggled.

Sam waved, sauntering up the sidewalk toward the gazebo, camera equipment in hand.

"Although cold, it's a great night for viewers to join us or tune in." Spencer looked up. "There's even light snow starting."

Jordyn followed his gaze when a flake landed in her eye. A laugh escaped, and she brushed her oversized glove across her lashes.

It didn't take long for them to set up and communicate with the tech team working at the WFRN office. Before the actual tree ceremony Jordyn had an interview with the mayor, and Spencer was going to greet a few people and ask them Christmas-related questions. After the lighting, the Horseheads Youth Choir would sing carols in the gazebo, and the reporters would sign off. It always looked good on paper.

Jordyn navigated the lavalier microphone wire through her coat as she sat on a bench in the gazebo. Her phone contained notes for the interview, so she was about to pull her cell out of her purse when she felt a tap on her arm.

"Jordyn, looking festive." Kent sat on the same bench, leaving little room for Jordyn to work. He smelled like smoke from the bonfire going on across the park by the pond.

"Kent. What brings you here?" On the bench, crowding her personal space.

He sidled closer. "Baker, Misny and Wheeler is sponsoring the tree lighting. Made sure the sign placement was prominent before you go live." His hand rested on her knee. "And to say hello to my favorite anchor."

Jordyn offered a weak smile, and placed her purse on top of his hand so Kent would be forced to remove it. "Hey. I hate to rush you off, but I really need to go over my notes." She dug deep past her wallet and lipstick, trying to feel the edges of the phone without removing her gloves.

"I bet you could interview the mayor blindfolded."

She nodded; her heartrate increased as she rooted for the device without success. "That's nice of you to say but I really need to prepare." Time to take off the gloves.

Kent didn't seem to take the hint as he didn't move. "Do you think you'll have time to interview me?"

If there was room, Jordyn was tempted to dump her purse. "Please, Kent. I need to find my phone. Why don't you get a hot chocolate?"

He bit his lip and stood. "Got it. I'll stand close by in case you need to fill time."

Where is the phone? She raked through the purse bottom, her breathing uneven. Words failed to form as Kent jogged down the gazebo steps. Thunder rang in her ears as she tried to swallow. She lost grip and the purse seemed to fall slow-motion to the gazebo floor. When Jordyn lifted a shaky hand to her forehead, a layer of sweat stuck to her skin. Her breaths increased and no words could form for her to call out. *I'm in trouble.*

. ♡ ♡ ♡

Spencer finished a couple live interviews with Sam and the two were walking toward the gazebo when he saw Jordyn. She was seated on a bench, her right hand across her heart, face crimson. He tapped Sam's arm. "Something's wrong with Jordyn."

Spencer reached her first. "Hey. Everything okay?" He knelt in front of her and noticed her erratic breathing and wide eyes. "Okay, I think I know what's going on. My college roommate had panic attacks."

She nodded. Her eyes darted to Sam, but she didn't speak. Probably couldn't.

Sam looked at Spencer and shrugged. He was a behind-the-scenes guy whether he was with a TV camera or not.

"Jordyn, I want you to find a focus point." Spencer sent a silent prayer and made sure his tone with her was gentle and reassuring. "It can be the tree, Sam's hipster beanie, my nose, whatever. Keep your gaze on whatever and concentrate on what I say. Got it?"

She nodded, but he couldn't quite tell if she was looking at or past him.

He scooched toward her. "Okay. Deep breath in, through the nose. Picture a balloon inflating in your core area. Keep going until you feel like you've blown it up as far as it can go."

Spencer thought he heard two inhales matching his. Was Sam participating too? "Now deflate the balloon through a mouth exhale. Take it as far as you can go until you feel it down in your stomach area."

"Better," Jordyn whispered before repeating the technique. By the sixth time, she had her hands on her lap and her breathing slowed. "Thank you."

Sam expelled the last of his air and whistled. "Wow, Collins. You should be a therapist."

"Not quite. Six o'clock anchor is as much drama as I want in my career, thanks." Spencer stood and felt his knees crack. "Are you okay, Jordyn?"

She stood and smoothed out her coat, then stuck her hand in a pocket, producing a phone. "This. I couldn't find my phone and I lost control."

Sam glanced at his watch. "The mayor is due here in five minutes. The tree lighting is in ten. Are we okay?"

Jordyn's jaw opened slightly as her eyebrows raised. She closed her mouth and took in another cleansing breath. When finished, she nodded. "I'm good. Let's do this."

Spencer stepped back but kept his gaze on her. "If it helps, I can join you for the interview. For support. I promise not to hijack your exclusive."

Jordyn broke the look and focused on her phone. "It's a kind offer, but I have my notes now." She approached the gazebo steps with care before turning around. "See you at the tree lighting."

Her smile carried the power to melt the snow. He watched her walk to the sidewalk area where the interview was scheduled. Sam nudged Spencer as he gathered his gear. "Dude, you've got it bad."

Before Spencer could feign innocence or defend his feelings, he spotted Kent Misny, who trotted up to Jordyn as if he'd been waiting for her the entire evening.

Anchored Hearts

CHAPTER SEVENTEEN

Jordyn bounded down the stairs with wool socks in hand ready to find the perfect tree for the Hart home. "Dad? You ready?" She stopped in the living room to put on her footwear and listened for sounds of downstairs activity. "Evan? Paige? Ryan's gonna have a fit if we're late."

Shelly entered the living room from the kitchen, to-go mug in hand. "Good morning, Jordy. Your father's looking for the rope from last year." She held the cup up. "I made this for you. My hot chocolate recipe. We'll need it in the woods."

Jordyn smiled as she accepted Shelly's kind gesture. "First time getting a tree off Ryan's property. Exciting times."

"Seems like yesterday he was dialing up the internet when I was over to help your mom when you all weren't even two years old." She laughed softly as she returned to the kitchen.

Jordyn followed and found an insulated bag full of the to-go containers. "Who would have guessed the Hart nerd would be the Navy vet and first homeowner of the six?"

"Good point. You were the only one who seemed to always know exactly what you were going to do and how to do it." Shelly offered Jordyn a motherly arm rub. "And look at you. Whether I'm driving in Corning, Elmira, Horseheads or Bath, there's at least one billboard or bus that has an *Early Rise and Shine* promotion displayed. You and Spencer are a big deal."

Jordyn thought back to her panic attack before the tree lighting two weeks earlier. She was anything but a professional with her heart palpitations and excessive perspiration. Spencer, though, was effortless in taking care of her and making the tree lighting a ratings hit against the other stations running repeats. Then there was Misny, mere feet away from her live shots, ready to pop in if needed. Which she desperately didn't want.

Shelly raised her eyebrows and cocked her head. "You okay? Seems like you're lost in thought." She picked up the beverage bag and placed the strap over her shoulder.

"Sorry. I kind of am. The viewers are amazing, but I struggled a bit at the tree lighting. I'm afraid it could happen again."

The two walked toward the garage, sounds of male voices filling the air.

Shelly opened the door as an icy wind blew in and scurried through the threshold. "Jordyn, I know we don't share common ground here, so I'll keep this brief. There is no burden you are meant to carry. Not even nerves."

Here she goes. Jesus talk. Jordyn paused on the top step to adjust her attitude and not roll her eyes. "I don't have nerves. Nervous is different."

Her step-mother kept walking toward the truck. She reached the passenger door and held onto the handle before turning toward

Jordyn. "Jesus can take care of everything you're dealing with. Past, present, and future."

With that, Dad hopped from the truck cab to the garage floor, immediately joining Shelly's side. "What's this about the future?"

Jordyn sighed and resumed movement, hoping this conversation would die along with the gas and oil smells coming from the old truck.

"Oh, reminding Jordyn that Jesus is ready and willing to take all her burdens, anytime." Shelly patted her husband's hand as he helped boost her in the vehicle.

"That He does, Jordy. Took me long enough to give my grief, worries, and sins to Him, but the peace Jesus gave in return, it's amazing."

Jordyn felt a stab in her gut. Sure, her parents shared a strong faith in Christ when she was a kid. But once Mom was gone, everything Jesus was snuffed from the home as fast as their mother's presence. And peace didn't seem achievable. Not without her mom. "Where's Paige?"

Evan jumped off the vehicle's back and climbed behind the driver's seat to the bench. "She got in late last night. Told me to go on without her."

Jordyn started to follow Evan when she caught Shelly looking her way. As soon as they exchanged glances, Shelly cleared her throat and broke off contact. She then focused on clicking her seat belt before nibbling on a thumbnail. For someone so at peace, Shelly sure looked—overwhelmed.

. ♡ ♡ ♡

Spencer drained the last of his coffee and put the faded Yankees mug in the sink. Dad was at the door, keys in hand, tapping his feet.

"I'm ready. Are you sure it's okay for me to visit the fire station?"

Dad's eyes brightened. "Cleared it with the Chief. Given my credentials as a retired fire fighter, I'm allowed to do just about anything." He chuckled. "Except start a fire."

Spencer laughed and his muscles loosened. The fire station invite was the latest in Dad's transformation. The two were spending time together most evenings chatting, and watching TV. He noticed more laughter between Dad and Carson. Now, Dad's pride in visiting the station where he was going out on volunteer calls shone. "Want to go to lunch after?"

Dad put on a blue stocking cap and nodded. "As long as you're paying."

The East Waverly Fire Department was a fraction of the size of the Elmira station where Dad spent years, but the brotherhood atmosphere was immediate as soon as the two entered.

A couple of men looked up from polishing the bigger fire truck's hood and spotted Dad. "Hey, Collins! There's no fire. What brings you by?" The taller man dropped his cloth and joined them, offering his hand to Dad for a handshake. The second guy waved as he kept cleaning.

"This is the day I told you I was bringing by my oldest boy. He's an anchor for that morning show."

The one who was working on the truck smiled. "Spencer Collins. Love your show. You and Jordyn Hart are like Kelly Ripa and Ryan Seacrest." The man invited himself to their circle and shook Spencer's hand.

"I don't know about that, but thank you."

Dad turned to Spencer. "Son, this is Tim Cramer, and the tall guy over here is Chief Wiggins."

Chief waved him off. "Just call me Pat. Pleasure to meet you. Your dad's brought a lot of structure to our little station."

Spencer nudged his dad in the arm and winked.

"Smitty helped too." Dad offered. "Do you mind if I show him around?"

The men shook their heads, but Pat answered. "Have fun. Cliff's in the kitchen making chili. We're cleaning up Scarlet today."

Dad chuckled and mouthed to Spencer, "The big truck."

An hour and a small bowl of chili later, Spencer faced his dad in their vehicle. "That was really impressive. That little fire department accomplished a lot for the community."

Dad turned the ignition and quickly lowered the volume on the radio. "I really like serving here. Your Mother would laugh at my life right now. We live in a celebrity home in the country, and I volunteer for a fire station. She thought I'd never leave Elmira or my green recliner."

Spencer bit his lip and nodded. "She really hated that chair."

They drove out of the lot and started for the highway when Dad sobered. "Is it okay if we stop somewhere before lunch?"

"Sure. Anything wrong?" Spencer narrowed his gaze and tried to get a read on his father. Nothing.

"Nope. Just thought I should share something with you."

Spencer shifted in his seat. Dad's tone reminded him of times when they were on errands and they found a way to sneak an ice cream stop in there, even if Mom had dinner waiting. "You're a man of mystery these days."

Dad kept his eye on the road, but gave a slight nod. "You'll see what I mean in a couple miles."

Sure enough, they pulled into a church parking lot and Dad put the truck in park.

"Okay, I'm confused. Why are we here?"

Seat belt off, Dad moved his back against the door. "I know you and Carson worry about whether I'm drinking or not. I'm not." He pointed to the small church with faded white paint. "And that's why."

Spencer looked around for a person, signage, anything that would help him understand. "I need a little more explanation, Dad. You're not drinking because of that church?"

With a shake of the head, Dad leaned across the seat and opened the glove compartment. "There's also this." He lifted a softcover book Spencer quickly recognized.

"That's Mom's Bible. I thought I left it at work or something."

The Bible rested between them. "One morning I was struggling and I was at the house alone. I paced around and found myself in your room. The Book should've had stadium lights attached to it. Seemed like the brightest thing in the room." He chuckled. "Son, it was like I had to take it. I was drawn to it."

Spencer considered the prayers and notes Mom wrote in the margins. He understood the need to read it. "So, you started reading it. And?"

"And your mother led me here. Well, God did, but her writings. She confessed how she couldn't do anything on her strength. That her church family was her spiritual battery charger. I know this isn't the same church she went to, but it's close by." He scratched his gray hair. "Pastor's been meeting with me. Thought you should know."

He pursed his lips together, trying to think of the perfect encouragement. After a few tongue clicks he lifted the Bible. "Thank you for telling me. I know after Mom passed, we all scurried away from what mattered most to her. Not that any of us were even close to where she was in faith."

A sad laugh filled the cab. "No, we weren't. But I know with the Lord's help, I can stay off the booze."

"I believe it." Spencer exhaled, relief filling him head to toe.

"Do you think you and Carson could come with me Sunday? You can say no."

Spencer looked to the Bible, the church, and then Dad. "I'm pretty sure we can make that happen."

. ♡ ♡ ♡

During the forty-minute ride to Ryan's property, Jordyn attempted to discern what Shelly was thinking about. Did she know something about Paige? Why did her expression change when Evan said their youngest sibling weren't coming along? Something was up. Journalist nose or sister intuition, Jordyn was ready to investigate.

Ryan was in his long gravel driveway, axe in hand, when they arrived. Still sporting the short, military style cut and no hat in the December cold.

"Hey, Son. Thanks for letting us chop down one of your trees." Dad was the first to exit the truck and walk over to the other side to open the door for Shelly and then circled to Ryan for a hug.

"My pleasure. Glad you guys are finally seeing the place." He glanced to the mint green ranch-style home. "Remember, it's a work in progress."

Evan was the last to leave the truck. "Aren't we all?" He chuckled.

Ryan led the four behind the house where his ten acres stood.

"This property had to have cost a chunk of change. Unless the house is a total dump."

Dad wasted no time responding. "Evan. How about we make this a quiet walk?"

Jordyn snickered. How many times had Dad asked for one of those when they went on the annual tree hunt?

While Dad and Shelly searched for the perfect Douglas Fir, Evan tried to find reception for his phone. Ryan hung back with Jordyn. "You're quiet. Everything okay?" He stopped and leaned against a bare maple.

Jordyn sighed, then shrugged. "I have a lot on my mind. Work. Paige."

Ryan straightened at their sister's name. "What's going on?"

She kicked at some snow. "That's just it, Ry. I don't know. Paige is never home. The rare time she is, all I hear from her is attitude. Now bailing on events like today."

Ryan's jaw tensed. "Think there's a guy?"

"A boyfriend?" Jordyn scoffed. "There's no way she could keep that quiet around the house. Or social media."

He nodded. "Keep me posted." Ryan glanced down the path toward Dad. "Before they need my axe, what's going on with work? How's Spencer?"

Jordyn's heart quickened at the mention of his name. Or was it the start of another panic attack? "I'm sure he's fine. Just like work. He's busy is all."

The two resumed walking toward the others. Shelly waved her hands. "We found it!"

Evan looked up. "Better reception? I have online stuff to check and it's impossible."

Ryan flicked the back of his younger brother's head as he often had when they were younger. "She meant the tree, Genius."

Once the group approved, Ryan laid down a carpet remnant and knelt on it, leaning over to cut the tree. Jordyn lined up the sled so once it fell, it would land right on the plastic transport. Out of the corner of her eye she saw Dad and Shelly talking.

"Okay Jordy, she's about to fall." Ryan announced, sawing back and forth at the base before it started to sway.

"Got it." Jordy tugged the fir toward the front of the sled, and Dad pitched in. "Evan, since you haven't done anything, you can pull the sled back to the truck."

While he obeyed, Jordyn planted herself between Dad and Shelly. "So, anything interesting going on lately? Have you heard anything from Scotty?" Talking about Shelly's nephew who lived with her during part of the sextuplet's childhood usually opened up conversation.

Not this time. Shelly shook her head and walked a few paces before replying. "I'm sure James is in touch with him, but Scotty doesn't answer my voicemail or texts."

Hmm. What other ways can I pry info out of her? "I'm sorry to hear that. I knew he had challenges, but I thought things were going well for him."

Dad placed an arm on hers. "Jordy. Let's drop it, okay?"

She nodded and kept moving, determined to figure out what Shelly knew about Paige. If not during the tree hunt, then the decoration.

Shelly perked up once the tree was tied down in the back of the truck. "Do we get a tour of the house?"

Ryan ran his hand through his short hair. "I guess. Just remember—"

Evan finished for him. "It's a work in progress. We know."

Ryan jogged up the wobbly cement steps that led to the door. A smell---more like a stench---assaulted Jordyn's nostrils before she entered. "What is that? Road kill leftovers?"

Shelly covered her mouth with her hand.

Dad took a few steps into the living room, floorboards creaking. "You're right, Ryan. This place needs a lot of TLC."

"I know. I repair and remodel as I can after work and as my budget allows. Something died in the chimney. A guy's coming out tomorrow to recover it. Sorry about the odor."

Jordyn sauntered into the kitchen. A greasy film covered the dated countertops.

Evan blew dust off the stovetop. "Seriously, Ry. Was this a drug house?"

Ryan leaned over and gave Evan a fist to the upper arm. "Hey, at least I live on my own."

This time Jordyn took offense. "Wait a second. It's not so bad, living at home." She glanced at Shelly.

Dad interrupted the bickering by starting up the wooden steps. "Let's see what's upstairs."

When they finished the tour on the small deck with rotting floor boards, Jordyn swallowed and tried to find the right words. Any words. *Something to make Ryan feel like he didn't throw his savings in the toilet.*

"It has potential."

They all nodded and murmured.

Ryan leaned against the plaid couch with scratchy fabric. "I know. It's a lot. More than I thought. But, Harts don't back down from challenges."

"Challenge? This is a nightmare." Evan moved his jacket over his mouth.

"Evan." Shelly chided.

"For once, Evan's right. But I'm going to make this a home. A showplace." He grinned. "And I could use free labor."

Now it was Evan who wore a different expression in his eyes. One Jordyn had seen before. And it was never good news.

Ryan declined following them back to the Hart home to decorate and enjoy dinner. After good-bye hugs, they made the trek back to East Corning. Once the tree stood inside with lights assembled, it was tradition for the Hart children to decorate. *Where's*

Paige? Evan is with Dad in the garage. Before Jordyn could search for her sister, Shelly was the first to choose a decoration from the box.

"What are you doing?" Jordyn raced to the tote filled with homemade decorations from across the years.

Shelly turned, eyebrows raised, holding a beaded candle Kelly made as a Brownie. "Helping. You didn't want to decorate this by yourself, did you? It's a big one."

Jordyn looked up at the tree, realizing it looked a lot bigger standing vertical. "We have an ornament we always put on first. One mom made when she was little. A cloth stocking."

Another facial change. This time Shelly paled. "Red?"

`Jordyn nodded. "I mean it faded a little over the years, but yes." She narrowed her gaze. "Why?"

Shelly placed her hand over her mouth again. "I'm sorry. I didn't know. Things were so chaotic last year with moving in after the wedding and all."

She put her hands on her hips. "What happened?"

"Please forgive me. I threw it away."

Jordyn felt dizzy processing the confession. "You what?"

Shelly swiped at the corner of her eyes. "I thought it was scrap material. It looked so beat up. I saw it in the tote when we took everything down and I thought—I thought it was garbage."

Jordyn now felt moisture pooling in her eyes, and a white, angry heat building. "Shelly, how could you? How many years were you over here? How many Christmas seasons did you witness all our stuff? Then you marry Dad and everything changes."

Shelly nibbled at her thumb nail before forcing her hands to her side. "It was an accident. I promise. I would never hurt you kids on purpose. You are like my own."

Jordyn refused to let her step-mother utter another word. "But you're not. You're just the neighbor help who latched onto Dad when he was lonely." She forced herself to keep her volume down so Dad and Evan wouldn't come running.

"That's an incredibly hurtful thing to say." Shelly's eyes were red, and she blinked faster than a windshield wiper during a torrential rain. "I never had any agenda except to help your parents, and then your father, with whatever they needed when it came to you kids."

"You could have started with leaving our traditions and things alone."

"I said I didn't know, and I'm sorry." Shelly's tone was clipped and tense.

"Shelly, if you really want to be a part of this family then you should know about the stocking. And how to really make green beans on Thanksgiving."

Her jaw opened, and it felt like minutes, not seconds, before Shelly replied. "Jordyn Bell Hart, I've tried with you. I have. But you aren't going to bully me. I'm here to stay. And if I'm so ignorant, how come I know what you clearly don't?" Her voice shook as she pointed toward Jordyn. "Paige is drinking to the point it's not just abusive, I think she's an alcoholic."

Anchored Hearts

CHAPTER EIGHTEEN

Spencer pushed the church doors open and held them for Dad and Carson, silently praying they didn't notice his shaky arms. Although this place of worship seemed smaller and more rustic than the one in Elmira they'd attended when Mom was alive, he hadn't stepped foot in a church since her funeral.

Dad passed through, patting Spencer on the shoulder, and then repeated the same gesture with Carson. "Thanks, boys, for coming with me. It means a lot." He led them to a pew in the middle and signaled for them to enter.

Carson sat first and slithered out of his jacket. He nudged Spencer. "Been awhile since—all of this."

Spencer glanced around. The carpeted altar. A simple platform with a drum set, guitar stands, and keyboards. A wooden cross to the side. He let out a nervous sigh. "Being here is helping Dad. It can help us, too."

Carson nodded. "Can't hurt."

Once the worship leader stepped on the platform, Spencer straightened and focused forward. Thankfully the words were on the big screen, because it wasn't a song he was familiar with. *Okay, this isn't scary. It's peaceful.* He glanced at Dad. The man was singing with an energy Spencer hadn't seen since he surprised Mom with a party for her fiftieth birthday.

By the time the pastor left his seat and sauntered up front with his iPad, Spencer's muscles were relaxed and everything about him was still. Church wasn't the enemy, although he'd felt that way since the funeral. Specifically, Spencer blamed God. Somehow, the anger vanished as he sat.

The pastor, a little younger than Dad, grinned as he shared a snippet of his summer vacation. "Jessica and I took the grandkids to Darien Lake. You know, the amusement park near Buffalo. Brandon wanted to drive the cars. They are the two-seaters that go around a wooden track, both seats have a steering wheel." He chuckled. "Brandon sat in what would typically be the driver's seat and boy, if speed determined flying off those tracks and racing through the park, that kid railed on that wheel like he was qualifying for NASCAR."

Dad nodded as he laughed along with the congregation. "You two were the same."

The pastor continued. "The reality was, Brandon had zero control over the car. He could have stayed in his seat all day, twisted that wheel every which way, and it would not have made any difference." He placed the electronic device on a stand. "It's the same for us."

Spencer felt a churn in his gut as the man talked about control. Whether a kid at the park, a teen worrying about college, or an adult up all night counting ceiling tiles, anxious because they want to know about the promotion, no one but God has control. Spencer lowered his head as the pastor prayed. *God, help me. Surrender isn't easy. Mom wasn't healed, and our unanswered prayers nearly ruined us. I've worried about Carson. Dad. Whether I ever anchor the six. Then there's Jordyn. It's Yours. I don't want to drive that car anymore.*

Dad stood first at dismissal. "So, what did you think?"

Spencer reached for his jacket. "Really good. The message was exactly what I needed."

Carson stepped closer. "Same here. I want to check out youth group on Wednesday."

Dad's smile brought a lump to Spencer's throat. "We all dealt with our grief differently. My way was the bottle."

Spencer took his keys out of his pocket. "I worried about both of you non-stop, feeling it was up to me to take care of everyone and everything." He looked up and Dad's jaw lowered, and Carson raised his eyebrows. "Thanks for inviting us. It's time for me to leave those burdens with God and not take them on anymore."

Carson cleared his throat. "Now that Spencer has his life on track, can we get lunch?"

The trio returned home and feasted on pizza from the local gas station. Carson texted while Dad viewed the Jets game on his cell phone. Spencer looked at his watch and realized it wasn't even three. *I could get some work done at the station while it's quiet.* "Hey guys, I'm going into work. I have some editing to do, and a bit of writing. I should be back before dark."

Carson didn't miss a beat. "Say hi to Jordyn for me."

Forty minutes later, Spencer swiped his badge and pushed through the employee entrance. Lights were on, but maintenance often took Sundays to clean the studio. He walked down the hallway and turned to the coffee machine, also on. He found his mug and poured himself a cup of needed caffeine. *Enough to get me through editing copy.* Spencer took a sip and turned toward the newsroom, running smack into Jordyn.

. ♡ ♡ ♡

Jordyn gasped as her chocolate bar hit Spencer square in the chest. "You scared me! What are you doing here?"

He looked down and swiped at the chocolate smudge. "Taking advantage of a quiet afternoon."

She cocked her head. "You could do that anywhere."

"I'm editing." Spencer enjoyed another sip. "How about you?"

"Same." Jordyn bit at her bottom lip, and then sighed. "That's a lie. There's work to do, of course, but I needed space to think." She looked at the floor before meeting his gaze, one that quickly left her weak in the knees. "You aren't here to listen to me and my drama."

Spencer raised an eyebrow. "That's up to you. I'm here, and willing to listen. If not, the editing bay is waiting for me." Before she could answer, he walked past her.

Think fast. He's a great listener. With amazing eyes. And a strong build. "Wait. Do you mind? Shelly threw me a bombshell and I need to process it." Her independent resolve vanished as soon as he stopped and returned to her side.

"Is the conference room okay?" His smile lit up her hurting heart.

Once they reached the door, Spencer opened it and Jordyn walked through. She picked up her pace and chose a seat across the room. *Would he sit next to me?*

Spencer shut the door and sauntered past the table, pulling out a chair next to her. "Since you mentioned your step mom, I thought maybe I should be close by." He cleared his throat. "To be supportive."

Jordyn nodded and folded her hands on her lap as they faced each other, apart from the table. "I won't take much of your time. Shelly and I got into an argument and she ended it by sharing Paige is partying. Not a little, but to an extent that's terrifying."

He mouthed a "wow," and sat without responding for a few moments.

"You have every right to make fun." Her voice was barely above a whisper and her chest felt tight. "I treated you—"

Spencer leaned forward and put a hand on her shaky knee. "Jordyn. That's not who I am. Remember, I grew up reading your family updates in the paper. Alcohol played a very traumatic part of your life."

His words were a healing balm to her broken soul. She let out a sob that was like the breaking of a dam. Tears came on so fast Spencer jumped up and ran to the counter for the tissue box. Her shoulders heaved as years of grief poured out.

It took five minutes before her breathing slowed and she was able to continue. "The woman had her daughter in the car. Mom was taking Kelly to a doctor's appointment that day. Paige and James were in the back seat." Fresh moisture spilled on her cheek. "I wasn't there. And Paige. How could she repeat the choices that killed Mom?"

Spencer scooched his chair closer and his even breathing warmed her wet cheeks. "Jordyn, you don't think the accident is your fault, do you? Whether you were in the car or not, the lady was still going to drive drunk and hit your family car."

Jordyn shook her head. "I could have done something. That's why I have my vow, to protect myself and my family." She sniffled. "But Paige's descent happened right in front of me and I didn't even see it. What am I going to do?"

Now both his hands rested on her knees. "It's not up to you to solve this."

She nearly burst out of her chair. "You want me to stand by and watch her drink herself to death?"

Spencer rose and reached for her shoulders. "You can't manage Paige. She's an adult. None of us have control. Can't you see?"

Jordyn shook her head. "Spencer, what if it was Carson? Wouldn't you want to take care of him?"

He looked as if she'd punched him. "It would be tempting. In fact, until this morning I would have probably inserted myself into every area of my little brother's life."

"What changed?"

Spencer dropped his hands to the side, but remained standing next to her. "I went to church with my dad and Carson. The message was about surrender." He grinned and lifted her chin. "Jordyn Hart, don't roll your eyes."

She swallowed hard. "Surrender isn't a word I'm accustomed to. Or church, for that matter."

He nodded. "I'm not going to push you to do anything you aren't comfortable doing. Church hasn't been part of my life for a few years, and even then, I was merely an attender at best. This time, it's real and personal." His hand moved to her cheek, where he swiped at a tear.

"Spencer. I'm so scared." *Of what's going to happen with Paige. The intimacy of this moment. Afraid of everything that could happen to those I love.*

His nod was slow as he took her other hand and circled her wrist with his fingers and thumb. "I know. Jordyn, we can work through this together."

She closed her eyes as he moved in, lips parted. The light brush against her mouth rattled her senses and sent her heart on alert. Her arms wrapped around his neck as she deepened the kiss before breaking it and stepping back. "Spencer, I can't. It makes no sense, I know."

He sighed. "Is this about your vow? Because I have an update."

Jordyn shook her head. "It's everything. My focus has to be on Paige."

"Honey, let me help you. We can work through this. Together."

Everything in her wanted to run to him but her limbs refused to move. Jordyn stood, shaking her head, hand on her heart. "I'm sorry."

Spencer had no issues with movement. He walked past her, but stopped, and turned to her. "Letting go is new to me, too. But already I have such a peace. When you're ready to explore freedom and surrender your need to handle everyone, let me know."

Jordyn watched him head to the editing bay through the small window in the door. Once she knew Spencer was out of sight, she slumped on the floor and continued to cry.

Anchored Hearts

CHAPTER NINETEEN

Mere minutes after the end of the last live *Early Rise and Shine* broadcast for the year, Joe Munson jogged up to Spencer as he was putting away his microphone.

"Collins, you never gave Sophia an answer about the company Christmas party."

Spencer looked up at his boss and sighed. "Not really my scene, sir."

Joe nodded and sat on the edge of the desk, facing Spencer. "I get it. The event isn't mandatory, but I have to tell you, Marcus Bright will be there."

Wow. The big boss. A man he had not yet met in his three years at the station. Spencer stood and brushed a piece of lint off his suit pants. "Marcus Bright as in he owns WFRN and twenty other television stations?"

Joe nodded. "That's him."

"Note taken. It's tonight, right?"

The news director slid off the desk. "Santino's at eight. Wear one of those ugly sweaters."

Spencer finished his workday successfully without running into Jordyn. Seeing her every morning pulled on his heart like an anchor falling, but he respected her wishes to remain platonic. Her family appeared to be in crisis and it wasn't right to insert himself. But it was tempting. Once home, he opened his closet and pulled out a pair of navy casual pants. Then the sweater that made him look like an elf. As he pulled it over his head, the memory of Jordyn's arms around him as they shared a seismic kiss returned for another round of emotional torture.

Once Spencer recovered, he left the bedroom and found Carson in the kitchen, holding up a paper. "What's that? Report card?"

Carson shook his head, smile wide. "Nope. It's called an acceptance letter to Syracuse University. Came today."

As soon as the words registered, Spencer rushed to his baby brother and picked him off the ground. "Congratulations! You worked hard for this." He returned Carson to standing position.

"Thanks. I look good in blue and orange." Carson smirked, put the paper on the counter, and then glanced toward Spencer. "But you don't look good in that green nightmare. You're wearing that on purpose?"

Spencer shrugged as he took the car keys off the counter. "Company Christmas party. Joe said to find something ugly."

"If there's a contest, you're a sure win." Carson snickered and backed up before Spencer could reach him.

"You're hilarious. Not sure when I'll be home. Do you work tonight?"

Carson sobered and nodded. "Friday night dishes. My hands will be in dish water until the end of the shift. I'll be home after midnight."

"Can't say I miss my table waiting days." Spencer opened the front door and offered a wave. "Be careful. Not sure who will get home first."

Thirty minutes later, Spencer opened the Santino front doors and discovered the entire restaurant was closed to the public for WFRN. A live band played a highly energetic version of *Rockin' Around the Christmas Tree* as it blasted through a huge speaker near the entrance. He strolled past the makeshift dance floor and found a couple reporters from his old Binghamton bureau near the punch bowl.

"If it isn't Spencer Collins, morning heartthrob." Christy Jenkins, crime reporter, gave him a playful nudge on the arm.

He rolled his eyes. "It's way too early each morning for anyone to think that way. We're just trying to inform and entertain the Twin Tiers."

Shay Walker, Broome County sports, crossed her arms against her chest. "Oh, c'mon. I've read the comments across social media. Sure, viewers enjoy Courtney visiting the new coffee shop in Big Flats, but they rave about you and Jordyn." She leaned in as the band's volume increased. "My television started to spark when you two went ice skating last week."

Spencer ran a hand through his hair wishing they'd talk about the weather, gas prices, anything but his chemistry with Jordyn. He wouldn't lie if they asked, because that segment at the Corning rink nearly melted the ice around them. "I'd rather talk about what's new at the Binghamton branch."

The two ladies exchanged a smile and then Christy grinned. "Okay, we get it. You don't want to talk. Seriously, *Early Rise and Shine* is a fantastic show. If there's ever a vacancy, remember me."

Shay's blonde curls bobbed as she nodded. "It's true, Spence. Anyone I talk to at the games first wants to make sure I know how much they love 'that morning show with that sextuplet and Spencer.'"

"You're both too kind. I promise when we have vacations and need a fill in, I'll speak up about you both." He turned and looked to the buffet table. "I should get something to eat. Good to see you."

Before Spencer could reach the long buffet tables, Rich Wakefield pulled him aside. "Dude, everyone is talking about the show. It's like we're celebrities here." His eyes were bigger than the piled pasta on the plate he held.

"We're new. I'm happy the ratings are strong, but these guys will forget our names by Groundhog Day." Spencer slid over to grab a plate.

Rich followed him, waving his fork in Spencer's direction. "I don't think so. Vince Tidwell was chatting it up with Marcus Bright. February is a sweeps month. They want something big."

Spencer scooped out sauce for the meatballs. "So you and Courtney try the bunny trail at that ski place in Cortland."

This time Rich moved ahead of him, blocking Spencer's access to the bowl of grated cheese. "Get ready, my friend. They are talking about Valentine's Day and wedding." There was a pause so Rich could enjoy a bite of penne. Once he swallowed, the fork became a pointing tool again. "You and Jordyn were the names I heard for the big event."

. ♡ ♡ ♡

For once Jordyn wished Evan was around so he could monopolize the conversation and she could sit and eat her lukewarm chicken parm. Everywhere she turned there was a reporter or someone from Bright Media gushing over not just *Early Rise and Shine*, but her and Spencer.

"A thousand dollars for your thoughts." Jordyn froze when a hand rested on her back.

Kent. *Of course he'd get an invite to this party.* "I thought it was a penny." She tried her best not to yell over the music.

He dropped his hand and chuckled. "Not in my line of work." Kent pointed to a table in the corner away from the food and music. "Care to sit?"

She looked at her untouched food and nodded. "Sounds good. I'm hungry."

Kent pulled a chair out for Jordyn and then sat across from her. His ugly sweater was a green knit with oversized dollar signs on the front. "Nice party. The owner liked my ideas."

Jordyn had a fork full of chicken heading to her mouth when she realized what Kent said. "What do you mean? Why were you talking to Marcus?"

His sigh had the potential to drown out the sax solo up front. "Jordy, the question is why wouldn't I talk to him? The guy is a media mogul. Baker, Misny and Wheeler want to expand throughout New York State. And beyond."

Seems innocent enough. She attempted to finish the same bite.

"He loved changing my segment from a few minutes at noon to a weekly feature on *Early Rise and Shine*. And an annual half-hour program, if we can hash out the details."

Jordyn swallowed the chicken and tried not to gag as she processed Kent's words.

Unfazed as always, he kept talking. "We'll have to pony up some real money for air time, but in return, it increases our exposure and I'll insist on you being my only interviewer."

She felt a pit growing in her stomach that was certainly not from food. "Kent, you can't make those kinds of decisions. Marcus certainly can, and he'll work with Vince and Joe."

Kent chuckled. "Dear, sweet Jordyn. With the money the company will be handing WFRN, I could ask for almost anything." He cocked an eyebrow. "Why refuse me? Anything I want will always have your name attached. These plans improve your brand as much as mine."

"Kent, I never asked you to involve me in your lofty plans. My goal was to work at WFRN the same as my mom did."

His laughter changed in tone, and sent a chill down Jordyn's spine. With the dark party lighting in the corner, he almost looked like a Disney villain in the shadows. "You want to stay in Elmira? Jordyn, there's potential for us both to go statewide, and then East Coast. After that, we could be household names across America." Kent tilted his head. "For reasons other than your birth story, that is."

She pushed her plate back as a rush of heat surged in her belly. "You can do those things without me, and do them well."

"True enough. But I'd have to work twice as hard. You're already a beloved name. I'd be a fool not to take you on my ride to the top."

Jordyn brushed at her brow as her emotions churned and stormed inside her. Kent made Evan look lazy and compassionate. She wanted to lob the perfect insult at him, but no words formed. The lead singer announced something that was muffled, but *What Are You Doing New Year's Eve* started with a definite slowdown to the previous tunes in tempo and volume..

"Excuse me, Ken, I promised Jordyn a dance." Spencer winked as soon as his gaze connected with Jordyn's.

"It's Kent." His icy glare didn't seem to faze Spencer.

"Right." He leaned in toward Jordyn and extended his hand. "Ready?"

Jordyn jumped up, her knee hitting the bar of the table as she stood. "Yes, Collins, you owe me that dance." Taking his hand felt like the most natural thing as he led her away to the dance area. "You're timing is amazing."

Spencer's arms wrapped around her waist and once again his sweet, woodsy cologne sent her into a heady emotional spin. He chuckled, "You mentioned once on the show that chicken parm is your favorite. I saw you weren't eating any, and the look on your face didn't appear happy. I'm glad you didn't think I was overstepping."

She fought the urge to rest her head on those broad tempting shoulders. "No. It was helpful. Kent was talking business, and I've heard enough of that for the day." She moved her wrist against the back of his neck and shivered when his grip tightened just a bit.

"That guy loves his job."

"It's an obsession, honestly." She paused to take in another slow breath. "Speaking of work, anyone else I've talked to tonight has raved about *Early Rise and Shine*. Vince told me he even has a vendor making WFRN merchandise. Shirts, mugs, keychains, all of it with our morning show logo."

Spencer stopped for a couple beats and stepped back, still holding her. "Okay, now I'm impressed. I figured everyone was excited but that it would die down."

"I hope not. We have something special, you know?" Jordyn initiated movement again, and Spencer quickly regained the dance lead.

"The six o'clock was my focus. Now, I can't imagine anything else but co-anchoring the morning show."

The song ended and most everyone left the dance floor. Another slow song began, one Jordyn couldn't recall, but it was swoony. Jordyn had avoided Spencer's gaze since his rescue from Kent, but this time when she looked up, all she saw were those soft features and very kissable lips. "We could dance again, but I don't want to bother you."

His hands fell to the side and he shuffled his feet as he looked to the floor. "It's no bother. It's just, you know, I don't want to send the wrong message."

To me? Our colleagues? What message? "Understood. I'll leave it up to you. No worries if you call it a night of dancing. With me."

Spencer stepped back, offering a healing distance between them, one that pierced Jordyn's hopes and dreams. "Just so you know, I could dance with you all night." His lowered voice left her shaky. "I also would love to take you to that quiet table in the corner and talk. Or not." Another wink.

Jordyn's laugh was as shaky as her footing. "As tempting as that is, it also probably means we should mingle."

Spencer nodded. "That works, too. Say, Rich said Vince and Marcus are planning February sweeps. Did you hear anything about our names and a wedding?"

Jordyn coughed until her voice weakened. "Did you say wedding?"

CHAPTER TWENTY

Spencer climbed out of bed thankful he'd ushered in Christmas with a midnight service. Sleeping in was a rare treat, but he figured it was time to start the coffee maker and maybe make scrambled eggs.

Dad beat him to the kitchen and had coffee brewing. "Merry Christmas. I'm so glad you don't have to work." His eyes were bright and a new joy radiated from his face.

"Merry Christmas to you, Dad. That makes two of us. My plan is to stay home and hang out with you."

Dad handed him a mug. "Perfect. We can enjoy a ham dinner, too."

The two sipped their java and talked about the show while they waited for Carson. Dad was still chuckling over Spencer misunderstanding the wedding plans for WFRN. "Haven't you watched those other morning shows? They feature a Valentine's Day live wedding. People write in hoping they will be picked so their nuptials will be paid by the network. The bride and groom have real tearjerker stories. Your mom always had the tissues out during those weddings."

That made much more sense. "Blame it on the party's loud music and late hour. I honestly thought Marcus and Vince meant Jordyn and I had to get married for the show."

Dad continued to laugh hard enough he snorted.

Carson sauntered down the hallway, rubbing his eyes. "For a minute I thought Santa was here with all that jolly noise."

He'd never been a morning person. Spencer returned to the kitchen to pour his brother a mug full of caffeine. "And Merry Christmas to you." He handed him the drink. "Dad was enjoying my confusion at the WFRN party."

"I didn't hear anything about it." Carson took a drink and stretched.

"Spencer thought when the boss men said they were planning a wedding at WFRN that involved him and Jordyn, that it meant they had to get married." Dad still chuckled.

Carson opened up the snack cupboard and pulled out a box of store-bought donut holes. He placed the bag on the counter after he popped one in his mouth. Once finished, he sighed. "That wouldn't be the worst thing in the world, would it? Deny it as much as you want, but it's obvious you're in love with her."

There's no way I'm debating that comment. Especially Christmas morning. "Let's open presents, shall we?"

Carson snickered. "Coward," and meandered to the living room where the five-foot artificial tree stood.

"I have a better idea. Let's bring back one of your mother's traditions." Dad's knees cracked as he moved from the kitchen to the couch.

The brothers glanced at each other, and both shrugged.

"You're making a big breakfast? I wouldn't have had the donut holes." Carson lamented, sitting on the floor next to the tree.

Dad shook his head and leaned across the couch to the scratched-up end table. "You'll have to talk to Spencer about making breakfast," He held up a leather-bound book. "Let's read from the Bible before we open gifts. Your mother insisted on it when you were kids."

The memories came over Spencer like Mom's smile. He could almost picture her on the couch, Dad's arm around her, as she read. "It was the second chapter of Luke, wasn't it?"

"You remembered." Dad's smile was contagious. "Care to do the honors, Spencer?"

He joined Dad on the couch and accepted the Bible, placing it on his lap. "Let me find it. My guess is it's one of the pages Mom dog-eared and highlighted years ago."

Carson nodded. "I miss her."

Sacred silence filled the room as Spencer found the passage. "Got it. She wrote in the margin to read Christmas morning through verse twenty-one." He looked up and noticed his brother leaning in, way more invested in the reading than Spencer could remember.

"Go on, Son." Dad's voice was soft and tender.

Spencer took a deep breath. "At that time the Roman emperor, Augustus, decreed that a census should be taken throughout the Roman Empire." At first, he didn't pause for fear of getting choked up. "Suddenly, the angel was joined by a vast host of others—the armies of heaven—praising God and saying, 'Glory to God in highest heaven, and peace on earth to those with whom God is pleased.'"

Dad's commentary was full of emotion. "Can you imagine the scene? I always listened to this out of respect to your mother, but this year, it's so real to me."

Spencer's throat carried a ball of regret and grief.

"An army of angels. That's insane." Carson shook his head.

The last line seemed to jump off the page as Spencer considered his faith journey. The daily prayer to surrender control. His growing feelings for Jordyn no matter how much he tried to deny them. "And peace on earth to those with whom God is pleased. That's amazing."

. ♡ ♡ ♡

Jordyn peeked out her bedroom window and found that a soft layer of snow blanketed the driveway. Not even Christmas morning could halt her morning car counting habit. Specifically, the check to make sure Paige was home. *Good. Her vehicle was parked.*

A quick knock followed by the bedroom door opening revealed Kelly. "Jordy? Ready to go downstairs?" Kelly piled her long, black hair on top of her head into a messy bun as she shuffled in wearing her pajamas and faded fuzzy slippers.

"Be right there."

Kelly turned to the door and took a few steps before pivoting back toward Jordyn. "By the way, Merry Christmas."

Jordyn narrowed her gaze as she tried to drop her worries about Paige and focus on Kelly being home. *For Christmas.* "Right, Merry Christmas, Kel. Let me get my robe."

By the time Jordyn descended the stairs, tantalizing bacon aroma filled the dining room. She resisted the urge to pick up a piece and entered the family room where the tree stood. The place where Shelly threw out the beloved decoration and revealed Paige was drinking. *Maybe hiding in the dining room with a plate of bacon is a better idea than staying here.*

"Merry Christmas, Jordy. How refreshing to enjoy a morning with you in person and not on your show." Dad hurried over for a hug she didn't realize she needed.

Evan joined the embrace. "When do you go back live? These repeat shows aren't the same."

Ryan approached Jordyn as soon as Dad and Evan stepped back. Instead of a hug, he reached for her hands and squeezed them. "Merry Christmas, Sis."

Jordyn glanced around to see if the other siblings were close by. James stood by Kelly, who was drinking orange juice. Shelly was at Dad's side. "Where's Paige?"

"I'm here."

One glance at Paige and Jordyn let out a sharp exhale. Paige's dark, long locks that matched Jordyn and Kelly's were cut into a wavy, blonde bob. Her glasses were gone. Something about her looked older than twenty-four and like a lost child at the same time.

"Wow. Your hair." Kelly beat Jordyn as the first responder.

Paige waltzed past them and sat by the tree on the floor, near the presents. "Did anyone volunteer to be Santa's elf?"

Ryan glanced at Jordyn, brow raised.

Dad led Shelly to the gift area as well, not giving any indication he was shocked or concerned at his youngest sextuplet. "No, Pumpkin Paige. It's your hat to wear if you want it." He reached across the tree and handed her the elf ears they had all taken turns wearing over the years.

Paige placed the oversized ears and felt hat on her head. "Well, are you going to stare all morning or come over here to open presents?"

I'm going to do both. Jordyn swallowed hard and took hesitant steps toward the tree. What on earth was Paige thinking, changing her hair and ditching glasses? She looked like a stranger.

Ryan sat next to her, eyes to the carpet.

"Any good elf knows you start with the stockings." Evan pointed to the mantle where nine crowded stockings hung together. "Better open the dog's first."

Shelly chuckled and walked to the mantle, pulling down each stocking. "Gigi can probably wait longer than you, Evan."

Laughter broke the awkward tension surrounding them. They each held their own over-stuffed decorated sock and waited for the signal to open.

Dad cleared his throat. "Before we tear into the stocking stuffers, I thought we'd bring back a tradition."

Jordyn narrowed her gaze. *Where was this going?*

"I wanted to start it last year but it was too chaotic with the wedding, Ryan being back from the Navy, and well, things seem calmer now." He nodded to Shelly, who returned to the mantle and picked up a book.

"You're going to read to us?" Kelly asked.

Dad chuckled. "I am." He gestured for Shelly to re-join him. "I'd like to read from the Bible."

Jordyn dropped her handmade stocking. "Why?"

"You guys might not remember, but your mom used to read it each Christmas morning. It was actually Shelly's idea to bring the tradition back." He looked to Shelly, who put her hand on his leg.

"Mom did read. I remember." Ryan was all in.

With no verbal objections, Dad opened the big book and flipped toward the back. His soothing voice made the story come alive. "All who heard the shepherds' story were astonished, [19] but Mary kept all these things in her heart and thought about them often.." When he stopped, Jordyn looked up and saw him swipe at his eye.

"Dad?"

He focused on Jordyn. "I'm okay. That line about Mary."

Shelly's voice shook. "It's so powerful."

"For me, reading it right now, it takes me back. It reminds me of when we learned your mother was pregnant. Doctors cautioned us with the risks in keeping you all. Your mother prayed and prayed. The danger to carry and deliver was great." Dad swallowed hard. "But she treasured you. And her faith and prayers convinced her to say no to the doctors in order to say yes to our family."

Selective reduction. Jordyn glanced around the room. Mom had been advised to abort some of her offspring. What a horrible conflict.

James bit at his bottom lip. "Thanks, Dad. I'm sure the choice wasn't easy."

"Actually, Son, it was. Sure, we prayed, but deep down we knew. By obeying God's way, we became the first family to deliver sextuplets to term in full health."

Paige fidgeted as Dad finished, but grabbed the present closest to her before he closed the Bible. "This one's for Ryan from Evan."

Jordyn considered the sentence about Mary as Paige passed out gifts. All those years Jordyn thought the Bible was simply a boring history book. Yet, what Dad shared about Mom made what he read so relatable.

"Jordy? Did you hear?" Paige's voice rose about Jordyn's thoughts.

"Huh? No. Sorry."

Paige pointed to the corner. "That sad wrapping job over there is for you from Ryan."

She looked next to the sectional and found wrinkled Christmas paper draped over what looked like an upright vacuum. Jordyn stood and walked over, pulling the covering off. "Ry, why did you get me a vacuum when I still live here?'

Ryan fidgeted with his shoelaces for a moment before facing her. "You won't always live here." He scrunched his eyebrows. "Will you?"

Why can't he ask Evan the same question? She crossed her arms against her chest. "No. So this is for my future?"

"And mine. While we all wait for you to get a life—" Ryan started.

"With Spencer." Evan coughed.

"Evan. That's enough." Dad shot his third child a cautionary look.

Ryan rolled his eyes at Evan and then faced Jordyn. "I bought it in hopes you'd help me clean up."

"Your house?" Jordyn's voice rose as she imagined this little upright sucking up the destruction known as Ryan's place.

James burst out laughing and Kelly covered her mouth before turning away, her shoulders shaking. Even Shelly bit down on her lip.

Ryan shifted on the floor. "Yes, Jordy. With your organizational skills, you'd do an amazing job getting the downstairs in shape."

"Dude, that's going to take an army and a load of sledgehammers." Evan chuckled.

Paige stood with a package in her hands. "Can we agree that a gift card would have been better? Let's move on." She read the tag. "For the Hart family. From Aunt Julia."

Dad scooted forward on the couch. "Go ahead. Open it."

Paige nodded and ripped the paper off the rectangular, thin box. "It's a note."

"What does it say?" Kelly asked.

"It says, 'turn around.'" Paige scoffed as she obeyed. "I'm facing the tree."

A familiar, female voice came from the kitchen, getting louder as the speaker walked closer. The rest of the family turned and found Julia entering the room. "When I asked your dad to set this up for me, I pictured you all on the floor facing the tree. Sorry, Paige."

The sextuplets rushed toward their mom's childhood best friend and surrounded her with a group hug.

"Merry Christmas!" Evan's orange juice breath blew on Jordyn's ear.

Julia chuckled. "Merry Christmas to all of you. The hugs are just as sticky and tight as when you were six."

The group backed off and gave Julia space for Dad and Shelly to greet her.

"So glad you pulled off the surprise. How does it feel to have time off?" Dad offered her his place on the couch while Shelly handed Julia a mug.

Julia gripped the mug. "Ah, coffee. You're a lifesaver, Shelly." She took a sip and looked to Dad. "Strange. It's been a long time since I've had time off where I didn't need to go somewhere else." She sighed and focused on the tree. "We can talk later. Go ahead and open presents."

An hour later, Paige took off the elf headgear and Dad packed the last of the wrapping paper into a third black garbage bag. Jordyn picked up her stack of gift cards, sweaters, and earrings to place them somewhere away from people and garbage.

Julia crossed the room and met Jordyn at the base of the staircase. "Jordy, I ran into Marcus Bright recently. That guy is seriously impressed with *Early Rise and Shine*."

"Vince told me at the Christmas party. The show's a bigger hit than I expected." Jordyn held her presents against her chest. "I did have an incident a few weeks ago. Wondered if I could talk to you about it."

Julia nodded. "I texted Spencer and he insisted I stay at the house. My boss sent me here on a company plane, and arranged a ride here. Do you mind driving me to my house? We can talk on the way."

Spending Christmas with Spencer? Sure, no problem.

Anchored Hearts

CHAPTER TWENTY-ONE

Spencer stacked the last of the dinner plates in the dishwasher and turned it on, stifling an after Christmas dinner yawn. With the meal finished, Dad and Carson reclined in the living room watching *It's a Wonderful Life*.

"Anyone want anything to drink before I join you?" Spencer called out, pouring himself a cup of coffee.

Silence. *Probably couldn't hear over the dishwasher.* He left the kitchen and stepped into the living room area. "Did you two—" Spencer looked out the bay window and saw a car coming up the drive. "That's Jordyn's car."

Carson turned with enough force his neck cracked. "Christmas keeps on giving."

'Dad chuckled as he rose from the recliner and took a gander for himself. "She's not alone." He turned to Spencer. "You didn't know she was visiting?"

Spencer shook his head. "No clue." He thought about his recent texts with Julia. "Unless Jordyn is Julia's transportation. This would be about the time Julia said she'd be here. I lost track of the day."

The trio watched the car park, and once the front doors opened, Carson bolted for the bathroom. Dad muttered something about putting on a fresh pot of coffee. Spencer rolled his eyes and headed to the entrance. "I guess I'll greet them."

He opened the door as Jordyn's index finger landed on the bell.

Her almond-shaped brown eyes widened. "Merry Christmas! Were you waiting for us?"

Julia stepped forward, and Spencer couldn't help but stare. America's anchor was mere feet away from him.

"Merry Christmas, Spencer." She turned to Jordyn. "With that big window I'm sure he saw us coming."

He swung the door all the way and gestured for them to come inside. Julia strode through with her long leather coat making squeaking sounds as she placed her luggage down. She removed her dark glasses and placed them on top of her short, black hair. "Spencer, it's a pleasure to meet you. I appreciate you moving in. I hated how the place sat unattended." Julia extended her hand and shook his.

Wow, that's a firm grip. "You did us a favor. I'm so happy to see you in person. I've been a fan for a long time."

Julia tilted her head as if every word he uttered carried significant meaning. Just like her interviews. "Thank you. Jordyn raved about your family. Where are they?"

Spencer looked around the room. "Dad said he was making coffee. I suspect Carson's making sure his hair looks good for you both."

Jordyn giggled. "Let's go in the kitchen. Julia, Mr. Collins loves to watch our shows. He's a sweet man."

Dad straightened and his jaw lowered once they entered the kitchen. "Julia Turmeric." He turned toward Spencer. "I can't believe she's in the kitchen. Her kitchen. This is crazy."

How fun to watch Dad fan-girl over a celebrity. Oh, wait. I acted the same. "Julia, this is my father, Ray Collins."

"Sir, thank you for keeping this home in tip-top shape. It's an honor to meet a retired firefighter." Julia's charm appeared to have melted Dad's heart as he stepped closer to her and pulled out a chair.

"You must be tired from your travels. Please sit and have some coffee. I'll have Carson take your luggage to your room."

Spencer raised his brow and faced Jordyn. "Time to find Carson. He'll come out of hiding for you."

She followed him out, leaving her puffy coat on the couch. Even in jeans and a long wine-red sweater, Jordyn still looked like she could grab a microphone and go live with no notice.

He approached the bathroom door and knocked. "Carson, your hair is fine. Be polite and greet the ladies."

Jordyn stood next to Spencer. "Merry Christmas, Carson."

There were a few seconds of rustling behind the closed door before it opened. Carson sprinted out in a fog of sprays and cologne. He shoved his hands in his pockets and leaned against the wall. "Hey, Jordyn. Did you have a good holiday?"

She bit her lip for a moment before grinning. "I have a few family details to iron out before I can answer, but there's hope." She curled her finger and gestured toward the kitchen. "C'mon, you need to meet Aunt Julia."

Carson let out a high-pitched laugh. "That's nuts that she's Aunt Julia to you. That's like calling Oprah your close friend or something."

Jordyn kept moving, her sleek hair bouncing with each step.

Carson sped up and nudged Spencer before they reached the kitchen. "This is mind-blowing. I can't believe we're spending Christmas with Julia Turmeric." He whispered.

"Try not to embarrass me." *If Dad hasn't already.*

Laughter filled the kitchen as they entered and found Dad sitting with Julia as if they had been acquainted for years. He stood and offered Jordyn his chair, then moved next to Carson. "Julia, my youngest son, Carson."

She rose and gave him a handshake and warm megawatt smile. "The football standout. I saw some highlights a few weeks ago."

Carson shook her hand with the energy of a child on a sugar rush. "What is happening here? The Julia Turmeric knows who I am." He looked down at his moving hand and released his grip. "Miss Turmeric, it's an honor."

"You're too kind. Can we take this to the living room? My vacation goal is to see a deer in the yard."

Dad helped her with the chair as Spencer led the way. Julia beelined for the overstuffed chair closest to the bay window. Carson and Dad returned to their recliners, leaving Jordyn and Spencer on the couch.

"While I'm on the lookout for wild animals, let's hear about *Early Rise and Shine*." Julia peeked out the window and then focused toward the couch.

Jordyn sighed. "Kent Misny showed his true colors at the Christmas party."

Spencer straightened. "He displayed those the first time I met him."

"He said his company plans to throw a lot of money at WFRN and land a weekly interview on our show. If that's not enough, his hope is to have a half-hour show. Both with me as host." Jordyn ran her hand through those beautiful black locks.

"Why is that so bad?" Dad asked.

Julia stretched out and crossed her feet at the ankles. "He's using you for your name with the hopes you'll move up the ladder and take him with you."

"How did you know?" Jordyn's mouth opened so wide Dad could have fit the leftovers in there.

"I've had it happen to me, and your parents fielded various opportunities on your behalf when you and your siblings were kids." She said it so matter-of-factly Spencer tried to hide his shock.

Carson shook his head. "That's terrible. Spence, you should tell the guy to back off."

If he only knew. "Not my job. Jordyn can handle it."

She turned to Spencer and smiled. "Not well. You were the one who rescued me at the party."

"Now we're talking." Carson rubbed his hands together.

Julia didn't have any problem joining in. "Rescue how?"

"Kent was going on and on about his plans to take over the state and then the country. He even mocked me for being content at WFRN."

Something in Spencer's gut tightened. The last thing he wanted to face was Jordyn leaving.

Julia stifled a yawn. "Funny that you said that about the station."

Spencer's neck hair stood at attention. "What do you mean?"

"Marcus Bright doesn't attend every station Christmas party. He's a busy guy."

Jordyn leaned on the armrest. "Aunt Julia, I don't understand."

"He owns a few stations in different sized markets. As sizzling as you both have been on *Early Rise and Shine*, rumor has it Marcus was checking out the potential of sending one or both of you to a bigger station." Julia glanced again out the window and pointed. "Yay! There's a deer."

. ♡ ♡ ♡

Jordyn looked around the room and realized while everyone was in shocked silence with Julia's bombshell, it was a cue to leave. Talking about Kent drained her, and she still had to catch Paige and talk to her before the party-girl darted off again. "On that note, I'm going to head home."

Carson piped up. "Spencer will walk you out." He looked around and followed up with, "To keep you safe. You know, because of the deer."

"Uh-huh." Spencer stood as soon as Jordyn did. "As capable as you are, Jordyn, it's the polite thing to do." He jogged ahead to open the door for her.

Jordyn zipped up her coat, turned and waved. "Nice to see you Mr. Collins, Carson. Aunt Julia, let's do lunch before you head back."

Spencer moved onto the sidewalk and waited for her to catch up. "That was a surprise about Marcus Bright."

She produced gloves from her pockets and put them on. "He wouldn't be a good executive if he wasn't watching the talent. Don't think too much of it. The show isn't a year old. My guess is he'll wait until our contracts are up."

"Then what? You said you like being at the show."

Jordyn reached the driver door and hit unlock on the key fob. "That's right. He'll probably approach you." *This conversation needs to end. No way am I confessing how much I despise the scenario.*

Spencer let out a nervous laugh and ran his hand through his hair. "Wow. My goal for the longest time was to anchor the six. I never considered moving to a bigger market."

Her throat threatened to close. Spencer sounded so casual and sure. How could he even consider leaving? Probably because she pushed him away time and time again. "Well, let's get through the new year, shall we?" She opened the door and slid in before Spencer had a chance to draw near.

He chuckled. "Thanks for coming out. It was good to see you."

Jordyn shut the door and started the ignition, her fragile heart beating with each rev of the engine. "Right. Enjoy your time off." Backing up and then leaving the long drive, Jordyn glanced at the rearview mirror as Spencer grew smaller. *Okay, no time to fight these feelings that are stronger each time we connect. However, Paige needs my undivided attention.*

Forty-five minutes later, Jordyn pulled into her designated spot, Paige's car still parked. She scurried through the garage and shed her shoes and coat in the mud room.

"Jordy? That you?"

Jordyn charged into the kitchen, nearly knocking Shelly over. "Sorry, I wanted to catch Paige before she went to bed." She recalled the truth Shelly lobbed at her about Paige's partying ways. "Or leaves."

Shelly's face showed no emotion as she pulled at a piece of rye bread. "Paige was on the phone earlier." After a bite, she continued. "Jordyn, we never addressed our conflict. I blurted something out about your sister that was not handled well. I'm sorry."

Jordyn slowed. The right thing to do was reconcile. But Paige could be planning her next escapade. "It's fine. I had every right to know. If you'll excuse me, I need to find her."

"You can't say the perfect thing and make her stop. Jordy, there's no way to control this. Honestly, it's something to pray about."

Okay, the Christmas story was nice. This faith chat is too much. "Point taken." Jordyn stretched and feigned a yawn. "Good night. I'm going to head upstairs." She jogged up the stairs before Shelly could respond. No matter what her step-mom wanted to say, Jordyn was set on confronting her sister.

Paige was leaving the upstairs "kid" bathroom wearing a gold sweater and black dress pants. Her lips were painted a bold red, something Jordyn didn't recall seeing before.

"You don't have to work tonight. The hotel restaurant has to be closed for Christmas." Jordyn stepped into the hallway, blocking Paige's attempt to use the stairs.

"It is. I'm not going there."

Jordyn took a deep cleansing breath. "Where are you going, then?"

Paige's eyes transformed from a calm brown to a dark, black storm and her face contorted to match the incoming thunder. "It's none of your business. Honestly, Jordyn. We're twenty-four. No one needs to check in, especially with you."

Jordyn's jaw clenched. "I ask because I'm concerned."

"Really. Because James and Kelly are living in another city going to college and you don't bother them with an interrogation." Paige took a step forward.

I'm not backing down. Jordyn crossed her arms against her chest and stood on her toes.

"Seriously, Jordyn. Move. I'm not explaining myself to you. Sorry you don't have friends to go out with because you're married to your work and smothering us."

Okay, that stung. "If you're planning on doing something dangerous, I think I have every right to speak up."

Paige rolled her eyes. "We have different definitions of dangerous. Unless you want me to raise my voice and alarm Dad and Shelly, it's time you let me through."

Where was Paige, the confidante and cheerleader when all the other siblings were bickering with Jordyn? The only girl on their soccer team that gave pep talks and shared snacks?

Jordyn's gut churned and the hall felt twenty degrees warmer with their exchange. Her heartbeat drumming like a hard rock band audition, Jordyn stepped aside.

"Have a nice night doing nothing." Paige scoffed, pushing against Jordyn's side as she passed her.

Jordyn watched the faux blonde hair bounce as Paige bounded down the steps, never looking back. Hot tears spilled and, with lips protruding in a pout, Jordyn wiped her face with the back of her hand as she moved toward her room.

Evan popped out of his bedroom and smiled wide as soon as he saw Jordyn. If he heard anything between the sisters, he wasn't letting on. Instead, Evan offered a tap on Jordyn's forearm. "Hey, Jordy. So glad you're here. We need to talk."

CHAPTER TWENTY-TWO

Spencer spotted Julia returning from her hike in the woods huddled behind a coat collar close to her face. *Hot chocolate should warm her up and give us a chance to chat.* He marched into the kitchen, determined to make her the drink before she ditched her winter gear in the foyer.

The front door opened and banged against the wall from a blustery wind that had plagued Julia's entire vacation in the Southern Tier. Spencer left the milk, sugar, and cocoa concoction heating on the stovetop and found Julia unzipping her boots.

"I forgot how cold it gets here compared to Manhattan. Clearly, I'm ill-equipped." Julia pointed to the sleek leather coat and chuckled.

"Good news. I saw you leaving the woods and made you a cup of homemade hot chocolate. It should be ready in a minute." Spencer gestured her to follow him to the kitchen.

"Thank you. That sounds heavenly. I wanted to circle the pond and back but that wind slapped me around like a punching bag." She pulled out a chair as Spencer turned off the burner and stirred the contents before pouring it in a Finger Lakes mug. "Join me. You've been a great host this week. I'd love to chat and get to know you better."

Spencer served her and sat across the island. "Being hospitable is the least I can do after you've let us live here rent free."

Julia took a sip and put her hand on her heart. "This is delicious. Reminds me of snow days when I lived in Big Flats. My mom always had cocoa ready for Jordyn's mom and me."

Jordyn's name sent a shiver through Spencer. Although he hadn't seen her since Christmas, he thought of her constantly. "I forgot you grew up in Big Flats. Do you still have family around?"

She shook her head. "No. My siblings are scattered across the country and my parents are gone. Lisa's parents were like my own, but only her mom is left. She moved down south once the kids graduated." Julia laughed. "Kids. They are twenty-four. I'm sure it didn't go fast for Paul, but the years flew by for me."

Picturing Jordyn as a child, Spencer had a feeling even then she was leading her siblings, keeping them organized and out of trouble. "If you don't mind me asking, do you plan on staying with *Rise and Shine* and *Wednesday Nights with Julia*? You've been at the network for a while."

"It depends on the day. There are times I'm ready to hand in my resignation and find a new purpose beyond anchoring. Then, other times I can't imagine myself anywhere but looking at the camera and sharing the latest with the world." She took another sip and wrapped her hands around the mug. "What about you? You must have goals."

Ugh. Not very ambitious ones. "Before *Early Rise and Shine* debuted, my focus was to move from Binghamton reporter to WFRN six o'clock anchor." He offered a sheepish grin. "Not anything lofty compared to what you've accomplished, but mom became terminally ill my senior year of college. All I wanted was to graduate and be close to her."

Julia slowly nodded as if she were processing memories. "The temptation to quit my job and return to the area when Lisa died consumed me. My life is busy, but lonely. She was my best friend. We talked every day, if only for a minute to say, 'Hey,' and then one of us got called away." She looked up for a moment. "You're blessed to have been able to spend time with your mother and stay local. There's nothing wrong with that. I can tell family is important to you."

Spencer glanced toward the living room, guessing that's probably where Dad was. "They've been through a lot. I was concerned for a while, but things are improving. Carson goes to college in the fall. It's like we made it through a storm and I can breathe." He smiled. "I'm sure you relate."

"My office should hold a plaque for surviving life's storms. Not that I don't appreciate my Edward R. Murrow award." She winked.

Spencer let out a slow whistle. "That's amazing. From Big Flats to award-winning national journalist. Who was your favorite interview?"

Julia rolled her shoulders back. "The answer most people want to hear is a former president or dictator." She tapped her fingers on the marble countertop. "Maybe even a beloved celebrity."

"Those famous interviews aren't the ones you want to be remembered for?" Spencer raised a brow.

"Nope. It's the sextuplets." Julia sighed. "They are my extension to Lisa. I certainly wasn't meant to leave my career and help Paul care for them after she died, but those annual interviews are everything." She flashed a sly smile at Spencer. "So, it's just us. Tell me, Spencer. What are your feelings about Jordyn?"

. ♡ ♡ ♡

Jordyn picked up her phone only to return it to her bed, and repeated the motion several times as she considered texting Aunt Julia. It was New Year's Eve Day and the last day of Julia's vacation. *Okay, you have to do this.* Jordyn held onto the phone and clicked Julia's message icon.

Hey, do you have time to meet? I have a couple things I want to run by you.

After Jordyn hit send, she noticed the bubble text pop up, showing Julia was typing.

Absolutely. Sorry I missed you when I visited yesterday. Come to my house. Let's ring in the new year.

Jordyn stared at the invitation. *New Year's Eve at Julia's? Would Spencer be home? Where would Paige be?* She sunk her face in her hands and groaned before responding.

What can I bring?

Junk food.

When Julia's long driveway came to an end, Jordyn noticed Ryan's truck parked behind Spencer's. Her breathing steadied as she considered her brother part of her conversation. He'd know what to do with Evan and everything else going on.

Mr. Collins greeted Jordyn with a warm hello and a quick hug. "So good to see you again, Jordyn. Come in."

Each time she saw him, the man seemed softer. No gruff responses or glassy eyes. Spencer never mentioned where his dad's sobriety was, but Jordyn sensed he wasn't drinking. "Thank you, Mr. Collins. Julia told me to bring junk food, so I have lots of snacks here." She lifted up her canvas totes.

His eyes brightened. "I insist you call me Ray. And I pray there are potato chips in there."

Jordyn set her belongings down and pulled out one of three potato chip bags. "Your wish is granted, Ray." She smiled, picked the snacks back up, and headed to the kitchen.

Julia sat at the island with Ryan, Spencer, and Carson. When Jordyn entered and placed the goods on the counter, Julia rose. "I know I'm back on air in a couple days, but chips are a must tonight."

Ryan also stood and walked over next to Jordyn, leaning close he whispered. "What a nice surprise. Are you here for Aunt Julia or Spencer?"

She wasted no time elbowing him in the gut. "Funny. There are things I want to run by Aunt Julia so she told me to come over. You should be a part of the conversation as well."

"Is it about Paige?"

"I don't even know where to start with her. It's Paige, Evan, and work stuff." Jordyn closed her eyes for a moment then opened them, wondering where the chocolate was.

Ryan didn't answer, but his slow exhale blew toward Jordyn.

"You two stop whispering and come on over." Julia waved the siblings over. "Jordy, you mentioned needing to talk. There's no better time than the present."

Jordyn swallowed hard and sat next to Ryan. "Are you sure you're up to this?" Spencer nodded. She let out a shaky laugh and focused on her handsome co-anchor. "I'm about to spill a lot about myself and my dysfunctional family."

. ♡ ♡ ♡

Spencer straightened in his chair as he drank in Jordyn's every word. There was something about her in Ryan and Julia's presence that lowered her invisible walls and displayed her vulnerability. He didn't dare look at Carson. Spencer's face would probably reveal everything his little brother had been saying all along. *I'm in love with Jordyn Hart.*

"What hurts about Paige is we were close. She used to tell me everything. Our last conversation was full of derision. I don't know how to reach her." Jordyn nabbed a wavy chip and nibbled.

Ryan slowly reached behind and rubbed the back of his neck. "Maybe you don't try. I hate what's happening too, but we're adults. She's allowed to live her own life, even if we don't agree with it."

Jordyn's eyes widened and she leaned in. "What if we do nothing and Paige gets hurt?" Her voice cracked. "Or worse?"

Dad broke the tension when he entered the kitchen with a cookie tray. "I thought the party would be in the living room." He chuckled. "And this doesn't seem festive. What's going on?"

"I'll take that." Carson rose and helped Dad with the tray, placing it in front of Jordyn. "Chocolate chip. It cures nearly everything." Carson winked.

That boy is a charmer. "Have a seat, Dad. Jordyn was sharing a situation regarding her sister. Paige is drinking a lot and acting out." Spencer stood and offered Dad the chair.

Julia reached for a cookie and pointed to the last empty seat next to her. "Ray, come on over here. I'd love to hear your wisdom."

"I'm not sure what kind of help I can be, but there's no way I'm turning down an opportunity to sit next to you, Miss Julia." Dad winked.

Oh, so that's where Carson's charisma comes from.

Dad looked around the kitchen island and took a bite out of a cookie. He chewed slowly, swallowed, and then faced Jordyn. "I'm not a doctor, but I say this from personal experience—those who drink to excess need to numb their pain."

Julia shook her head. "Paige can't be drinking because of the accident, right? Years ago, I set up Paul and the kids with therapy."

"It's possible. The Navy brought out childhood trauma I had not dealt with." Ryan stared at the bowl of chips before taking a handful.

"So, what do I do?" Jordyn looked to Ryan. "What do we do?"

Spencer's heart hurt seeing the pain etched across her face.

"Pray." Dad's blunt response brought a collective gasp from Julia, Ryan, and Jordyn. "Seriously. My wife was on her knees every morning praying for us, even when she was dying. I went off the rails in grief and used alcohol as my comforter, but it wasn't any help. Finding her Bible and praying, that was key for me. Everyone who loves Paige has to surrender her and believe God has got her."

Jordyn blinked back tears.

Spencer grabbed a napkin and handed it to her. "I know this isn't an easy answer, but it's helping me. My way of dealing with grief was to jump ahead and try to solve everything. It's not a way to live."

She nodded and offered a small smile. "Thank you. I'll take everything that's been said into consideration."

Ryan blew out a sigh. "Dare I switch gears and ask what's going on with Evan?"

Carson stood and picked up the cookie tray. "I've seen enough of him on TV to know we need to move to the living room. This conversation will take a while."

Ryan smirked and joined Carson, a bowl of chips under his arm.

Spencer waited for Jordyn, extending his hand to her arm. "Hey, Paige will be okay."

"I want to fix her. Is that so wrong?" Those chocolate saucers of hers nearly cut him at the knees.

He shook his head. "Loving your sister isn't wrong."

"Spencer, what you aren't saying speaks volumes. You still want me to trust God with her. I hope you're praying."

"Of course I am. Why?" Spencer rubbed her shoulder in a circular motion.

"Because it's going to take a miracle."

It was eleven-thirty before the group hashed out all the scenarios regarding Evan's confession that he had a premise for the reality show Julia suggested for their twenty-fifth celebration. Restore Ryan's home.

Julia leaned back in her overstuffed chair. "It has potential."

Carson chuckled. "Jordyn, I have to see you take a sledgehammer to a wall."

Spencer bit his lip before taking the plunge. "She might do that with or without a show." The more he pictured the siblings working on Ryan's dilapidated home, Spencer considered what it would take to make the show binge-able. A must-watch. "You'd need a hook that sets you apart from other reality shows. I don't think being sextuplets is enough."

The group sat in silence for a few moments, except when Julia stood and helped herself to a cookie.

Ryan paced the living room perimeter. "Aunt Julia, you know I hate Evan's constant scheming to bring the family publicity."

"Consider this, though. From what I've heard, you've got more than a fixer-upper. A reality show brings financing and repairs." Julia turned toward Spencer. "But it's true, there has to be something special to set it apart from any other home improvement shows."

Dad glanced at the wall clock. "Five minutes till midnight. Let's think on it while we get some sparkling cider together for a toast."

Spencer returned to the kitchen to grab glasses. When he turned toward the fridge, Jordyn had snuck in behind him, standing in front of the doors. "You should wear a bell, Jordyn. I didn't know you followed me in."

She held up two sparkling cider bottles. "You were too busy creating a reality show."

He searched her face for a reaction. Did she love the idea? Resent him? "Should I be quiet?" The glasses clinked together. "Will Ryan toss me in a snowbank?"

Jordyn's giggle was an invisible ribbon wrapping around Spencer's heart. She backed against the door, but didn't open it. "Your input means everything to me. At work. Here. I might disagree, or even be scared of what you say." She took a deep breath and locked eyes with his. "But Spencer, I love that no matter what conversation you're involved in, you're always trying to help and improve things. Please never change."

With that, she pivoted and returned to the living room.

Spencer paused to get his heart back in alignment, jolted back to reality by Carson pointing to the clock. As they poured their drinks, Spencer stole another look at Jordyn. There might not be a kiss at midnight, but Jordyn's encouragement was pretty close.

Dad turned on the television and the famed Times Square ball started to descend. "Raise your glasses, it's almost time."

Jordyn held her drink in her right hand, moving her hair behind her ear with the left.

There has to be a way I can stand by her to ring in the new year.

"Hey, Spencer. Can you hand Jordy a cookie? I can't see her starting a new year without chocolate." Ryan jutted his head in his sister's direction, so Spencer took the few steps to pick up a napkin and a cookie.

He weaved past Dad with hopes to land at Jordyn's side as the clock struck twelve.

"Five. Four. Three." The television countdown added to Spencer's stress to reach Jordyn.

Just as the new year shouts and music blared from Times Square, Carson moved and ended up next to Jordyn, a slow grin evolving into a wide smile. "I've got it. The perfect reality pitch. How about blending two premises together?"

Everyone held their glasses mid-air.

"Let's hear it." Julia treated him like a valued colleague, not a high school senior.

Carson stood a little taller. "Before the siblings work on the house, start with a matchmaking aspect. Perhaps that's how you find a crew. Have people apply to be matched with you."

Spencer dropped the cookie. He bent down to retrieve it, silently praying. *Don't let my face show how much I don't want Jordyn being matched with strangers.*

When he straightened, Dad tipped his glass toward Julia's. "Happy New Year!"

Anchored Hearts

CHAPTER TWENTY-THREE

Jordyn stared at the suitcase she'd nearly tripped over on her way up the stairs to her room. Evan raced over, picked it up with a whistle and spring in his step.

She huffed as he moved the obstacles. "Where are you going? Visiting James and Kelly in Cortland?"

Evan scoffed and patted the hard-shell luggage. "It's way more important than seeing them. I'm going to Manhattan."

Her ears perked up at the mention of the big city and Aunt Julia's homebase. She placed her hands on her hips. "Evan, why are you going there?"

"Aunt Julia invited me. It's not like I have any plans for Valentine's Day, and she wants me to meet with the agent she secured for the reality show. Plans are moving forward." He sang in a sing-song voice, producing his phone from his pocket. "I'll be back in a couple of days."

Jordyn's stomach churned. She'd been so busy at work with *Early Rise and Shine's* live wedding that their twenty-fifth birthday reality show idea fell to the wayside. *Ugh. Evan needs a supervisor. This idea has disaster all over it.* "What are the plans, exactly?"

Evan checked his phone. "Jordy, I have to go. Trust me. Everything about the trip will be great." He leaned over and offered a quick peck on the cheek. "Enjoy your Valentine work wedding."

His loafers scuffed against the tile and the luggage wheels trailed behind. Jordyn stood at the bottom of the stairs as the mud room door shut and the garage door opened.

"Hey, Jordyn. Everything okay?" Shelly approached her as though she was a wounded cat.

The two never hashed out their Christmas conflict, and each time they ran into each other pressure built in Jordyn's head. *For Dad's sake, we need to get along.* But work, Evan, Paige, and Spencer were ahead in Jordyn's priority line. "Evan's New York City trip surprised me."

Shelly nodded. "He's gung-ho about this reality show. What are your thoughts?" Her kind blue eyes matched her button-up sweater. "Maybe it will help you get out of using that vacuum cleaner Ryan bought you."

Jordyn offered a small smile and shook her head. "Worst Christmas present ever."

They shared a chuckle and then Jordyn ambled up a couple stairs. "Do you think Aunt Julia can prevent Evan from creating a disaster with this show? This is Ryan's house at stake. I'm also sure none of us want to be the country's laughingstock."

Shelly pursed her lips for a moment and looked toward the stairs. "Evan's a wild card, but he did graduate with a business degree. He's got the chops to create something memorable that honors your unique birth story and special day."

"I suppose." Jordyn reflected on the times Shelly came through for them with last-minute trips to the store for school supplies. Late nights sewing costumes for dance recitals. The numerous football practices she drove Ryan and James to when Dad had to work. "Thank you, Shelly, for sharing your opinion."

Shelly's shoulders slumped in a relaxed pose and she placed her hands on top of her heart. "You're welcome. I'm glad I could help. Are you going to bed?"

"I am. This week is beyond busy with the wedding. Tomorrow I work a full day and then we film the *Early Rise and Shine* bridal shower at Santino's. Spencer's schedule is even worse. He hosts the bachelor party at the hotel restaurant where Paige works." She raked her hand through her hair, wondering if anything about the live wedding was messing with his emotions. *Because my thoughts for Spencer are all over the map.*

"That does sound busy. I'll let you go so you can get some rest. Good night, Jordy." Shelly's voice was as calm as a peaceful brook. She locked eyes with Jordyn. "I love you, sweet girl."

Jordyn's balance wavered as she processed the declaration. "Um, thanks. Good night." She coughed, silently praying the same words could magically spill out of her. Instead, Jordyn continued up the stairs, the stabbing pain in her forehead nagging at her.

The next afternoon, Courtney and Jordyn skipped lunch to prepare for the bridal shower. The viewers chose maroon and pink as the colors, so Natalie lined up colors for the anchors.

"Please tell me we're allowed to eat at this event. It can't be all work, right?" Courtney entered the women's restroom suite with a garment bag draped over her arm.

Jordyn followed, choosing a private dressing area close to the door. "That's the fun aspect about today. We're part of the experience. Sure, we have to interview Brianna and the bridal party, but we also sit with the guests." She unzipped the vinyl bag without looking at the contents.

"I can't believe Vince ordered that the viewers vote on our dresses. What if some angry person puts me in a prairie dress to get revenge for something I did on air?"

"All the choices were modern, so that's good." Jordyn swallowed. "Okay, I'm ready to look at mine. How about you?"

Court's booming voice bounced off the suite walls. "The bag's unzipped. My eyes are closed. Here we go. Three. Two. One. Look."

Jordyn instantly recognized dress number two as the winner. A maroon, long-sleeve lace dress with a wide horizontal neckline, and crochet overlay sleeves that included exaggerated cuffs. The skirt's interior lining hugged her figure, and the same overlay pattern hung a couple of inches past it. Feminine, yet a little sexier than she was used to.

"Well? Do you like it?" Courtney called out as her garment bag dropped to the floor.

"It's number two. I'm afraid I'll drag these sleeves through my plate, but it's beautiful."

"Nice. I remember that choice. Viewers also voted for the first one. Mine's a carnation pink wrap-around mini dress." Courtney's chuckle sounded shaky. "Emphasis on the word 'mini.'"

Jordyn left the changing room first and walked over to the wall of lined chairs, a long countertop, and plastic containers labeled with each anchor's name. She pulled a curling iron out of her basket and plugged it in. *Okay, dress. You need to be longer.*

Courtney's sigh filled the suite. "Get ready for the big reveal."

"Let's see it. We have thirty minutes before we leave for Santino's."

The little cubicle door opened, and Courtney sashayed behind Jordyn, the wall-length mirror displaying the red-head's every move.

Jordyn stood to face her. "That's super cute on you, Court."

The early morning reporter bowed like royalty. "Thank you. Your dress is fire. Seriously, Spencer's going to need to take a cold shower."

Jordyn pulled on her outfit in an effort to lengthen the underskirt. "Oh, stop. It's not what I'm used to wearing. If anything,

Spencer and Rich will hand me a pair of leggings and tell me to put them on for modesty's sake."

Courtney's green eyes glinted as she smiled. "Make that two pair of leggings. I wish I'd listened to Rich's weather forecast. It can't be windy tonight." She picked up the thin hem. "If this dress flies up, that's the end of anyone taking me seriously."

Thirty minutes later, the women exited the suite in their dresses and matching heels. Jordyn transformed her straight locks into ebony ringlets. Courtney gave her auburn bob a beachy wave look. With a few power strides, the duo entered the newsroom.

Joe was the first to clap, followed by Natalie.

Rich cleared his throat. "Ladies, you look beautiful. I hope you have dress coats. My forecast calls for gusts up to twenty miles an hour."

Courtney nudged Jordyn and mouthed, "Told you."

"Rich is right. You're both stunning." Spencer focused on Jordyn. "Those curls. Wow."

Jordyn's nerves didn't carry enough steam to act steady through the party and interactions with Spencer so she smiled and reached for her purse under her desk. *Probably smart to grab a couple candies from the drawer, too.*

"We're off to Santino's. You two have fun at the WFRN sponsored bachelor party." Courtney winked.

Spencer raised a brow and waved.

Would a morning show bachelor party be wild? Would the bridal shower? Jordyn sighed and tugged on the dress again.

. ♡ ♡ ♡

A waterfall greeted Spencer when he entered the fanciest of the Corning hotels lobby. He remembered attending a family reunion there, but it had been years. Right above the bar was a huge banner welcoming WFRN's *Early Rise and Shine* Bachelor Party.

"Spencer Collins?" The front desk clerk brushed her hair behind her ear and giggled. "I watch the show every morning."

He walked forward and shook her hand. "That's impressive, especially if you work the night shift."

The college-aged girl shook her head. "Actually, I volunteered this shift. The wedding is big talk around here. It's got everything. The groom was the high school jock but then went into the military. He returns home a wounded hero." She sighed. "And then there's Brianna. She went to the same school, same time, but they never crossed paths. The two meet and fall in love when Brianna is assigned as Brian's therapist. It's so romantic."

Spencer nodded. Every interview he'd given tugged on his heart as much as the viewers'. The young couple had already overcome many odds. "We're excited at *Early Rise and Shine* to give them a beautiful wedding. Could you tell me where the bachelor party is?"

The girl straightened. "Of course. In fact, your camera person is already here. Ballroom A. Walk past the bar and turn right down the hall. First room on the left."

He mumbled a thanks and trekked to the location, his blazer sleeves moving with every step. A black balloon arch stood over the ballroom threshold. Spencer stepped through and found Sam up front, setting up the tripod.

"Hey, Sam. Is the groom here yet?"

"No, the limo we rented for the groomsmen is on the way. Joe wants you to interview each of them, including Brian's dad."

Spencer nodded. *Sounds easy enough.*

"He also wants footage of you dancing with the guys." Sam took his hands off the tripod and faced Spencer, chuckling.

"Why did I choose a career in front of the camera?" Spencer rubbed at his neck, ready to get this party going.

By the time Brian and his guests arrived, the DJ had the Rolling Stones playing and the wait staff had salads distributed. Spencer signaled Sam and grabbed the microphone. *Time to knock out those interviews before the alcohol starts flowing too freely.*

Spencer maneuvered to the head table and leaned in front of the groom. "Hey, Bri. Can I interview you for the show?"

The Army Ranger vet nodded and slowly rose, reaching for the back of the chair. "I'm still moving slow." He shuffled a few paces. "But I will walk Brianna down the aisle."

When Sam gave them a thumb's up, Spencer took a deep breath and held up the microphone. "Brian, the big day is almost here. Viewers want to know—what advice would you give the men out there who are considering popping the question?"

Brian's steel-gray blue eyes narrowed as he considered the question. After a few seconds, he looked at the camera. "Do it afraid. As a Ranger I faced terrorists, took gunfire. My parachute failed over enemy lines. Through it all, I wasted the most time worrying about marriage."

Spencer furrowed his brow. "How so?"

"After the friendship Brianna and I built, there was no doubt I was in love with her. But with my injuries I wondered if I would be less of a man to her. Did she pity me? Could I make her happy?" His voice shook, "Were we too different?" Brian raked a hand through his short hair.

"How did you get from those concerns to where you are now?"

The groom's smile spoke volumes. "I was alone for all my other challenges and fears. Brianna taught me so much about love, healing, faith. After all those nights worrying, I decided to pray. The answer gave me complete peace. As scared as I might be about failing her, I would never be alone. She's my safe landing."

Spencer felt the growing lump in his throat. "Brian, congratulations. We'll see you at the wedding."

Through all the bachelor party interviews, Brian's stuck in Spencer's mind as Sam packed up and Rich got lost among the guys on the dance floor. Through the months Spencer gave Jordyn space to surrender her vow. Why didn't he persist? "Okay, God. Give me clear direction like you did with Brian. I can't imagine my life without Jordyn."

Although the room was reserved until midnight, Spencer knew at ten he had to leave in order to function with an alert mind and energy for the morning show. He said his goodbyes and passed the arch. The bar area was nearly full and the lights dimmer than when he arrived.

The bartender raised a tall, clear bottle. "Have a nice night, Mr. Collins."

Spencer waved, moving toward the lobby. He heard a woman's giggle and turned his head. A woman who was probably a couple years younger than him with dyed blonde hair sat on a man's lap. She threw her head back in laughter, one of those exaggerated, drunken outbursts. The man, at least fifteen years her senior, kept a hand on her waist as Spencer walked by. This time when she leaned in to whisper in the stranger's ear, her balance shifted and as Spencer walked by, she started to fall.

"Hey, where are you going? That floor isn't as comfortable as I am." The man slithered, hoisting her upright.

As the woman straightened and pulled down on her short skirt, she locked eyes with Spencer. Her glassy brown eyes widened at the same time as Spencer's jaw lowered. Her features matched Jordyn's.

"Are you Paige Hart?"

She slid off the man's lap and wobbled to a standing position. "Oh, no. Spencer Collins. Don't tell Jordyn. Please."

Anchored Hearts

CHAPTER TWENTY-FOUR

Jordyn pulled the WFRN-viewer-voted dress over her head and pushed her arms through the long sleeve cuffs. The dusty pink lace mock neck trapeze outfit had a cute sheer heart overlay that fit just right. *Thank you, viewers.*

Courtney knocked on the suite door. "Joe texted from the church. The bridal party arrived. He's having a fit we aren't there."

"Gotcha. Be right out." Jordyn looked at the mirror. Her classic bun was wedding ready. Her makeup routine was complete, and she stuffed her heels in her work bag in favor of boots for the fresh snow. She breathed in and nodded. Live wedding time.

Twenty minutes later, Jordyn entered the sanctuary as Sam switched on the camera lights. The wedding would be over, and national *Rise and Shine* would be broadcasting with Aunt Julia before sunrise. Jordyn adjusted her eyes to the light and stepped on the aisle runner, noticing Joe was up front with Brian and the groomsmen.

"Beautiful night for a live wedding. Or is it actually morning?"

Jordyn turned and nearly ran into Spencer's broad chest. Once she regained her regular heartbeat, she smiled. "I have to say this is a first. Not even four-thirty, and we're going to watch Brian and Brianna marry. Crazy."

"It's also new to attend a reception at nine. I don't think I've had brunch that early." He chuckled.

The two walked the runner together toward the front. Jordyn's legs shook with each step. Spencer looked so gallant in his gray suit. She'd never seen Joe dressed up, but his navy pinstripe ensemble only made him look like an angry executive as he bellowed commands to Sam and Natalie. When Jordyn overheard Brian's mom asking the best man if he had the rings, Jordyn nudged Spencer's arm. "Do you think this is going to work? Live is risky."

He bent down and reached into the case carrying the wireless microphones. Spencer grabbed two and handed one to Jordyn. "Actually, life is risky. We air live all the time. This will be great."

Jordyn looked to the ground and sucked in a breath. "Right." She glanced up at Spencer, his smile and gaze a perfect combination of comfort. "See you after the wedding."

Spencer left first, taking his place up front where the groomsmen would enter. Jordyn gripped the microphone, took an earpiece, placed it in, and power-walked to the back, just outside the sanctuary. Rich was stationed outside near the entrance, interviewing guests as they arrived. Courtney and Natalie sat in the nursery ready to live stream and reply on social media. Jordyn executed a voice check with the studio and discovered the flower girl twirling in the corner.

Joe boomed through Jordyn's ear. "Groomsmen are up front. Priest is ready. Music is a go. Jordyn, Sam's coming to you. Get a quick reaction from the bridal party."

Viewers had chosen a sheer lace long-sleeved ball gown wedding dress, and when Brianna walked up the stairs from the basement changing area, Jordyn gasped. "You look stunning."

Brianna managed small steps to reach Jordyn, beaming the entire way. "I feel like a princess."

Sam completed set up and made sure the station was ready to go live. He gave Jordyn a thumbs up, and a red light turned on.

"It's wedding day at *Early Rise and Shine*. Welcome to the nuptials of Brianna Clark and Brian Walker. I'm Jordyn Hart, and we'll get things started with the bridal party." A bobby pin started to dig into her scalp, but she cleared her throat and continued. "First up, our beautiful flower girl, Elena Clark, the bride's niece."

With each interview, Jordyn's throat felt like she was swallowing sand. *The Wedding March* started, and Brianna's father linked arms with the bride.

Joe piped in her earpiece. "Jordyn, wrap up and throw to Spencer."

Jordyn watched Brianna start her trek to Brian. The guests stood and focused on the bride.

"Hey, Hart. You're live." Joe's voice rose.

Her neck suddenly felt captive in the lace. She looked at her chest and noticed how rapidly it moved. Her grip on the microphone loosened with all the moisture in her palms.

"Well, ladies and gentlemen, it's Courtney Tate and I'm ready to reply to your social media comments as Spencer gives us a quick take on how Brian is faring. Spencer?"

"Courtney, I've got a fantastic view of Brian and his Army Ranger buddies, and they are wedding-ready in their tuxes this morning. They have been subdued and emotional. Brianna has now reached the front, so we're going to let the wedding continue without our commentary. We'll re-start once the bride and groom exit the sanctuary."

As soon as Sam confirmed audio was off with the station, Joe roared. "Jordyn Hart, where are you?"

Jordyn opened her mouth, but could only gasp. Her eyes widened and she looked around. Footsteps sounding like heels on the concrete headed her way.

"Joe, I've got eyes on Jordyn. She's having, um, technical difficulties. We'll fix it for the exit footage." Courtney came through the earpiece and into Jordyn's view as she bent over and struggled to breathe.

"Jordyn, it's Courtney. My earpiece is out, so it's just us. I'm going to walk you to the bench, okay? Here we go. One step at a time as we breathe in big, and let it out. And again." Courtney's soothing voice guided Jordyn's breathing and pacing to a seat. "Now look at me and focus as you inhale once more, and then exhale. Okay, let's do those three more times."

At the end of the third exhale, Jordyn sniffled and looked at her trembling hands. "Thank you. I don't understand what happened."

Courtney leaned back on the bench. "It's okay. It happens."

"Joe's going to need an ambulance for the stress I'm putting him through." Jordyn took another deep breath and closed her eyes. *What is happening? I can't keep losing control like this.*

Courtney opened the palm of her hand and replaced the earpiece in her ear. "He'll be fine. Do you feel like standing?"

"I need to." Jordyn put pressure on her thighs in an effort to stand, but her legs were as wobbly as Jell-O. She let out a small cry. "I don't understand. This can't happen."

"I'll run and get you a glass of water. That should help."

Jordyn nodded and listened to Court's heels clip-clop down the hall to the kitchen. In a minute, the sound returned until she was next to Jordyn, handing her a small cup of water.

"Any better?" Courtney asked, walking to the sanctuary doors. "They're doing the unity candle."

Jordyn sighed and attempted to stand. "Better. Still shaky." And terrified.

Courtney returned to the bench. "If you're able to walk, we'll trade. The nursery is a few steps away. You sit and share your thoughts on social media. I'll complete the exit interview with Brian and Brianna."

Jordyn nodded. Seems easy enough. She rose and took a step without faltering. "My strength is coming back. Maybe I can finish after all."

"I don't mean to be blunt, but you look deathly pale. Viewers will notice. Go on to the nursery." Courtney pointed toward the door.

Jordyn tried to argue, but realized she only had the energy to debate or walk, not both. She sighed and shuffled to the nursery. Looking back, Jordyn observed Courtney turning the microphone back on and positioning herself for the crowd about to join her.

Did Courtney help me or push me out of my job?

. ♡ ♡ ♡

Spencer's focus darted between the back doors and Brian. The groom stood without assistance, a testimony to Brian's faith, resolve, and Brianna's therapy technique. He slid the ring on Brianna's hand. With a quick glance, Spencer looked for signs of

Jordyn. She never missed a cue. What was the technical difficulty? Was she okay?

"Get ready for audio. Spencer, you're first." Joe's instructions rang through the earpiece.

"Will do."

The priest announced the couple as Mr. and Mrs. Walker, and the guests jumped to their feet, cheering. Brian and Brianna held hands and raised them over their heads. They stepped past the parent pews, Spencer's cue.

"And there it is, ladies and gentlemen. I'm Spencer Collins, and you're seeing Brian and Brianna Walker for the very first time. Jordyn? They're heading your way. Care to share what you're seeing?" He paused, ready to hear her sweet voice.

"Actually Spencer, it's Courtney Tate. The bride and groom are heading toward me, and I can see the wedding party making their way. There's only one way to describe what I see. Pure joy. What a beautiful celebration of love."

Spencer heard the all-clear as soon as the last of the guests went outside and Rich started his round of interviews. It took seconds for Spencer to take out the earpiece and return the microphone so he could jog to the back and find Jordyn.

"Hey, that went well, right?" Courtney greeted him with a wide smile.

"Where's Jordyn? Is she okay?" He ran a hand through his hair as he looked around.

A door squeaked open and Jordyn stepped out. Her face looked pasty at best. "I'm here." Her voice didn't sound too strong, either.

He dashed to her side, searching her eyes to discover what had happened. "Did you get sick? Why is Courtney in the lobby?"

Jordyn's sigh sounded angry as she marched toward Courtney. "I had an anxiety attack. But I recovered."

Spencer tried to keep up as she quickened her pace.

"Yet Court insisted on taking my place. And I have to wonder, was it out of concern, or to push me out?"

Courtney's face contorted. "What? Jordyn, you were in trouble."

"I could have finished things up."

"You looked sick." Her lips trembled. "You're still pale. I didn't want viewers alarmed."

Jordyn shot a look toward Spencer.

He shrugged. "Courtney is right. You don't look yourself."

Courtney's face was blotchy as she approached Jordyn. "I have zero designs on your job. Jordyn, please believe me. I was helping. Truly."

Spencer bit his lip, unsure of Jordyn's reaction.

"I'm sorry, Court. You really saved me. Forgive me for thinking anything else. The pressure got to me, I guess." Jordyn opened her arms in a rare display of affection, the two women hugged and wiped their tears.

"Glad that everyone is okay." Spencer saw movement from the sanctuary. "You might want to freshen up. Joe's coming."

The news director worked steady with his emotions unless it was sweeps month. Ratings meant everything. Mistakes were forbidden.

"There were six seconds of dead air." He pushed his stubby index finger on his watch. Six. Seconds."

Jordyn stepped forward. "Joe, that was all on me. I blanked. Courtney realized it, and stepped in. It wasn't intentional, and from viewer feedback, they didn't realize it. Everyone is too busy finding more tissues."

Joe dropped his hands to his sides. "Viewers are responding?"

Courtney nodded. "It's the most feedback I've ever seen. We're even trending for the region. Maybe beyond."

With that blockbuster proclamation, Joe loosened his tie and faced Jordyn. "Are you okay?"

"Yes. Promise. I'm so sorry."

"Okay then, Rich should be finishing up outside. We're heading straight to the reception. The wedding party wants pictures at Harris Hill. That gives us time to set up at the hotel." Joe swiped at his brow. "By the way, good job everyone."

Spencer waited for Joe to exit the church. Once the heavy wooden door closed, he ran his hand across his forehead. "We did it. Now let's have fun at the reception."

Ninety minutes later, Spencer sat in between Jordyn and Rich, holding his iced water glass. "To *Early Rise and Shine.*"

Rich, Jordyn, and Courtney raised their glasses. After a sip, Rich chuckled. "To sleeping in this weekend. Getting here earlier than usual was brutal."

"The good news is we each only have one live segment. While Brian and Brianna leave for their honeymoon, we can all go home." Courtney pretended to fall asleep with her head resting on her arms.

Spencer offered to interview Brian during his segment. Something about the newlywed Ranger caught Spencer's attention. He met up with Sam for camera set-up and microphone check, then waved the groom over. "One last interview. We have ninety seconds."

Brian's grin could have powered the banquet hall. He scratched his beard and patted Spencer on the back. "Thank you for everything. This wedding is beyond anything Brianna and I could have imagined."

"I'm so glad you were the winning couple. You both have an inspiring story. Don't be strangers." He caught Sam's countdown. "Okay, follow my lead." After a pause, Spencer lifted the microphone. "Good morning, WFRN family. We're still at the Walker reception and here with me is the groom, United States Army Ranger veteran Brian Walker." He tapped the groom's shoulder. "Congratulations. How does it feel to be a married man?"

Brian turned toward Spencer and eyed him more than the camera. "Spencer, this day means everything to us. But Brianna and I are excited about tomorrow, the day after that, and the day after that. We planned a wedding, but we're prepared for marriage." His voice started to catch. "After my accident, we know how precious life is. We're going to live each day to the fullest."

After the segment concluded, Spencer watched Brian return to his bride and greet her with a kiss. Hand in hand, the two took to the floor for their first dance. *I don't get how this tough solider reduces me to tears every time we talk.*

He observed their whispers and giggles, and remembered what Brian shared at the bachelor party. Do it afraid. The DJ announced the dance floor was open to all, and Spencer turned toward the table. Jordyn was sitting alone.

. ♡ ♡ ♡

Jordyn looked at her phone screen and discovered a text from Evan. She opened it and sighed.

Having a great time. Aunt Julia says hi.

No real update. Then again, Evan most likely planned it that way. Anything he had to share would probably frustrate Jordyn further.

She looked up to see Spencer standing near her.

"May I have this dance?" He ditched the suit jacket, and the crisp white shirt laid taut against his chest.

Jordyn offered a demure nod and placed her hand in his.

Spencer navigated through the crowds and found a small area free from other couples. He placed his arms around her, and his gentle touch sent lightning shivers up Jordyn's spine. Without thinking, she rested her head against him as they swayed.

His chuckle was just as tender. "Tired?"

Jordyn swallowed hard and shook her head. "Safe."

Neither spoke until the end of the song. A popular dance craze was the next tune. Jordyn stepped back. "That I'm too tired for."

"Same. Want to take a walk? I didn't see the koi pond when I was here for the bachelor party."

Jordyn looked down and realized they were still holding hands. "Sure. Paige said a lot of people come to see the fish, even if they don't stay at the hotel, or bar."

Spencer bit his lip and picked up the pace as he escorted her out of the banquet room and down the hall. Before they reached the walking bridge that extended over the pond, he stopped and pulled her to a quiet corner where no one could see them.

"What's going on? Is it Paige? Did something happen at the bachelor party?" She felt the orange peel wall texture brush against her back as Spencer leaned in, his arms above her on the wall.

"Jordyn, Brian said something at the party I can't shake. He's been through so much and he said his biggest fear was disappointing Brianna. The fear held him back until he chose to live afraid."

Anyone else and she would have ducked out and run. Jordyn parted her lips.

He took one hand and rubbed at his neck. "That's how I want to live. Unafraid. Full of faith."

"That's great Spencer. Very admirable." Her throat was so dry she could barely utter words.

Spencer returned his hand to the wall. "Jordyn Hart, I'm done fighting it. No more denying." He took a breath and swallowed. "I'm absolutely, completely in love with you."

Jordyn felt her knees start to give. She braced herself against the scratchy wall. "Spencer."

"I'd like to take you out on a date. And another. And another. See where this might go."

She searched his eyes. Do it afraid. Spencer didn't drink. His dad had been sober for months and was a lovely man. Spencer forced her to work better and harder. Although Natalie was a great work friend, he was her best friend.

"Jordyn?" His probe felt like a layer of velvet against her melting heart.

"Yes. I'd love to go on a date with you. And hopefully another. And another."

CHAPTER TWENTY-FIVE

Spencer picked the roses up from the passenger seat and glanced at the Hart home. It had taken a week to hammer out a first date with Jordyn, and now that he was parked in the driveway, he took a deep breath. *Maybe Jordyn was right. We probably should have left for our date from work.*

Flowers in hand, he passed the cement signatures on the sidewalk and jogged up the steps to the front door. A yappy dog started barking, sending Spencer's already stressed heart into palpitations. He put a closed fist onto the door frame, ready to knock, when it flew open.

"Spencer, hello! Are you ready? Let's go." Jordyn took his hand and joined him on the porch, probably breathless from talking so fast.

"Whoa, Jordyn. What's the rush? You didn't even let me give you these." He extended the bouquet toward her.

Her worry lines softened, and she reached for them. "Thank you. They're beautiful."

"We should probably get them in water." He turned toward the house.

Jordyn paused, then her tone elevated to a high he had not heard before. "I mean, they can survive a few hours without water and a vase, right?" She moved her hair behind her ear.

Spencer looked inside the window and found at least three Hart family members standing, smiling, and definitely paying attention to them on the porch. "Oh, I get it. You're nervous about me meeting your family."

Jordyn let out a breath she'd clearly been holding for too long. "I mean, I've never brought a date inside before. Sure, prom and homecoming stuff, but not as an adult. Dad will be all dad. Then, there's Shelly. Don't get me started on Evan." Her words started rushing again.

"It's no problem. We need to get the flowers in water. It won't take long." He placed his hand on her back and led her inside.

"I don't know about this." She whispered.

"Remember? Do it afraid." As Spencer spoke his new mantra, he felt his joints stiffen.

Jordyn marched into the living area where the three curious adults had been watching out the window. "Dad, Shelly, Evan, this is Spencer Collins. Spencer, my family."

Mr. Hart held the spunky dog. "Spencer, it's a pleasure. Paul Hart." He glanced at the dog. "And Gigi."

Shelly's kind smile confirmed everything Spencer had read about what a neighborly help she was when the sextuplets were younger. "Hello, Spencer. You're a fantastic anchor. I really enjoy watching you and Jordyn."

Evan was on his phone and looked up. "Hey, Spencer. Good to meet you."

"Those are gorgeous roses, Jordyn." Shelly pointed at the bouquet.

"Someone means business." Evan murmured, prompting a glare from Jordyn.

So far this isn't torture. "It was nice to meet you all. We're going to get these flowers in water and head to dinner."

Mr. Hart stepped forward. "Have a great time, you two. Be careful."

Before Jordyn left for the kitchen to find a vase, she glanced toward the stairs. "Is Paige home?"

Evan shook his head. "She said she closes tonight, and then she might go out with friends."

Spencer coughed. The moment he discovered clearly intoxicated Paige on a man's lap, her glassy eyes pleaded with Spencer not to tell Jordyn, flooded back.

"Okay. Well, good night." Jordyn waved and ushered Spencer to the kitchen. She opened the cupboard under the sink and reached for a wide, crystal vase. "This was a wedding gift for my parents."

Spencer's eyes widened. "Wow. I don't think my little bouquet is worthy enough."

Jordyn filled the container with water and placed the flowers inside. "Let me be the judge of that." She turned and looped her arm through his. "Shall we?"

The dinner reservations were at Annette's, a bistro about twenty minutes away in the village of Addison. Courtney featured the restaurant in one of her segments, and Spencer hoped the recommendation wouldn't disappoint.

"I never would have thought about dinner here. It's beautiful, but out of the way." Jordyn accepted his hand as they walked up three wooden steps to a quaint entrance with a rustic motif.

Spencer noted the sign that invited customers to seat themselves. The booths were tall, private, and almost pew like in seating, with sewed in cushions. The tablecloth was red and white check. Very simple establishment. *Something Mom would have loved.* "I like finding hidden gems. Most places are in Corning or Elmira. Annette's came to mind after Court spent one morning shooting here."

Jordyn's eyes brightened at the mention of Courtney's name. "That's right. Annette spoiled us rotten with baked goods she insisted the crew take back to the station." She opened the menu. "I can't wait to see what she offers for dinner."

Annette recognized the couple and insisted on taking their order herself. The woman looked to be in her early fifties and greeted them with a broad smile accented with a light lipstick. "Our business increased twenty percent since *Early Rise and Shine* featured our little restaurant. It's a pleasure to meet you two."

"That says as much about your work as it does the show." Jordyn closed the menu. "What do you recommend?"

The owner put her hands on her hips. "Why, Jordan Hart, that's like asking me which one of my children is my favorite."

Spencer chuckled as he perused his menu. "You offer such a variety. Pizza. Deli sandwiches." He glanced at Jordyn. "Do you like seafood? There are a few choices. Lots of Italian dishes, too."

"Now we're talking. Chicken parm. That sounds heavenly."

Ah, a girl who isn't afraid to eat on a date. "I'll have the Pasta Alfredo."

Once Annette left for the kitchen, Spencer couldn't help but gaze at Jordyn. Soft lighting still highlighted her long hair, with no sign of curls from the wedding. Her black sweater sparkled. She glanced at her phone before casting it to the side, catching his gaze. "What?"

Spencer shrugged. "Nothing. You look radiant. I can't stop staring."

Jordyn lowered her eyelids and offered a flirty smile. "You're as charismatic as your brother."

He lifted his hands. "Guilty as charged. Tell me, what's new with you and your siblings? Work has been so busy I haven't had a chance to ask."

"It's been rather calm, actually. Evan said his trip to meet with Aunt Julia and the agent went well. He returned home with work to do."

Spencer leaned back. "Really? Like what?"

"He needs to write a formal pitch. If they start with a matchmaking premise, he has to format that concept. If the show moves forward with home improvement work, that's a documentary style, and is basically a completely different program. They don't think that's been done. Evan has to figure all that out and produce a synopsis."

"Wow. Sounds like it's not about turning a camera on and seeing what happens."

Jordyn chuckled. "Listening to Evan, there's not a lot of reality in the shows."

Spencer considered that tidbit. "Does that mean the matchmaking aspect won't be authentic?" *And that Jordyn won't have to participate?*

Before she could answer, Annette returned with their meals, and once they started eating, Jordyn turned the conversation toward work. "Did you notice in Joe's last email he wants us in Corning and Rich and Courtney in Elmira to co-host the St. Patrick's parades? That's on a Saturday."

Spencer swallowed a bite of pasta. "Goodbye weekend."

Jordyn swung her empty fork in the air. "I love that the show is doing so well but getting up early on a Saturday to stay outside for a parade…."

"Here's the good news. You can go to Vince and Joe and tell them that, and still keep your job. I'm not sure the rest of us could."

Jordyn stabbed a piece of her chicken. "The show might have started with the 'Jordyn, the sextuplet' angle, but we're an ensemble." She placed the food in her mouth.

"True enough. We're a team." And a really good one.

Instead of driving Rte. 86 back to the Hart home, Spencer decided to extend the evening by taking old roads through small hamlets and villages like Erwin, Coopers Plains, then on to Painted Post and downtown Corning. It was after eleven as headlights showcased a few flurries dancing through the velvet black sky.

"I wish it were a little warmer outside." Spencer turned on the left signal for West Market Street. All the trees that lined the touristy street were full of white lights illuminating the area.

"How come?"

"So I could park and we could take a nice walk." With his confession, he felt a small hand touch his knee.

"Hopefully another night." Jordyn leaned forward, pointing. "Looks like some activity ahead. Maybe an accident or something."

Spencer noticed the red lights to his right. An ambulance and two police cars. "Praying no one is hurt." He passed the scene and continued on for another ten minutes until they reached Jordyn's home.

"Lights are on inside. I was kind of hoping everyone would be in bed." Her soft titter floated around the front seat.

Spencer turned off the ignition and unbuckled his seat belt. "You don't want an interrogation?" He opened his door and slid across the snow in his loafers to the passenger side.

Jordyn stepped out. "I'm waiting for one of them to use Gigi as a prop to take outside to spy on us."

"That dog is assertive enough to come out on her own." He chuckled, then sobered, lifting her chin. "I better not take too long saying goodnight."

"There's nothing wrong with the adage 'short and sweet.'" She whispered and parted her lips.

Spencer leaned down with eyes closed, barely touching her when the garage door whirred to life. He jumped back as the motion light threw a spotlight on them.

"Unbelievable." Jordyn muttered, arms crossed against her chest.

Before she could share her frustration further, Mr. Hart and Shelly ran out of the garage toward them.

"There's trouble with Paige."

. ♡ ♡ ♡

Jordyn glanced over at Spencer as he pulled out of her driveway, with Dad and Shelly in the backseat. "Thank you for offering to drive us." She whispered.

He nodded, leaving the development for the highway toward Corning. "Whatever I can do to help."

Dad's voice carried a slight shake. "Paige only said she was at the police station. What could be happening with her?"

"Let's not jump to conclusions, Paul. We'll get there and hear her out." Shelly expelled a long sigh, betraying her own encouraging words.

The police station was on Houghton Parkway, a block from where Spencer had turned for their earlier drive down Market Street. He pulled into an adjacent lot and hit the unlock door button. "I can wait here until you are all done." Spencer offered.

Jordyn reached for his hand. "Please come in. Please."

They reached the front doors only to find them locked. Shelly pointed to a sign. "It's after hours. We have to be buzzed in."

As soon as the group had access inside, Dad took the lead and walked up the half a dozen marble steps to the reception area. An officer looked up, bags under his eyes as if the late hour was new for him.

"Hello, my daughter called. Paige Hart?"

The officer looked at his computer monitor and scratched his mustache. "She's in lock-up. I'll page Officer Taylor."

Two minutes later, a man in uniform who was probably in his forties ambled out, and his expression was all business. In a monotone voice he introduced himself to Dad. "I'm Officer Jay Taylor. We apprehended your daughter on Caton Road, her vehicle still running, in a ditch."

Shelly put a hand to her mouth. "Is she okay?"

He continued as if he had not heard the question. "Ms. Hart was in the driver's seat, passed out. We performed a sobriety test, and she measured 0.08."

"That's a DWI." Spencer rubbed the back of his neck.

Jordyn swallowed hard. Her ears started to pound. Everything she worried about with Paige was playing out.

"Can we see her, Officer Taylor?" Dad's face looked like it had aged ten years in minutes.

"While we waited on the tow truck, we noticed damage to the car beyond what a drive into a ditch could accomplish. It was established that Ms. Hart's vehicle fit the profile of an accident that took place on Market Street. A hit-and-run."

Jordyn hid her face against Spencer's coat. *Please don't let anyone be dead.*

"The victim suffered minor injuries. It happened close to Ms. Hart's place of employment, so we allege that she barely had time to accelerate given she most likely had just left the premises."

Dad's hands trembled as he rubbed at his temples. "I can't believe it."

"Can she go home?" Shelly's eyes widened and she blinked. A lot.

Straight-laced Officer Taylor raised a brow as if Shelly spoke in a foreign language. "She was arrested at the scene for DWI and leaving the scene of an accident. Her court date is Monday."

Jordyn turned from Spencer to face the officer. "Paige has to stay here until her court date?"

The man nodded, but pointed to Dad. "You can see her if you'd like."

Dad bit his lip and shook his head. Shelly reached for his arm, but he started for the steps, shaking off her arm as if he were forsaking everything about the night and the station.

Jordyn scurried to catch up to him. "Dad? You aren't going to see her?"

His hand grasped the metal door handle. "No."

No one spoke during the drive home. Jordyn stared out the passenger window, yet saw nothing in the bleak night. How was Paige holding up? Would the other person sue? Jordyn's stomach felt like she ate brick for dinner the more she considered Paige's plight.

Dad and Shelly marched into the house in silence. Jordyn moved in her seat to face Spencer. "Thank you for everything. I'm sorry you had to be a part of this."

"Sweetheart, I hate you're going through this. When I saw Paige, I really prayed she'd make better choices."

Her mouth flat-lined as she processed his words. "When did you see her?"

Spencer turned off the ignition and inched closer. "I'm sorry. She begged me."

Jordyn unbuckled her seat belt and narrowed her gaze as she refused to look anywhere but straight in his eyes. "Tell me everything. Now."

"It was the WFRN bachelor party. I was heading out and I walked past the bar. There was a loud giggle. It was Paige. She sat on an older man's lap, and she was unsteady. Almost fell. We locked eyes and recognized each other."

Jordyn's jaw was in locked position. "Was she drunk?"

Spencer sighed. His reply was barely audible. "Yes."

She released the seat belt and threw open the door. "How could you keep that from me? You know what a trigger alcohol is for me. It's my sister, Spencer!" Her voice cracked as she fluctuated between rage and betrayal.

"I'm sorry. You would have worried and there was nothing you could have done."

"That's not for you to say. I could have handled it and she would have avoided what is now her reality. No thanks to you."

Spencer leaned across the seat in a failed effort to reach her outside the car. "Jordyn. Please."

She ducked back in to make sure Spencer heard her and forever remembered the steel resolve etched across her face. "We're done. This relationship is over."

CHAPTER TWENTY-SIX

Winter refused to fade away from the Finger Lakes Region even though the calendar announced spring. The irony wasn't lost on Spencer as things remained icy around his office space. After Jordyn ended their romance weeks ago, she built an emotional wall of distance that with any attempt to overcome, Spencer fell short.

"Hey, I got an email from Brian, the newlywed. Have you heard from them at all?" Spencer leaned over near her chair as Jordyn typed.

She didn't even look his way. "Brianna texted me last week."

"They seem to be doing really well." Spencer silently prayed his gaze would affect her and Jordyn would turn around.

"He's a stand-up guy. I'm pretty sure their marriage will be an amazing one." Jordyn paused typing, but only gave a slight turn in his direction without any eye contact. "If you don't mind, I have copy to work on."

Point taken. Spencer sighed and rose from his chair, the need to walk off his anxious energy growing with each glance Jordyn's way. He walked to the conference room, pacing around the chairs.

"Is there a meeting?" Natalie popped her head in with a furrowed brow.

Spencer stopped and grasped the top of a chair. "No. Thinking things through."

She stepped all the way in and crossed her arms against her chest. "About Jordyn."

"Wow. That wasn't even a question, but a statement." He wheeled out the chair and sat. "Is it okay if we talk? You've known her a long time."

Natalie sighed and took tentative steps to the chair across from him. "She's my friend, and we're all professionals. I don't plan to act like we're in high school with this conversation."

Spencer felt a flutter of hope rise in his chest for the first time in over a month. "Thanks so much. I appreciate any insight you have." He raked a hand through this hair, noting it was time for a trim. "Not telling Jordyn about Paige wasn't a smart move, but I don't understand why she has closed herself off from everything and everyone."

A minute passed before Natalie put her arms on the table and leaned in. "What she's going through is added trauma. Few understand the wound she carries from losing her mother. That pain runs very deep and into every aspect of her life. The last thing Jordyn wants is anything that comes close to that hurt."

Spencer lowered his head, eyes closed. *I failed her. The grief we shared in missing our parent was a thin thread. I thought we had so much in common with the loss of a parent.*

"You had a piece of information about Paige that she believes could have prevented what happened had Jordyn known. Probably not true, but that's her thought process." Natalie sat back in the cushioned chair. "Now Paige is national news. Not even Julia Turmeric could stop the consequences of Paige's hit-and-run DWI. The family is imploding."

Spencer returned to an upright position and faced Natalie. "And Jordyn can't stop it."

Natalie's eyes widened. "But she's going to kill herself trying."

"What can I do?"

"Be supportive without being patronizing. You're a good guy, Spencer. I think Jordyn needs you but she doesn't realize to what extent." Natalie stood and faced him. "And pray."

Spencer nodded and rose, pushing the chair back to the table. "Of course."

"Because Jordyn will need it when she hits that emotional bottom and realizes she can't control anything—past, present, or future."

. ♡ ♡ ♡

Jordyn hung her purse on the mud room coat hook and kicked off her heels. The goal was to be home before dinner to learn how Paige was doing and the latest with her legal case. Instead, Joe called her in for a quick meeting that ended up longer than promised.

Shelly turned as soon as Jordyn entered the kitchen. "How was work? I saved dinner for you. Spaghetti and meatballs."

"Ah, the meal we always begged for when Dad told us Shelly Hoffman was the neighbor in charge of making our dinner that night." Jordyn grabbed a plate and scooped out her serving.

"I was sure your dad could have made it better than I could, but you guys always requested it. It was a pleasure to make you kids happy whenever possible." Her voice faded toward the end as she looked to the floor.

Jordyn bit at her lip. *What part of my body isn't completely exhausted by the devastation?* "Is Paige home?"

Shelly shook her head, worry lines creased across her forehead. "That man she calls her boyfriend picked her up a couple hours ago."

Pain shot through her stomach. "Does Dad know?"

Shelly's silence spoke volumes.

"That guy isn't her boyfriend. He's her supplier." The mere thought of Paige spending time with that social bottom-feeder accelerated the churn in her stomach. "How could you let her leave after all we've learned? Do you remember the lawyer Aunt Julia hired revealed Paige was more than a social drinker and also taking prescription meds 'to take the edge off?'" Jordyn pounded the counter. "She should not be out of the house, let alone with him."

"We can't force her to stay home." Shelly cleared her throat. "We can't make her do anything."

Jordyn narrowed her gaze. "Maybe you can't, but I will." She marched toward the stairs with her dinner. "I have to."

The next afternoon, Jordyn finished a taped interview with Kent Misny.

"We make an amazing team, Jordyn Hart. Let's grab a coffee and strategize future promotions." He straightened his tie and grinned.

"I'm sure you're aware our family is going through a difficult time. I need to be at home."

Kent scratched at his day-old-beard. "Honestly, Jordyn, that sister of yours is toxic. I'd stay away from her. She's ruining your brand."

Jordyn rolled her eyes. *Did he have any compassion in him? Any family that cared about him?* "Kent, I'm not a brand. I'm a person. With a family. That needs me."

He gathered his briefcase. "Paige has these issues, not you. *Early Rise and Shine* can't afford you taking on her problems. The scandal will attach to you, and I know you don't want to think this way, but sponsors are big business. If ratings drop, ad revenue plummets. That's business." He jingled his keys and offered a weak smile. "What you have here at WFRN is good, I believe this can be a stepping stone to an amazing national career. For both of us. Be careful."

Jordyn pushed Kent's advice to the back of her mind as she drove home. *Paige probably just woke up thanks to losing her job and another late night with that sketchy creep.* When Jordyn pulled into her parking spot, she closed her eyes for a moment and sighed.

After ditching her purse and shoes, Jordyn climbed the stairs and threw open Paige's bedroom door without warning. Paige, still in her pajamas, had her old black frames on, and her hair was in a headband. She sat upright and placed her phone on the comforter. "What are you doing?"

Jordyn stalked to the bed, hovering over Paige's side. "Checking on you."

She scoffed. "I'm fine."

"Uh-huh. If that were the case, you would have been home last night." Jordyn stood over her, arms crossed.

Paige threw the covers off the bed, watched the phone fall, but ducked past Jordyn, marching to the other side of the room. "I'm not under house arrest. It's okay for me to leave as long as I don't drive." She opened the closet door with a huff and pulled out a hoodie from her high school track years. "Besides, it's none of your business."

"That's where you're wrong. Your foolishness affects us all. And there's no way that pusher you call a boyfriend will be your driver. Or your anything."

Paige marched back near the bed and stabbed at Jordyn's chest with her manicured index finger. "Where do you get off? No one, not Dad, Shelly, not even Mom's will put you in charge when she died. You aren't even an hour older than me. So stop."

Jordyn gasped and stepped back. "I'm trying to help."

"It's not wanted or needed. I made a bad judgment call and I'm dealing with the consequences. Wyatt has been a great support through it all. Just because he doesn't have a job where he has to wear a suit doesn't mean he's creepy." Paige dropped her hand to her side, but stayed in Jordyn's face.

"Does he buy drinks for you? Provide pills?"

"I'm over twenty-one. I'm a big girl."

"With a DWI and hit and run. Way to go." Jordyn offered a slow-clap.

"Jordyn, I mean it. Stay out of my life. Get one of your own." Paige's breathing was erratic and her neck turned blotchy.

"What's it going to take, Paige? Are you going to keep this up until you plow into another car and kill a driver with kids in the car?"

Paige's hand smacked Jordyn's face, the contact fast and full of fury. The slap didn't just make noise, it bounced off Paige's walls.

The sting sizzled across Jordyn's face at the same time tears sprung down the affected area, and she stumbled back. Jordyn held her cheek and lowered her jaw to speak, but no words came to mind.

Paige stood still. Her gaze narrowed. Silence filled the room.

Jordyn turned and scrambled out, marching to her room. She fell on her bed face down, and sobbed.

CHAPTER TWENTY-SEVEN

Spencer took advantage of the mild April afternoon and drove to lunch with the truck windows down. The fresh air after the long winter sparked new energy in him. Sure, Jordyn maintained her invisible wall, but Natalie's advice helped. Spencer also had a lot to be thankful for. Dad loved his volunteer work and wasn't drinking. Carson had a couple months left before graduation. *God is good.*

Rich beat him to Santino's and waved him over to a small table. "You must have hit every red light, Collins. I've been here for ten minutes."

"That's exactly what happened. If you weren't going home after lunch, we could have car-pooled." Spencer opened the menu and scanned the lunch specials.

"Our work day is done. Why you insist on going back and putting even more hours in is a mystery. We could golf." Rich raised his eyebrows to accompany his grin.

The guy would make an excellent salesperson. "I have loose ends to tie up. It's better to finish and start tomorrow without extra tasks."

Rich sipped his ice water. "Would staying late have anything to do with Jordyn?"

"You've been around the last couple of months, right? We co-anchor the show, and return to our cubicles. That's it." *And it hurts.*

The waitress took their orders and returned with their drinks. Spencer drank some of his iced tea hoping Rich would talk about the weather. Even golf. Anything but Jordyn.

"You know, Spence, Jordyn will come around. She's hurt and scared." Rich's low tone was genuine and discreet against the white noise of the restaurant.

Spencer nodded. "Natalie helped me understand that Jordyn losing her mom isn't anything close to my grief. She was a child. It was public. Her family became the news for all the wrong reasons."

Rich slipped his straw into his third drink, a lemon-lime flavored pop. "Wow. That's a lot. I never considered that either. No wonder Paige's legal troubles caused Jordyn such an emotional spiral." He stabbed at the ice. "Any word on what's going to happen with that situation?"

"Paige?" Spencer sighed, remembering her defiant look that night at the police station. "Only what's been reported. Jordyn barely gives me answers that go beyond yes or no, so she's definitely not sharing anything personal about her or her family."

"That's rough."

The waitress returned with their meals, placing the pasta plates in front of them. Once she left, Rich extended his napkin across his lap and glanced at Spencer. "I still say your story isn't over when it comes to Jordyn. I'm rooting for you."

Spencer drove back to WFRN tempted to join Rich for a round of golf, but he knew he had to finish his segment on the team's latest likes feature. Each month Spencer struggled to find something he personally used, an object that viewers might not be aware of. This month was no different. As he locked his truck and walked toward the employee entrance, someone sat on one of the steps. Jordyn.

"Hey, soaking up some sun?" Spencer approached her as cautiously as he would a lion exhibit at the zoo.

Jordyn looked up, her face wet with tears. Those chocolate-colored eyes he fought staring into each work day were bloodshot. She didn't even react to his presence.

Spencer immediately bent down to her level. "What's wrong? How can I help?"

Jordyn's lips parted, but no words formed. Spencer moved to the step, sat next to her, and she let out a sob that sounded like it came from the core of her soul.

He turned and placed a hand on her knee. "You can talk to me, Jordyn. Don't keep it in."

She nodded, and her eyes widened as she reached for her chest.

Spencer noted her erratic breathing and color change in her cheeks. *Fire engine red. Not good.* "Sweetheart, focus on my eyes. We're going to breathe together, like the time at the gazebo."

Her inhalations were louder than gasps, but her gaze locked on to his.

"Let's breathe in nice and slow." He didn't dare blink. "And out. Really let that air out so you feel like your stomach is a completely deflated balloon."

Jordyn followed his every instruction until her breathing recovered. She looked down at Spencer's hand on her knee and said nothing. Within seconds, her warm hand eased on top of his. "Thank you."

"Do you want to talk about it?" He swallowed hard. "With me?"

She worked through another deep breath. "It's amazing you still want to talk to me. I haven't treated you well."

Spencer used his other hand to grasp hers. "No matter what happens between us, your welfare means everything. You can always talk to me."

Another nod. "Do you have any meetings or anything I'm keeping you from?"

"There's little stuff I want to tie up, but it can wait."

Jordyn offered a small smile. "Spencer, I'm terrified. Things with Paige are such a mess. No one tells me anything. Worse than that, I seem to be the only one who's disgusted with this Wyatt person Paige keeps spending time with. He's trouble."

Her words reminded him of the time Dad had to open a hydrant in Elmira. Water gushed everywhere.

"That has to be so difficult. You are such a close family."

Jordyn scoffed. "We were." She pointed to her right cheek. "Her handprint is gone now but a few weeks ago I tried to talk to Paige. We got into an argument and she slapped me. We haven't talked since."

"I'm so sorry. What can I do?"

She squeezed his hand before letting go. "It helps to talk to someone. I can't give you any promises about us. Not now. I feel as though I'm standing under an arch and my entire life is piled on it." Jordyn swiped at the corner of her eye. "And that arch is crashing down on me."

Spencer couldn't shake Jordyn's arch image for the rest of the afternoon. After he shut down his computer and left the building, Spencer took his time leaving the lot. With his head laid back on the driver's head-rest, he closed his eyes and prayed aloud. "God, I definitely need Your guidance. You know the pain of loving and not stepping in to take the hurt away. Give Jordyn Your strength to help her surrender everything to You. Her fears, her family." Spencer fought the lump in his throat. "I love her. I have to surrender her. We might not have a future beyond co-anchors. Direct my steps, God. Thanks for always being available. Amen."

. ♡ ♡ ♡

Jordyn walked into the living room later that evening with a glass of water and ibuprofen in her hands. *These anxiety attacks have to end. They are becoming way too frequent.* She looked for a vacant seat and sat, swallowing the bitter pill.

Dad glanced over. "Rough day at work, Jordy?"

She bit her lip as she considered her reply. "Rough everything."

Shelly reached for the remote and the game show on television suddenly had no audio. "What's going on?"

"Did you know Paige isn't talking to me? I'm trying to help her." Jordyn placed the glass on a coaster and folded her arms against her chest.

Dad closed his eyes for a moment. "Honey, that's not your job. It's mine." He looked over to Shelly, sitting cross-legged on the couch next to him. "And Shelly's."

Jordyn's stomach was ground zero for the acid to start doing laps. "Don't we get a say as siblings in what her legal situation is? Or what should be done with this Wyatt?"

"I'm sorry, but I don't see it that way. If you were battling with something private, the last thing I would do is call a meeting that involves your brothers and sisters." Dad's answer came fast. Too fast.

"Paige's struggle is far from private. It was not only on our newscast; it was on *Rise and Shine*. It's national, Dad." Jordyn's voice rose in tone and volume.

Shelly clasped her hands together. "Knowing it's a story should make you feel relieved not to be a part of it. That way you can do your job without a conflict of interest."

Ugh. She doesn't even understand news. Or family. Jordyn turned to Dad. "Why didn't you visit her that night in jail?"

Although his volume didn't change, his tone sharpened. "Jordyn. I'm only going to say this one more time. What's going on with Paige doesn't include you. It was a mistake that you went to the jail. I was in shock and Spencer offered to drive us. I should have put a stop to your participation right then."

Jordyn's breathing betrayed her. She focused on the wall clock above Dad and Shelly. *Do not lose control. Slow, deep breaths. This isn't the time to fall apart.* "Dad, I've always been involved. I don't understand why you're pushing me away. Especially when you need me more than ever."

Dad and Shelly exchanged a look before Dad rose. "I love you, Jordy. More than my life." He strode toward the stairs before turning toward her. "But I never asked you to take care of all of us. Maybe I should have spoken up after your mom died, but everything was so traumatizing for all of us. It was too shell-shocking to do anything for a long time."

Shelly expelled a long sigh. "You've given everything to everyone as long as I've known you. Jordyn, Paige is going to be okay. It will be a hard battle, but your Dad and I are working it through." She gave a thin smile. "Sweetie, it's time for you to live. Enjoy your life. Don't worry. We've got this."

Jordyn sulked in the chair long after the two headed upstairs. No mean words were exchanged yet she felt like two daggers landed square through her heart. She grew up being the one who packed snacks for Ryan's baseball team. Who else made sure the other siblings got on the right bus in elementary school? *I was even the one who gave that bully Fletcher Wheaton a black eye when he dared tell Evan a "Your Mama" joke.*

She leaned back, and tried to pull the daggers out, one at a time, when her phone vibrated. Jordyn looked at the text notification. Evan.

Hey, Jordy. Need to meet with you and Ryan. Talk show stuff. Make it soon

CHAPTER TWENTY-EIGHT

Spencer saved his staff notes in his app and looked across the conference room toward Jordyn and Rich. "So, what do you think of the big feature for all of us? Summer vacation destinations on a family budget?"

Rich polished off the last of his bagel and shrugged. "Joe doesn't believe in letting us stay idle, that's for sure. Easter wasn't even a week ago and already there's a plan to send each of us on these excursions across the northeast."

"I like the idea." Courtney sipped her iced coffee and stood. "No one pitch Niagara Falls for their trip. That's where I want to go. Viewers will love watching me on Maid of the Mist."

Jordyn snapped her fingers. "Nuts. That's a good one. I'll have to think about my destination." She sighed and played with her charm bracelet. "Too bad there's not an unlimited budget. I'd be tempted to go on a cruise and never return."

"You'd miss us." Rich sang and left his seat for the door.

Spencer joined him, with Courtney and Jordyn behind.

"You're right, I would." Jordyn cleared her throat. "I'm not sure anyone would miss me."

Once they left the meeting room, Spencer walked back to his office and waited for Jordyn to sit in her adjacent space. "Hey, I take it things aren't better at home?"

Jordyn shook her head. "Not really. Dad and Shelly formed this marital front where I'm apparently not needed." She turned her computer monitor on and opened her not-so-secret chocolate drawer. "After work I'm having dinner with Ryan and Evan. Something about the reality show. At least those two are talking to me."

"I hate that I had to read the update on Paige." Spencer looked to the floor. "I'm sorry you had to watch the interview with the district attorney."

She unwrapped a small candy bar and popped it in her mouth. Once Jordyn finished, she wiped the corner of her mouth. "Obviously I don't have the whole story, thanks to no one telling me anything. My only hope for peace with Paige is Aunt Julia's lawyer. He's a beast, I guess."

Spencer sobered as he watched her take another chocolate out of the drawer. "I've been praying."

Jordyn looked over at him, her face a blank slate for a moment. Then she gave a slight nod and smile. "Thank you, Spencer. That means a lot."

Before he could reply, Joe walked up to their area. "Collins, I need to see you in my office."

"Sure thing." He stood, looked at Jordyn and shrugged. *What's going on?*

The few feet it took to reach Joe's office felt like a trek to the principal's office when he forged his mom's name for a permission slip. Spencer racked his brain trying to think what, if anything, was wrong with his work. By the time he sat across from Joe, his palms were moist and his throat felt as hydrated as a desert.

Joe loosened his tie and scooched his leather chair with wheels closer to the desk. "What do you think of *Early Rise and Shine* summer vacation feature?"

This feels like a trick question. "Good, Sir. I look forward to finding a destination viewers will enjoy."

"No worries. We have it." Joe held up a hand. "Your segment is customized. No need to come up with a plan. It's already done."

Spencer raised his eyebrows as he straightened in his cushioned chair. "I'm confused."

Joe chuckled and placed his arms on the desk. "Your assignment comes from Marcus Bright. And as you can imagine, when the station owner offers input, we make it happen."

Even Spencer's lips felt dry. He tried to lick them, but it didn't help. "Where does Mr. Bright want me to travel to?" He pictured an exotic location like Hawaii, but Joe's pregnant pause forced him to consider other locations. Gulf Coast? New England?

"Cleveland." Joe's monotone delivery didn't help Spencer's let down.

"I'm sorry? Cleveland, Ohio? That's the mandate for my summer vacation segment?" Spencer tried to understand Marcus Bright's process, but nothing made sense.

Joe sighed. "You and Jordyn both signed a one-year contract for *Early Rise and Shine.* That ends in September. However, there's some legalese that could potentially affect you and Jordyn's career. If Marcus desires to move the on-air talent within the network of stations he owns, then Marcus can exercise that right." Joe pointed his index finger toward Spencer. "And that appears to be what his intent is with you, Collins."

"I'm being transferred to Cleveland?" Spencer voice squeaked out the words he sounded. *What about Dad? Carson? Jordyn? Early Rise and Shine?*

"Spencer, slow down. He wants you to go to Cleveland to cover the different attractions a family can enjoy on a budget. There's the Rock and Roll Hall of Fame. *The Christmas Story* Museum. Not too far from there is Presque Isle in Erie, or even Cedar Point amusement park in Sandusky."

Okay, that actually sounds fun. "How come he picked me?"

Joe picked up a pen and tapped it on his desk calendar. "Marcus owns a station there. It's a bigger market. He'd like you to visit the station and interview for reporter and weekend anchor. That trip could actually result in a promotion for you."

. ♡ ♡ ♡

Jordyn entered Santino's and looked around the restaurant for Ryan and Evan. Their vehicles were in the adjacent lot, so chances were good Evan was already chatting away about the reality show. She cruised through the central aisle toward the back room and noticed Evan waving from the place where she had filmed the *Early Rise and Shine* promos with Spencer. *Seems like years ago.*

"I ordered a bucket of wings. It's not the annual interview dinner celebration, but we're talking about it, so wings are in order." Evan announced, helping Jordyn with her seat.

Ryan appeared gobsmacked as he shrugged. "I can't believe we agree with something. I'll never turn down Santino wings." He slid a glass of ice water toward Jordyn. "How's work?"

"Busy. We had a staff meeting and already there are summer plans and a rough agenda for the fair."

Evan whistled. "I still have candy left from the Easter basket Shelly gave me."

Ryan rolled his eyes. "You're spoiled rotten. I didn't get one."

Now it was Jordyn's turn to be surprised to side with Evan. "You should have joined us for Easter dinner."

"Touche." Ryan gave her a mock salute. "Was Paige there?"

Evan looked to Jordyn, and back to Ryan. "No. It's like she doesn't exist unless we hear Spencer talking about her on the news." He returned his focus to Jordyn with a narrow gaze.

"Hey, it's his job. I can't report it, so that lands on Spencer." She lowered her voice. "Evan, does Dad say anything to you? I don't see her. She locks her room so I can't visit."

Ryan snickered. "You mean burst in."

I'm not going to win a debate against Ryan. "Whatever. Everything is just a mystery. I'm worried she's living with her drug pusher."

The words hung in the air like storm clouds. Ryan clenched his fists and cracked his knuckles. Evan checked his phone. Jordyn sipped her drink.

Ryan was the first to break the silence. "Let's change the subject. Evan, you said you had an update on the reality show."

At the mention of show, Evan sat up from his slouch with a grin. "I asked to meet because anything our family plans, the success rests with you two. Ryan, everything I have to share involves you." He turned to Jordyn. "And Jordy, you're the organizer. If you're on board, the rest will follow."

Evan bent down, fumbled inside his briefcase resting on the floor, and then returned to the table with two folders. "One for each of you. This is what has transpired since I met with Aunt Julia's contact, the agent." He handed them the packets. "Go ahead, open them. I wrote it."

Jordyn's red folder had a simple label with a text title on the cover.

Hart Sextuplets Turn 25

Format and Docuseries Reality Shows Celebrate Their Milestones

Jordyn looked up. "It says shows. As in more than one."

"It's never been done. That's why Arthur, our agent, thinks it's an easy sell." Evan could barely sit still.

She opened the folder and perused the synopsis. In short, their 25th year celebration would kick off with a reality show split in two. The first half was formatted, a matchmaking show featuring Ryan.

"Hold on. There's no way I'm signing up for that degradation." *Ryan apparently read the same line.*

Evan wasn't deterred. "Ry, this is how you get a home and not the death trap you're living in."

Jordyn raised a brow when Ryan didn't argue. She continued reading. *The concept allows Ryan the opportunity to meet different female contestants through challenges to find his construction manager. Once chosen, she oversees everything about the overhaul of Ryan's home.*

"I get it." Jordyn lowered her folder. "You start with Ryan choosing his woman via a construction job, and then the series flips to watching the winner work with Ryan and her crew re-building the house."

Evan clicked his tongue. "Kind of. Because it's also about us turning twenty-five, we'll be involved with both shows."

The waitress emerged with the wing bucket, plates, and a stack of napkins. Jordyn was about to set her information aside when Ryan shook his head and tossed his folder back at Evan.

"No way, Evan. I'm not doing this."

Jordyn glanced down at the rest of the synopsis. "Oh, Evan." She kept her finger on the alarming sentence. "Do you mean to tell us that there will be a couple women planted in the show who will be faking their experience? They won't even work in construction?"

Ryan picked up before Evan could respond. "This is my home, Evan. You're going to train those plants like a circus act, so hopefully one of the fake managers win only to watch everything fail when the re-build starts? That's cruel." The vein in the middle of Ryan's forehead popped out.

"This is TV gold. Even if the fake one wins, the crew is legit. They will get the job done despite what she tries. It makes for excellent entertainment, and hey, a possible love match too." Evan grabbed a wing and gnawed at it like a hunter after a successful kill.

Jordyn looked over at Ryan, who reached over to retrieve his packet and kept reading. "You okay, Ry?"

He grunted, and she knew enough to let him finish.

"Okay, don't hog the bucket. I'm ready to eat." Jordyn placed the folder in the empty seat next to her. She moved the bucket away from Evan and closer to her.

"I ordered Jerk sauce." Evan lifted up a meaty wing to show.

Ryan muttered as he kept reading. "Sounds fitting."

Jordyn giggled as she grabbed a chicken piece for herself. "Bring on the Jamaican fire." Although her own orders were always mild, she refused to be bested by Evan. After her second bite, the spicy paste burned with each swallow.

"I tried to warn you." Evan reached for yet another wing as Jordyn grabbed her ice water and gulped for a few seconds.

Before Jordyn could complain about the sauce heat, Ryan closed the folder. "Evan, count me in."

Anchored Hearts

CHAPTER TWENTY-NINE

Spencer looked across the living room to see if Dad or Carson had any reaction to his Cleveland announcement. Dad scratched at his silver hair. Carson played with the strings on his Syracuse hoodie. "Anyone going to say anything?"

"Son, it's a wonderful opportunity. It's a bigger market."

"I never pictured leaving Elmira." *My goals were to anchor the six. This is bigger. And without Jordyn.*

Carson fidgeted on the couch. "Because you were worried about us."

Dad nodded. "That's no reason to stay, Spencer. Your brother will be away at college soon."

"All the more reason for me to continue at WFRN." He sighed and raked a hand through his hair. "I don't want you to be alone."

Dad chuckled and leaned forward. "Boys, I'm not alone. The gang at the firehouse looks after me. It's a brotherhood. There are also the folks at church. Everyone is good to me. God's got this, Spencer. What phrase did you keep saying a couple months ago? 'Do it afraid?'"

Ugh, bested by my own advice. "You're right. I will definitely pray about it. If I like it at WDMF, WFRN plans to use the segment to announce my departure." Just saying it felt like a baseball bat to the gut.

"You aren't going to miss graduation, are you?" Carson straightened.

Spencer shook his head. "Absolutely not. Joe thinks I'll leave before Memorial Day. Too bad you have school or I'd invite you to join me."

Carson shrugged. "Slater says Pittsburgh is better."

Joe followed through with trip details the next week. Spencer and Sam would drive to Presque Isle for a quick shot of Lake Erie and the popular tourist spot filled with hiking, beaches, and boat tours. From there they would travel to Cleveland for a two-day stay with a few museum visits and of course, the interview. After that, the duo would move on to Sandusky and cover a day at Cedar Point amusement park before driving back. *Just looking at the itinerary is exhausting.*

"One thing, Spencer. Your time at WDMF is confidential. Don't share details with the rest of the team."

Spencer sighed. *Easier said than done.* "They already feel like Cleveland is an odd place to travel for a summer vacation."

Joe scoffed. "It's not. Your angle is to sell a trip on a family budget. You can do it, Collins. You have to."

Spencer left Joe's office with his head down and shoulders slumped. *How can I keep this news from Jordyn? Rich and Courtney are also more than colleagues, they're friends. I feel like a traitor.* He returned to his desk and found Jordyn typing away in her little nook.

She looked up and smiled. "Someone doesn't look very happy. Did Joe have a problem with you sharing another app as part of the 'I Like' segment?"

"No, but that conversation is probably coming. Looks like my summer vacation is squared up. Cleveland, here I come." Spencer knew his enthusiasm attempt fell flat. "How about you? Did you pitch the Thousand Islands?"

Jordyn rolled her eyes. "I did. It seemed like a winner to me. Joe sent an email after today's show that said no, and he wants to see me."

"That's odd. Rich's trip to Scranton was approved. He's going to do a tour of the area based on that show he loves, then he's also covering the Poconos. Seems like your excursion would have as much potential if not more."

"I know, right?" Jordyn shook her head. "Anyway, if you're done in his office, I guess it's my turn." She picked up her WFRN mug, phone, and stood. "Send help if I'm not back in an hour."

Her laugh floated around and landed right on Spencer's heart. *It's so good to see her smile. Thank You, God, that Jordyn's talking to me. Please don't let this job interview ruin everything.*

. ♡ ♡ ♡

Jordyn slid into the warm seat Spencer probably occupied minutes before. "What's so bad about the Thousand Islands? My parents honeymooned there."

Joe chuckled and tapped his desk with his pen. "You never waste time getting to the point, do you, Hart?"

She crossed her legs and leaned back in the chair. "Not when I think something's going on."

"You should be an investigative reporter, you know that?" He took a drink from his mug, swallowed, made a face, and pushed it away. "Ugh, that coffee tastes older than my tie."

Jordyn bit her lip. *Don't laugh, girl. Be professional.* "So, I'm right. You can't approve my trip because you already have something else planned."

"Correct. Vince and I were tossing around ideas and this is what the viewers want. You in New York City."

"What? I've never heard that feedback." She furrowed her brow.

Joe reached for the mug but let go. "Let me be specific. Viewers want to see you with your Aunt Julia, America's anchor. We're going to have you two attend a Broadway show. She's going to give you a tour of *Rise and Shine*. Vince is even working with her producers to have you co-host with her one morning."

Jordyn felt all air go out of her. "That's a lot. I thought viewers would be satisfied to see me on a boat cruise." *The once-a-year interview is all the national news I'm willing to perform.*

"Nice try. Julia's viewers and ours have watched you grow up. If I could get the funding, I'd make a way for all of you to join in."

"You aren't making this pitch sound any better, Joe." Her head started to pound at the thought of joining Aunt Julia on *Rise and Shine*. Her mom's goal.

Joe checked his phone and grunted. "I have a meeting in Binghamton. Consider New York City a done deal, not a pitch. We're working to schedule you. Looks like mid-May so we can kick off the series with you. Sweeps month and all." He rose and pushed his chair against the window. "Once I have details, I'll email them to you."

"Great." She followed her boss out of his office and meandered back to her chair.

Spencer stopped working and tilted his head. "How did it go?"

Jordyn pulled open her sweets drawer and grabbed a handful of chocolates. "I'm going to New York City."

Jordyn's internal doom stuck with her for the rest of the day. By the time she reached home, all she wanted was to do was change into pajamas and climb in bed. The only car in the driveway besides hers was Paige's, but that was the case since her accident. *Maybe it's time to talk to her again.*

"Paige? It's me. Can we talk? I hate this." Jordyn knocked on the bedroom door, but no reply. In fact, she didn't hear any movement. "You in there?" After a few more raps without response, she jiggled the knob. Nothing.

I don't think she's in there. Jordyn turned and headed into her room where she kept a small tool kit. "Where's that flathead screwdriver?" After digging through a small hammer and pliers, Jordyn found the appliance needed to gain access to Paige's room. With a few steps, she returned, picked the lock, and pushed the door open.

"What on earth?" Jordyn marched in with hands on hips. Paige's bed appeared hotel-stay ready. Her bed was made and the comforter didn't show even a slight wrinkle. Jordyn threw open the closet drawers. Nearly everything was gone. Her heartbeat started working double-time. "Dresser. Please let there be clothes there." She ran across the room and opened one drawer after another. Empty.

Jordyn sat on the bed, a large lump forming in her throat. *Paige is gone.* She stayed on the comforter for a few minutes thinking of all the places she could be. One sprang to the top. "Oh, God. Please don't let Paige be living with Wyatt. And that Dad and Shelly aren't doing anything about it."

The garage door hummed and a vehicle pulled in. Jordyn stood up and smoothed out the bed. She raced down the stairs and entered the kitchen as Dad and Shelly came in from the garage.

"Jordy. What a surprise. We thought you'd still be at work." Shelly placed her purse on the counter and produced a bag. "There's extra chicken from The Poultry House."

"No thanks, I'm not hungry." Jordyn turned to Dad. "I have a question."

He walked over and rubbed her shoulders. "Sure. What's going on?"

She took a deep breath. "It's about Paige." Her voice shook. "Where is she?"

Dad let go of her shoulders and moved in front.

Shelly cleared her throat and glanced toward Dad. "Paul. She deserves to know."

The thought of Paige living with an older man gave Jordyn a headache. "Did she move out? Did you force her to leave?"

Dad waved her toward the living room. "Let's sit down."

What's going on? Jordyn felt bile rising in her throat. She followed him in, turned the standing lamp next to the chair on, and sat. "Is Paige with Wyatt?"

Shelly took her usual seat on the couch next to Dad. She placed her hand in his.

"Paige is not with Wyatt and we didn't force her to leave." Dad cleared his throat. "Julia's working with us to craft a statement we can release."

"I don't understand." Jordyn's legs trembled in sync with her heartbeat.

"Your father and I met with the DA." Shelly looked to Dad.

He let go of her hand and focused on Jordyn. "The lawyer Julia provided also was involved. The hit and run charge was dropped, and Paige avoided jail time." Dad lowered his head into his hands.

This is bad. Something terrible is going on.

Dad's back shook, although Jordyn couldn't hear him cry.

Shelly moved closer and massaged the area where he shuddered. "Paige is in a long-term care facility. It was the only way the DA would sign off. She loses her license for a year, and has severe fines to pay." She shared the information as if they were talking about the weather.

Jordyn felt a shiver light up her spine.

Her step-mom continued. "We made the arrangements for her after Easter. Our hope was to sit the rest of you down soon to tell you, but everyone has been so busy. In a way it helped because no one realized Paige wasn't around."

"When will she be back? Can we see her?" The thought of Paige in some lonely room away from family sent Jordyn's headache to level nine.

Dad shook his head. "The minimum stay is six months. We're pushing for twelve." He sighed. "She can't have visitors for six weeks. Even then, it will be limited."

"Paige can have phone calls after a month." Shelly offered the only hope Jordyn could discern in the conversation.

It was Jordyn's turn to bury her face in her hands. "She has to be scared."

No one answered. The only sound beyond the tick of the wall clock was intermittent sobs. Whether from Dad or herself, Jordyn couldn't tell. She lifted her head and glanced around the room. Even in the heavy grief of missing mom, the house was always full, Now, everything was bleak and empty. *I can't believe Paige is in rehab.*

CHAPTER THIRTY

Spencer took one last inhale of his seasonal nasal spray and blotted his eyes. Nothing like the May lilac and tulip bloom to send his allergies into hyperdrive. He opened his email and clicked on the subject that grabbed his attention. A press release.

IMPORTANT NEWS RELEASE, PLEASE REPORT AFTER MAY 7.

He double-clicked to open the message. It was from Julia Turmeric on behalf of Paul and Shelly Hart. *Jordyn's family. What's going on?* The first line delivered the answer. Paige avoided further court dates by agreeing to a deal with the DA. She's at an undisclosed long-term addiction rehabilitation facility. The family asks for privacy. Spencer sighed. *How long has Jordyn known?*

Spencer wrote the copy and emailed Natalie so she could place it in the morning's show. *Rise and Shine* would most likely report it during their broadcast, so he'd do the same. With that task completed, he looked at the clock. Four-thirty. Almost show time.

Jordyn scurried to her desk, muttering. "I overslept. Sorry."

"It's all good. If you need hair and make-up, go ahead. The show's set up."

She turned to him, letting out a sigh. "Thank you. I definitely need to go to the ladies suite and cover the bags under my eyes."

Spencer looked at his monitor. Seeing the press release was a stark reminder the show would update the viewers regarding Paige's legal situation. "Hey, before you go, there's something I need to tell you."

Jordyn bent over and slipped off her casual shoes and strapped on what she called her "show heels." "Can it wait? I'm definitely not camera ready. I'll meet you on stage."

Please give me time to tell her Paige is in the news today. "Okay, see you there."

Spencer was at his *Early Rise and Shine* seat listening to Natalie on the earpiece when Jordyn rushed to her seat as fast as her heels would allow. Less than a minute until they were live. She ran the lavalier microphone through, offered a few words for volume check, and placed her ear piece in.

Jordyn nudged Spencer with a smile. "I can't make a habit out of this. I can barely breathe."

He started to open his mouth to reply when Sam started the countdown. *Oh, no. There's no time to give Jordyn a warning.*

"Have a good show, everyone." Natalie's calm voice rang through his earpiece.

Spencer felt like a layer of bricks just laid foundation in his stomach. *I do not want to deliver this news without giving a head's up to Jordyn.*

"Good Morning, Southern Tier. It's time for *Early Rise and Shine*. I'm Jordyn Hart."

"And I'm Spencer Collins. As always, Rich Wakefield has the weather, and Courtney Tate is our on-the-go reporter. Let's get started with our top news stories for the day." He steadied his breathing as Jordyn read the latest on the restaurant fire in Horseheads.

Natalie placed the Hart update as the third story. Spencer didn't dare look Jordyn's way to see if she read ahead. Probably not given her late entrance. *Would that make things worse?* Sam pointed to Spencer.

"WFRN has learned that Paige Hart, the youngest of the sextuplets, is receiving care at an undisclosed long-term facility in an attempt to avoid jail time. In a plea deal with the Steuben County district attorney, Miss Hart lost her license for a year and has fines both for her DWI charge and for costs involved with her hit-and-run accident earlier this year."

When Joe called commercial, Spencer moved his chair so he could face Jordyn. "I'm so sorry, I didn't want to spring news on you like that. Are you okay?"

Rich also wheeled his chair closer to them. "Sorry about all that's happening with your sister. That's rough."

Jordyn blew out a slow breath but managed a flat smile. "It's okay. I've been so busy with this summer vacation project and making sure everything is okay with my dad that I forgot to tell you about the press release. I knew it was coming."

Spencer felt an instant weight loss. Thank God. "How is Paige?"

She shrugged. "I don't know. There are pretty tight restrictions right now. She is in a detox phase." Her voice faltered for a moment. "I found out in a weird way, but it's helped Dad be more communicative. He sat Ryan and Evan down to share the news, and I helped set up a video chat with James and Kelly. We'll get through this."

Spencer heard the thirty second call. He gave her arm a slight tap. "You're amazing, Jordyn Hart. Never forget that."

After the show, Joe had yet another update to Spencer's travel plans. He was pretty sure he'd worn an imprint into the chair inside the news director's office.

"Brace yourself, Collins. Big change."

Spencer tilted his head. "Let's have it."

"Marcus called while you were on air. A reporter turned in their resignation last night in Cleveland. He wants you to interview this week. You leave for Erie in the morning." Joe glanced at his phone. "Rich will take your place until you return."

"Tomorrow?"

Joe nodded. "You'll be fine. Tie up your business here and get on home."

Spencer stood, his mind racing and body numb. *I need to talk to Jordyn.* He jogged back to the offices and stopped when he realized she wasn't at her desk. He spun to see if Courtney was back. Yes. "Court, where's Jordyn?"

She looked away from her monitor. "The last thing I remember her saying was she was off to lunch. One of her brothers. The goofy one."

Probably Evan. "Did she say where?"

Courtney returned to the keyboard and started typing. "Santino's? Honestly, I wasn't paying close attention. I need to finish the June schedule for my roving reporting, ha ha."

Spencer raked a hand through his hair and mumbled a thanks. "If Jordyn returns before I find her, tell her I'm trying to meet up." He turned and dashed out to the employee lot before hearing any reply. *Knowing how distracted Court was, Jordyn wasn't probably going to get the message.*

. ♡ ♡ ♡

After watching Evan polish off a small chicken wing bucket and a bowl of ziti, Jordyn couldn't believe that they were related. His stomach was a bottomless pit, breakfast, lunch, and dinner.

"Sis, you haven't answered. Did you talk to James and Kelly about the reality show? If one says yes, you know the other will. Those two are more like twins than anything else." Evan shoved another forkful of pasta in his mouth.

That's the most accurate statement I've heard from Evan. "No. You need to get your ducks in a row first. Ryan and I read a synopsis. That's it. You have a lot more work to do, the least of it getting a network to sign you. Once that happens, then we'll need coaxing to participate." The more Jordyn talked, the more his shoulders slumped.

"Always the taskmaster. I'm working on it."

Jordyn offered a smug grin. "Awesome." She sipped her ice water. "One more thing. Ryan and I will have nothing to do with this celebration of yours if Paige is involved."

"That will probably be the thing executives will want." Evan rested his fork on his plate. "But I understand, Jordy. I do. Her health comes first."

The authenticity in Evan's reply brought tears to Jordyn's eyes. "Thank you." She was about to reach over for a quick hug when movement near Santino's front door caught her eye. "Spencer?"

Evan turned. "Well, well, well. This should be good."

Spencer marched toward them like he was on a mission.

"Don't do anything stupid. Remember, you need me for your show." Jordyn's warning to Evan came through clenched teeth. As soon as Spencer reached their table, her tone changed. "Hey! What are you doing here? I would have asked you to join had I known you were hungry."

Spencer pulled up a chair and sat between the siblings. "I was called in to Joe's office. My trip was moved up. I leave for Pennsylvania tomorrow."

That dropped a boulder on Jordyn. "Oh, no! That isn't a lot of notice. Are you pulling an all-nighter?" She wiped the edges of her mouth with a napkin.

Evan smirked. "Don't you news nerds stay up all hours anyway?"

Jordyn shot him a glare.

"I hope not, but it's a possibility." Spencer leaned in toward Jordyn. "Could we talk?"

Evan cleared his throat. "I have some business to take care of. Jordyn, keep me posted." He looked to Spencer. "On everything."

"Remember what I said, little brother."

Evan stood, waved, and moved toward the register to pay. Spencer adjusted his seat so he faced Jordyn.

"What's going on? You seem so serious. Did the date change for Cleveland really throw you off?"

Spencer balled his hand into a fist, and then stretched out his fingers before speaking. "Yes, but there's more. Something big is happening in conjunction with the trip and I want to share it with you." He slid one of his hands over and grasped hers.

Seismic vibrations pulsated down Jordyn's spine. She gazed at him with a raised brow. "Is it one of Joe's ideas? He paired up with Vince and did the same with me and New York City. It's why he rejected the Thousand Island trip."

"Wow. I didn't know. Are you okay with it?"

"I have to be. My name and birth story still brings recognition so viewers crave what they watch. I go where I'm called." She sighed. "I was really excited about the boat cruise, too."

He squeezed her hand. "You have a great attitude. That doesn't surprise me, though."

"I'm learning I can't control everything." Jordyn drained the last of her water and chuckled. "Slowly. Definitely have a ways to go before I've completely surrendered."

. ♡ ♡ ♡

Spencer drove home without streaming his playlist. He needed to create a mental checklist for the trip. Instead, all his thoughts were about Jordyn. *Was she interviewing in New York? Sure sounded like it. And for that, there was no way he would confess the same agenda awaited him in Cleveland. No chance he'd ask her to define their relationship. How could they be anything if they were in separate states?*

He pulled in the driveway and noticed Ryan's truck was there. That was a surprise. Spencer clicked the garage door opener and found Jordyn's brother inside.

"Hey, Ryan. Wasn't expecting you to be here." Spencer closed the truck door and walked over to shake Ryan's hand.

"I got out of work early and thought I'd drive out and check the lawn. Looks like you men have been busy."

Spencer chuckled and looked over at the newly mowed lawn and fresh mulch under the trees. "My guess is that's all my dad. We try to do as much work as we can because we're so thankful to be here."

"It takes a load off me, but you aren't obligated. I promised Aunt Julia I'd look after the property." Ryan scratched at his chin.

"How about this? If we run into trouble, we call you? Otherwise, we're happy to help. Dad loved doing outdoor work with Mom. I think he enjoys helping here."

Ryan nodded. "Deal. Just make sure you save receipts. Julia would kill me if you weren't reimbursed." He moved the gas can back to the shelf and then turned back to Spencer. "So how are things with my sister?"

A fresh stab numbed Spencer's heart. "We're both getting ready for our summer trip segments. I leave tomorrow for Cleveland. There's a lot riding on this trip." He sighed. "And I sense Jordyn feels the same about her trip to New York."

Ryan laughed. "She's not excited. Jordyn probably has more class than the rest of us, but she loves living in the country. New York City isn't her favorite place."

That's odd. Why would she agree to an interview if she hated The Big Apple? "She has to at least be looking forward to co-hosting thirty minutes of *Rise and Shine* with Julia."

"Not really. Jordyn's obsessed with remembering that task was mom's goal—to go national with Aunt Julia. She feels a lot of pressure to do well." Ryan wiped his hands on his jeans and moseyed to the driveway.

"I wish Jordyn knew how talented she was. That girl could turn New York upside down with her skills."

Ryan leaned on his truck and smirked. "You are so crazy for her. Why don't you do something about it once and for all?"

"I've done nothing but pray about that. I love her. But with both of us on job interviews as part of our trips, it's no use." *And I hate it.*

"Wait. What?" Ryan straightened and narrowed his gaze. "Jordy isn't interviewing. At least that's not what she shared with me. It truly is Broadway and co-hosting that half hour with Aunt Julia."

Spencer felt like he was hit in between the eyes. *She wasn't talking about an interview during our time at Santino's?*

Ryan shifted his weight and his stare toward Spencer. "Now what's this about you going on an interview?"

Anchored Hearts

CHAPTER THIRTY-ONE

Jordyn wasted an entire commercial break staring at Rich. He was a valued member of the *Early Rise and Shine* team, but to see him in Spencer's chair seemed wrong.

"What? Is my deodorant too strong?" Rich sniffed his underarm. "You have a weird expression on your face."

She swept her bangs back and shook her head. "No, it's not you. It seems odd not having Spencer here."

Rich nodded. "I get it. Each of us will have moved on at some point. It's going to look different, I'm sure."

"Right." Jordyn heard the fifteen second call and swiveled her chair back toward the cameras. She pictured Spencer stacking his papers during the countdown. The cute way he sat so straight at the anchor desk. "So different."

Joe didn't wait too long after the show ended to call Jordyn in for a meeting. Even with an iced coffee caffeine boost, she still dragged to the familiar chair.

"Hart, you looked like a lost puppy out there. Even social media is talking about it."

Jordyn glanced around as she considered her options. If she feigned surprise, there was a risk Joe would call her out on it. Confession didn't feel appealing, either. "You're right, I'm sorry. I couldn't focus. Everything felt odd, out of place today. It won't happen again."

"Good. That wasn't the real reason I called you in. One of the *Rise and Shine* producers called. They plan to send Julia to DC to cover some of the primary results and gather the pulse of the American people."

"Okay. How does that affect me?" Jordyn pinched the bridge of her nose. *There's not enough iced coffee to spike her energy.*

Joe chuckled. "It changes both our schedules. You leave for New York Wednesday. I'm down both lead anchors for *Early Rise and Shine*. Looks like I'm calling in one of the Binghamton reporters to cover for you."

"Wow. They want me to film my summer segments before Julia leaves?"

He nodded. "Bingo."

She mumbled his word all the way home.

Jordyn passed a taco shell to Dad during dinner, still in shock that both she and Spencer would be out of town. Because of Julia's upcoming travels, Vince and Joe shortened Jordyn's time in the Big Apple. *Whether that's good news or not, time will tell.*

"That all sounds so rushed. You get into the city, tour *Rise and Shine,* watch a Broadway show, and then go back the next morning to co-host? I hope the station gives you time to recover." Shelly noted, sprinkling cheese on her taco.

"I doubt it. Spencer won't be back until next week. Joe will want me on air as soon as I return. I'll sleep through the weekend." Jordyn laughed.

"It's tempting to worry about you." Dad admitted.

Jordyn thought of Paige. She had no idea what anyone going through detox might look like, but all she could picture was her sister, alone. "I'm fine. Worrying isn't healthy, but keep your thoughts on Paige."

He nodded. "I'm doing a lot more than that. We are praying. A lot of people are."

She bit into her shell, still not comfortable talking about things with faith at the level her Dad and Shelly did. "Sounds like that's exactly what Paige needs."

Shelly cleared her throat. "Jordyn, we pray for each of you. Not only when we know you're having a tough time, but every day."

Jordyn shifted in her chair, but didn't hate the admission. "I appreciate it." She pushed her plate back. "In fact, I have something specific you could pray about."

"What's going on, Jordy?" Dad wiped his mouth and placed the napkin on his plate.

Spencer's mantra danced around her mind. *Do it afraid.* "I keep having anxiety attacks. When things feel out of control, my breathing increases. I get hot. Sometimes there's heart palpitations." Her voice cracked. "I'm afraid it will happen when I'm co-anchoring with Julia."

Shelly put her hand on her heart. "Oh, Jordyn. Thank you for telling us. Of course we will pray."

"Honey, I didn't know you were struggling. I've been so preoccupied with Paige—" Dad's voice caught.

Jordyn shook her head. "I didn't want you to know. It was embarrassing."

The three sat in silence for a few moments before Shelly broke the quiet. "How have you worked through it?"

Spencer helping in the gazebo at the tree lighting comes to mind. "Breathing exercises. Finding a focus point. Spencer taught me."

The worry lines across Dad's forehead relaxed. "He's a good man."

The best. "I hope he's having a good time."

Shelly smiled and pat Jordyn's hand. "We'll pray for him, too."

. ♡ ♡ ♡

Spencer pulled into the parking lot for Lyons Beach, also known as Beach 6, at Presque Isle State Park. Even though it was before the traditional start of summer, there were several hikers and bikers along the peninsula paths.

"Did you bring a coat? My dad said Lake Erie wind is brutal." Spencer turned off the ignition and looked at Sam.

Sam shook his head. "I've got my WFRN hoodie. It should be good enough." He unbuckled his seat belt. "We should capture great footage here. From what I read there are bike rentals, a lighthouse close by, and lots of trails."

"Up that sand hill I can see some folks on the beach. I doubt they're going in the water, but at least we can interview them and ask what brings them here mid-May."

The two unpacked the camera, tri-pod and microphone gear and scoped out the area. "Since it's early evening, let's go to the beach first. Between the wind and fading sunlight, it's smart to start there." Sam initiated the trek uphill.

Spencer interviewed a retired couple who admitted they only visit Beach 6 and do so each week from late spring to winter. He then talked to a ranger about the appeal of Presque Isle.

"We have everything here. The peninsula offers amazing fishing and swimming. Biking, walking. There's history. The War of 1812 had action right here on Lake Erie. Today it's a honeymoon destination. People drive from New York and Ohio to see the sunsets." The ranger grinned. "Like I said, Presque Isle offers it all."

Spencer glanced at Sam, who gave the thumbs-up sign. "Thank you for your time. Our viewers will want to jump in their cars and drive right here."

The ranger drove off on the ATV, Sam swung the equipment around so the camera faced the beach. "Hey, I'm going to video the sunset. You can walk around if you want. I'll be a few minutes."

"Sounds good. Text me when you're ready to go to the hotel." Spencer walked along the shore, waves bringing in branches before gently pulling them back into the lake. Far off in the distance a boat zipped across the horizon.

Spencer found a large piece of driftwood away from the water that offered a full view of the surrounding beaches and the pink sky. He sat and watched a seagull fly overhead and land nearby. Everything was still, and his thoughts drifted like the branches. Jordyn. *I wonder how she's doing. Did the show go well? How much chocolate did she sneak out of her desk drawer?* He smiled picturing her and the handful of candies. "I love her, God. I have to tell her when I get back. Help me find a way."

Spencer enjoyed thirty minutes praying and listening to the water crash against the manmade rock walls before Sam texted that he was ready to go. The trek back against the sand was quite the workout.

"Did you see that sunset? It was a palette of colors. Pretty amazing." Sam clicked the hard-shell case and picked it up. "I started to think I'd love to live here. Then I remembered how brutal winters can be."

"Dad has a friend who doesn't vacation here in the summer, he waits until winter. Smitty says the ice fishing is amazing." Spencer couldn't imagine the beautiful water frozen over with people camping out for the day with their fishing gear. Especially with the lake winds.

Sam chuckled as he shuffled through the sand down to the parking lot. "Let's be thankful Joe thought of this for May and not January."

The two checked in to the hotel and received their keys. Although the drive from Elmira was under four hours, Spencer felt drained. He turned the ceiling light on and found a huge fruit basket on the kitchen counter. "What's this?"

Sam walked over and raised his eyebrows. "Is it WFRN thanking us for being the first to provide an *Early Rise and Shine* summer vacation?"

"Not sure." Spencer shrugged and lifted the cellophane packaging. "Here's a tag." He pulled the label toward him. How odd. It was from a station, but not WFRN. The Marcus Bright-owned station in Cleveland.

Spencer,

We hope you enjoyed your time in Erie. See you soon for another Lake Erie gem, Cleveland.

Sincerely,

WDMF News Department

Sam grabbed a banana. "Vince spent some money for a change?"

"Not exactly. Remember when I told you there's a block of time where you can explore and get street shots?"

He nodded, slowly chewing through the sweet fruit.

"I have an interview for weekend anchor and daily reporter at WDMF." Spencer held his breath as he waited for Sam's reaction.

Sam swallowed the banana. "No offense, but I never pictured you leaving Elmira."

"Me either. Marcus Bright set it up. There's an opening and he can exercise the option to transfer me before my contract ends." Spencer rubbed his eyes. "I'll know for my next contract to close that loophole."

Sam kicked his shoes off and lay on the side of one of the double beds, propped up by his elbow. "Do you see yourself in Cleveland?"

Spencer went to the mini fridge and grabbed a bottled water. "No, but I recently started praying and making faith part of my every day. I think I want to stay in Elmira, but God might have another plan."

"I respect that." Sam stared at the ceiling for a bit. "If you moved there maybe the Browns would finally be a winning team."

"Stranger things have happened." Spencer chuckled, taking a swig of his drink.

. ♡ ♡ ♡

Jordyn boarded the Corning Incorporated jet with a suitcase and a bundle of nerves. WFRN arranged the flight with executives who traveled to New York City for business. Aunt Julia promised to meet her at JFK so they could enjoy a steak dinner before *Hamilton*.

Although the flight was short, it gave her plenty of time to think about Spencer. How much she enjoyed his laugh, his touch. The fact he'd only communicated with Joe. All she knew about his travels was that he was constantly busy. Joe told everyone in the newsroom that it was a great trip. Yet, Jordyn had so many questions. One floated to the top. *Does Spencer miss me as much as I miss him?*

Nine hours later, Aunt Julia opened the door to her penthouse guest bedroom and turned on a light.

"You'd think I'd get used to you being a national anchor, but this is so fancy." The white walls were a modern motif, and black shelves showcased Steuben Glass pieces.

Aunt Julia laughed, "You know I didn't do any of this. I've visited palaces and war bunkers. I'm happiest with that chair at the Waverly house where I can watch the deer." She pointed across the penthouse. "This is all an interior designer's vision."

What a life she's had. "Do you think Mom would have kept her career and followed you here?" Jordyn sat on the edge of the king bed.

"That's a great question." Aunt Julia sighed and pulled out an ergonomic chair with wheels that was near a simple work station desk. "Honestly, no."

Jordyn's mouth dropped. *That wasn't what I expected to hear.*

"Let me explain. Your mom was a great reporter. People flocked to her because she was so warm and nurturing." Julia chuckled. "If things had been different, she would have been an amazing talk show host. But her heart wasn't in journalism."

"But you said she was good at her job."

Aunt Julia nodded. "She was. But when she met your dad, it was clear what her real purpose in life was. Journalism was my dream and as kids, and then young adults, we couldn't imagine life without each other. We were the best of friends. After Paul entered her life, it was clear a career in news was my goal. Lisa Bell was meant to love your father and each of you."

Wow. "Are you saying it was easy for her to resign from WFRN and marry Dad?"

"We talked a lot after she left the job and I moved on. Your mom had no regrets. Zero." Julia rose from the chair. "You know how early our day starts. Time to get some sleep."

Jordyn nodded. "Right. Goodnight. Thanks for everything. I had a great time today."

Aunt Julia walked out, but held the door. "I'd do anything for you all. Love you, Jordy."

"Love you, too." Once Jordyn was alone in the room, she prepared for bed and relaxed under the silk sheets. She tried to picture her mom working with Aunt Julia at *Rise and Shine*, but the image didn't fit. The only place her mom seemed to succeed in Jordyn's mind was loving Dad and their crazy six. *Am I like Mom? Did I become a reporter to honor her memory? Do I really belong in this field?*

Anchored Hearts

CHAPTER THIRTY-TWO

Spencer wiped his hands on his dress pants as Jacinda, the WDMF receptionist, led him to the conference room. He caught a glimpse of his reflection as they walked by offices surrounded by glass walls. *The puffy bags under my eyes tell quite the story. I've been way too busy these last few days.*

"Mr. Collins, Charles Perrott will be conducting the interview. Can I get you coffee or bottled water?" Jacinda gestured him inside the conference room, twice as big as WFRN's. A bright room with a sterile long table and hanging black lights. Chairs to match. There was a video screen embedded the whole length of the opposite wall.

Impressive. "No thank you. I'm all set."

Jacinda nodded and closed the door, the sound of her heels faded as she walked away.

Spencer sat at the table's center and pulled his phone out while he waited. No important emails or timely messages to return. He opened up the text screen and started to type in Jordyn's name. Before Spencer had a chance to enter a message, the door opened and one of the tallest men he'd ever seen without a basketball uniform strode inside. Spencer stood with a rising heartbeat.

"Hello, I'm Charles Perrott, news director. Spencer, we've heard a lot about you from Marcus Bright." He extended his hand and offered a firm shake before they both sat across from each other.

"Nice to meet you, sir. Mr. Bright is very kind."

Charles moved his chair against the table and folded his hands. "I watched *Early Rise and Shine*. You have a good screen presence. You're the morning show host, are you also a reporter?"

Spencer pushed his phone aside. "*Early Rise and Shine* takes most of my time. We write a lot of copy, edit segments, there's quite a bit of promotion." He swallowed. "Before the morning program, I was a reporter for the satellite office."

"I see. What are your goals? Specifically, where do you see yourself in a year? Five years?"

"To be honest Mr. Perrott, I'm not sure. My family is in Elmira and for a time, I was concerned about my dad's health. He's doing better, but…" All Spencer could think about was *Early Rise and Shine*, and Jordyn in the chair next to him.

Mr. Perrott raised his eyebrows. "Is it correct then that I heard there's nothing keeping you in Elmira. Do you aspire to anchor a bigger market?"

Focus, Spencer. This isn't the time to daydream. He blinked a few times. "I haven't given it a lot of thought." He scratched his head. "The bigger market, I mean."

"Interesting. I admit, you're the first candidate with an answer like that."

Spencer realized as he left the building twenty minutes later that the highlight of the interview was his first vague admission. He didn't have any goal to anchor in New York, LA, Miami, or even a smaller market like Cleveland. *I wasted that man's time. And Marcus probably won't be pleased.*

He returned to the hotel and found Sam watching a basketball game. "Hey, how did the interview go?"

Spencer collapsed on the sofa. "It's safe to say I won't be asked to interview anywhere outside of the Finger Lakes region."

Sam whistled. "Did you bomb on purpose? You're the calmest guy I know."

"I didn't go in the room thinking I'd give terrible answers, it just happened. Elmira is my home. That's not what another station longs to hear." Spencer chuckled.

"Looks like our time in Cleveland is almost done. Ready for the roller coasters in Sandusky?" Sam turned his attention back to the television.

Spencer looked over to his luggage. Cedar Point was their last excursion. *What a long journey. Not just by car, but also the emotions.* The interview proved what his heart already knew. There were too many miles between him and Jordyn.

. ♡ ♡ ♡

Jordyn swiveled in the hair and makeup seat next to Aunt Julia. "You've spoiled me. We do our own at WFRN, unless there's a special event. "

"Oh, I remember. There are memes out there with my frizzy hair and tart makeup." Julia sat still for the makeup artist to apply eye shadow. "Those were the days."

An assistant breezed in and handed Aunt Julia pages of notes. The entire time they had been getting ready for the show there wasn't a second of stillness. The college-aged girl smiled as she glanced at Jordyn. "What a fun day. Julia Turmeric works alongside one of the Hart sextuplets."

Jordyn closed her eyes as the stylist applied hair spray to Jordyn's new waves. "It's different being on the same side of the camera with her, that's for sure."

Aunt Julia thumbed through the pages but spoke up. "Co-hosting with Jordyn is going to be much more enjoyable than my DC trip."

Once live, Aunt Julia navigated the two through their thirty minutes by bragging on Jordyn and her siblings. "If you're a regular viewer of *Wednesdays with Julia*, each year I interview the sextuplets. It is an absolute honor to have Jordyn at my side this half hour."

Jordyn started to touch her hair to move it behind her ear, but it was so stiff from spray she put her hand down. "The pleasure is mine. Because I co-anchor *Early Rise and Shine* in your hometown and mine, I don't get to catch you here. This is a treat."

"So tell me, Jordyn, I've watched *Early Rise and Shine* and read the comments on social media. Your show has the potential to knock me right out of the ratings. What's your secret? Why do viewers get up at 5 a.m. to watch you and your team?" Julia shifted in her chair, clearly in interview mode.

Good question. Now to think of a dynamic answer. "It's the same reason your show beats the legal programs and game shows that run in the same slot as *Rise and Shine*."

"Which is—" Aunt Julia's smile disarmed Jordyn's remaining nerves.

"Family. *Early Rise and Shine* is a family. It's Courtney Tate and Rich Wakefield. Spencer Collins and myself, together with the viewers. We all experience life together. There's trust between us all. Viewers appreciate genuine people. They consider us family, and it's mutual." The more Jordyn spoke, the straighter she sat. The connection they all shared was beautiful, and it was easy to talk about it.

After the show there was a three-hour gap between *Rise and Shine* going off air and Jordyn returning to the airport. Julia changed into clog-shaped slippers and waved Jordyn to follow her. "Are you hungry? I can ask craft services to bring us something."

"No, thanks. I'm too excited. That was fun."

Jordyn entered Aunt Julia's spacious office, taken aback by its massive size. Six of Joe's offices would fit. Her assistant was already inside with phone messages and a cup of tea. Julia scanned the communications and thanked Ava for the drink. Once they were alone, the two sat on the leather couch. Behind them was a city view that was most likely part of the Thanksgiving parade route.

"You survived *Rise and Shine*. It wasn't so bad, was it?" Julia blew on the tea.

Jordyn sat back and nestled in the soft cushion. "No. Of course, you make everything easier. You're the best to talk to. You always were."

"I'm glad you think so." Julia bit her lip. "There's another interview about to take place."

What is she talking about? Jordyn sat up. "Not a job, right? There's no way I'm ready for this every day."

Julia shook her head. "No, nothing like that. It's kind of the opposite."

"I don't understand." *A donut would hit the spot. Or a cupcake. Anything chocolate.*

"Jordyn, I've been thinking a lot about our talk last night. And your answer this morning. You remind me so much of your mom. But, you're not her." Julia sighed and took a sip of her tea. "Let me backtrack a little."

Where is this going? Jordyn clasped her hands together in hopes she wouldn't fidget.

"Okay, here goes. There isn't a lot of time that I have left here at the network. I've put in over twenty-five years. There are younger talents who can do this job."

Jordyn swallowed hard. "You don't mean me, do you?"

Julia sobered. "Honey, is journalism your passion? Is this what you truly want to do? I'm preparing for life after retirement. And I think you're a big part of it."

"You have my attention. What are your plans?"

"Watching all of you grieve through the years, and then knowing about Paige's troubles, I want to create a foundation to help families recover from crisis. The greater Elmira area is my home. I'd like to set that up there."

What a fantastic idea. Aunt Julia definitely has the funds to start a project like that. And the heart to help others. "I love it. There are a lot of hurting families out there."

She nodded. "I know. And you are the perfect person to help find them."

Hours later, Jordyn sat on the Corning jet waiting for other executives to board. She pulled out her phone and tried to call

Spencer. *Straight to voicemail. Once my contract ends, could I leave Early Rise and Shine? Am I the best person for Aunt Julia's foundation? Was I only at WFRN to honor mom's memory?* "Where are you? It's Jordyn. I'm heading home from New York City. There's so much going on, I need you, Spencer."

CHAPTER THIRTY-THREE

Spencer held up his cheese on a stick and took a bite. "Rich Wakefield, I could see you eating these every day." He smiled. "This Cedar Point delicacy is just one concession the amusement park is famous for. As for me, I'm a little nervous to finish this and jump on the fast rides."

Sam clicked off the camera. "Smart man. What time do you want to pack up and head to the hotel?"

"This life out of a suitcase is not for me. I miss my bed." *I miss Jordyn.*

"Let's interview a few people and then get you on a few of those high intensity rides. The sooner we can wrap up our last assignment, the sooner we can think about heading back tomorrow." Sam pulled down his sunglasses off the top of his head. "It also means the sooner we get to edit all this footage into a summer vacation package."

Spencer found the first bench after Sam finished taping the last Lake Erie sunset of their trip. *How many roller coasters did I ride?* He took in a deep breath and reached deep into his pocket for his phone. Both a missed call and voicemail from Jordyn. Spencer pushed play.

"Spencer, where are you? It's Jordyn. I'm heading home from New York City. There's so much going on, I need you, Spencer."

Sam walked over with the equipment. "What's going on? You have a weird look on your face."

"Jordyn left a message. I don't quite understand it, but she has to talk to me." Spencer felt like he consumed ten drawers full of Jordyn's chocolate. "Sam, how long would it take to drive home?"

Sam's gaze narrowed. "You aren't suggesting we leave tonight, are you? We're both tired and that's nearly six hours." He sighed. "Why don't you call her back?"

Spencer rubbed at the back of his neck. "I can if I have to, but seeing her would be so much better."

"So let's get a good night's rest at the hotel so you'll be fresh for her tomorrow." Sam didn't look like he was going to debate, so Spencer hit dial for Jordyn's number.

"Ugh. I don't have signal."

Sam walked toward the park exit without saying a word.

Lord, help me be patient. Next to You, Jordyn's the only one I want to talk to.

. ♡ ♡ ♡

Jordyn stifled a yawn as she pulled in the driveway. The last twenty-four hours sucked her as dry as an empty juice box. Aunt Julia and her career proposition. The deep, growing ache missing Spencer and not being able to reach him. A whirlwind trip where she had enough time to get off the jet, go home, sleep, and start back at *Early Rise and Shine.*

She slogged into the kitchen where she found Shelly on her phone.

"Oh, Sweetheart, you too. It's so good to hear your voice. Yes, we love you and are praying for you. Bye now." Shelly pressed end and gave Jordyn a wide smile.

"Welcome back, Jordy. Guess who that was?" Shelly opened the mud room door and reached for Gigi's leash.

She shrugged, her eyes feeling heavier by the moment.

"Paige. She earned a call. It was so good to hear from her." Shelly snapped her fingers and the little fluff ball with paws landed at her feet.

Jordyn's senses came to life, as well as the hairs on the back of her neck. "You talked to Paige?"

Shelly nodded, and connected the leash to Gigi's collar.

"My sister. Paige has one call to make and it's you she talks to?" Jordyn knew she was speaking louder than necessary but why would Paige call Shelly?

"Jordyn, she knew you and your dad were at work. There wasn't a lot of time. Paige knew I was available." Shelly opened the mud room door and released enough leash for Gigi to race down the sidewalk.

That's not good enough. I needed to hear her voice. I need to know she's truly okay. "I think you should have ignored the call."

Shelly dropped the leash but turned toward Jordyn. "Why would I have done that?"

Jordyn crossed her arms against her chest. "So she would have called someone who is really part of the family."

Shelly stepped back as if Jordyn had slapped her. Her face contorted as the pain moved through. She bit at her lip. "When does it stop Jordyn? You were little and when I'd come over to help, I couldn't get you to leave my side. As soon as I married your father, I became enemy number one. I don't understand."

Jordyn brushed away the moisture from the corner of her eyes. "I was supposed to take care of everyone. Before you started batting your eyes Dad's way, I filled his cholesterol medicine. Evan came to me for math help. Shelly, you waltzed in and took over when Dad was the only one who invited you in."

Shelly shielded her arms against her chest. "Do you think I'm out of line?"

Finally, she gets it. "Yes." Jordyn blew out an angry breath. "There's a special bond between us and Dad. You were the neighbor who signed up to help relieve the burden our parents had taking care of six kids. Then you were a key member of the volunteer team after mom passed. But that doesn't give you the authority you've taken."

"Jordyn Bell Hart, you need to open your eyes and look at the facts. My last name is Hart now. The second I married your father, that gave me authority to act as a member of this family. Because I am." Shelly's mouth trembled, but her words still delivered a huge punch.

"You took over. We didn't even talk. One second you're the neighbor, the next, you're making meals and checking Dad's medicine."

Shelly tilted her head, her features softened. "Those were jobs you never should have done. Not as a child. When I moved in, my goal was to take that burden off you. Give you the freedom to live your life. My heart broke watching you all those times take the lead with the family to make sure they were okay. Once we married, it was my priority to relieve that pressure. You never got a childhood, and I didn't want you to miss being an adult, too."

Jordyn wiped her face with her sleeve. "Shelly, it was never a burden to me. I only did what I thought mom would have wanted." She sniffled. "But once you married Dad, I should have stepped aside. I'm sorry I felt threatened by you."

Shelly let out a sob and grabbed Jordyn for a tight hug.

This feels so good. Why did I fight this for so long? Jordyn stepped back and glanced around the sidewalk. "Wait. I should be tripping over a leash. Where's Gigi?"

"Oh no. I didn't realize…" Shelly's words faded as she marched out into the rain.

Jordyn followed her, brushing past the landscaping, bending over for peeks in the taller bushes for any sign of the dog. "It's my fault. I'm so sorry, Shelly." She looked down the driveway. *There's the development to run to. Beyond that, there's the highway. No way would that scenario have a happy ending.*

"I need to get my keys." Shelly mumbled, but didn't move. *Were those tears or rain on her face?*

"No. Let me run down the drive. Gigi couldn't have made it too far." Jordyn didn't wait for an answer. She dashed down the curvy pavement, wet drops stinging her face the faster she ran.

By the time Jordyn reached the end of the driveway, she'd called for Gigi several times. No response. Not even a flash of white fur running by. She doubled over, breathless. Her back spasmed from the sobs flowing out of her faster than the rain falling. *Okay, God. You've got my attention. There's so much emotional carnage. Paige. Dad. Shelly. Spencer. I can't control anything and I have to stop trying. That's Your job. Spencer's shown me the true way to peace. That arch I kept picturing with my life piled high on it, and it ready to collapse? It's because I've been trying to hold it together on my own strength. You need to take over. I surrender.*

. ♡ ♡ ♡

As soon as Spencer unpacked the WFRN vehicle, he looked around the employee lot for Jordyn's car. *She probably went home.* He sent a quick text, happy to finally have signal.

I'm back in town. Heading to your house.

Spencer tossed his suitcase in the truck backseat and turned on the wipers. *I thought April was the month for showers, not May.* He accelerated onto Route 86. Only four exits until Jordyn's development. Few precious moments before they could talk. Spencer steadied his breathing. *Time to pray.*

"Heavenly Father, I need You to direct my steps. I don't know what Jordyn needs to tell me, but help me be at peace. If I'm supposed to declare my feelings, give me the words. Don't let me do one thing without You."

He was about to pull off the exit when something small darted in front of his truck. *Is that a dog? Wait. That looks like Jordyn's step-mom's yappy pet.* Spencer pulled over and turned his flashers on. The rain increased and made it hard to see, but Spencer ran toward the grassy area before the guardrail and highway. "Gigi? Come here, girl. You definitely don't want to go any further."

A flash of white fur dashed near his side with something long trailing behind. Spencer raced over and noticed it was a leash. *If I can get to that, I can step on it and grab her.* With a few strides Spencer plopped his shoe down on the black nylon attached to the dog. Gigi stopped and Spencer scooped her up. "You are a wet mess. I have a feeling there are a few Hart family members looking for you." He snuggled her to his chest and jogged back to the truck.

"Gigi! Gigi, please!"

Spencer heard a female voice calling out. He placed the dog in the passenger seat and shut the door. Squinting, he could see someone with long black hair heading toward the exit. "Jordyn?"

The figure stopped and wiped limp strands of hair out of her eyes. "Spencer?" Her voice trembled as if she had been crying. She picked up her pace toward him.

His shoes squeaked as he sprinted on the pavement. "I'm coming."

When they were within feet of each other, Jordyn stumbled toward him, sobbing. "Gigi."

Spencer stepped forward and reached for Jordyn, holding her. "I have her in the truck. She's fine."

The news brought on another sob. "Thank you. I was so scared." She looked to the sky. "Thank you, God. You answered my prayer."

"Let's get you to the truck and I'll drive you both to the house. You look soggier than the dog."

Shelly was pacing the sidewalk, her blonde curls saturated by the heavy rains.

Jordyn raced out of the truck with Gigi curled in her arms. "Spencer found her. She's okay!"

The women hugged, the dog yapping as the two cried.

"Hey, let's go inside. Everyone is pretty wet." Spencer jogged ahead and opened the front door for them. Once he escorted them out of the weather and into the kitchen, Spencer blew out a relieved breath.

Shelly unleashed Gigi and accepted sloppy kisses from the soaked dog. "I'm going to give her a bath. Spencer, thank you so much for finding her. You're a hero." She smiled and left, leaving Jordyn and Spencer alone.

"Shelly's right. You're a hero. I started a fight and we didn't notice Gigi ran off." She looked to the floor. "If anything had happened—"

"It's okay. Everything worked out. Shelly doesn't seem upset. Maybe you and Gigi will become friends after all this." Spencer nudged her arm and grinned.

Her shoulders relaxed and she chuckled. "I have to look frightening. My mascara probably streaked." She reached for her strands of hair. "This is a wet mess."

Spencer stepped closer and locked eyes with Jordyn. "I think you're stunning." He swallowed. "I got your voicemail. Before you say anything, there are things you need to know."

"You too? I have a lot to share. Is something wrong?" Her eyes grew wide as her voice quieted.

"Only that it's taken this long for me to tell you how I feel. Jordyn, part of my summer trip segment was to go on an interview in Cleveland because Marcus wanted me to. The entire time all I could think of was you. How much I love being around you. Working with you. We've been through a lot, and I don't want another moment to go by before confessing how much I love you."

Jordyn gasped. "Spencer."

He took her hand and kissed it. "Don't be scared. I promise to be there with you through everything with Paige. We can be a couple. An amazing one."

She shook her head. "I am scared, but I'm surrendering the fear. I prayed and confessed all my controlling ways. There's something you need to know, though."

"What? Is it Paige? Your Dad?"

"Aunt Julia." Jordyn walked over to the table and pulled out a chair, waving Spencer to join her. "After my *Rise and Shine* segment, she invited me to her office and talked about her future."

Spencer sat next to her, searching her eyes. Droplets from her hair fell onto the tabletop. "Is something wrong with her?"

"Aunt Julia is setting things up for her retirement. They involve me."

Where is this leading? Is Jordyn moving away?

"Talking with her helped me see I became a reporter for the wrong reasons. It's not my passion. Aunt Julia's going to start a foundation here for families in crisis. She's asked me to be the executive director."

Spencer cleared his throat. "You're leaving *Early Rise and Shine*?"

Jordyn reached for his hand. "I'm not re-signing my contract. It's terrifying, but I'm so excited. It's my job to start the foundation, get it off the ground, Then I'll find the first families to help. Once Aunt Julia moves back, she will participate but wants me in the daily workings. Does it change anything about us knowing I won't be at the anchor desk this fall?"

He leaned over, and offered his reply with a kiss.

Anchored Hearts

CHAPTER THIRTY-FOUR

Spencer grabbed a bottled water before returning to the WFRN fair booth. The August humidity wasn't playing fair and he wished he could be anywhere with air conditioning.

"Hey, Collins. Tell me your 'I Like' segment involves something other than an app on your phone." Joe entered the tent wiping his forehead with a cloth.

"Promise. What's the next live shot?"

Joe lifted the clipboard and flipped the paper. "Here it is. Courtney interviews Kent Misny in front of the farm buildings."

Spencer cracked a smile. "How did Jordyn get out of that gig? And who planned for it to take place close to where the cows are housed?"

Jordyn walked into the tent with her new shoulder length haircut, "That would be all me. Since it's my last day at WFRN, it's only fair my replacement take care of Kent. He's pouting, but Courtney can handle him." She grinned. "His company is also a major fair sponsor, so I told Sam to make sure the interview is near one of the Baker, Misny and Wheeler signs. And the cows are chatty."

Spencer walked over and put his arms around her. "You're amazing, you know that?"

She rubbed his back. "Ready to do our last broadcast together?"

He glanced at Joe. "Definitely."

Rich arrived last and checked out the green screen the tech crew set up for his weather forecast. "I think today will break attendance records. I had a terrible time parking."

Jordyn put in her ear piece and sighed. "This is one packed show. The like segment, Kent's interview, animal time." She raised her eyebrows. "Natalie? What's this? Did you add in animals?"

Spencer heard Natalie through his audio. "We're at the fair, Jordyn. You know we had to feature animals."

"You couldn't wait until after I left the show?" Jordyn's voice rose, but then she took a breath. "Never mind. I can do it."

"Are you sure?" Spencer whispered.

She nodded. "I can't control the animals, but I can control how I react to it."

Natalie started a countdown, which ended the animal chat. Spencer watched Jordyn prepare before her final broadcast. She truly didn't seem upset about handling animals. *Thank You God, for healing her fears.*

"Good afternoon, Southern Tier, and welcome to a special edition of *Early Rise and Shine*. I'm Spencer Collins and we're at the Chemung County Fair broadcasting for Jordyn Hart's last day at WFRN."

"I'm Jordyn, and don't you change that channel because you don't want to miss our fair food taste test, Courtney's interview with Kent Misny, the latest weather with Rich Wakefield, and an animal exhibit."

Spencer looked over to Jordyn. "Don't forget, we're also doing a fair edition of 'I Like.' That means viewers, stay tuned."

After news highlights, Courtney sailed through her first interview with Kent. While the broadcast was focused near the cow barn, Natalie offered direction. "Spencer, Jordyn, head to the next building. The 4H director has animals lined up for you to meet."

Spencer nodded and looked to Jordyn, who offered him a flat smile. He took her hand and they followed the sidewalk to the Vitrix Building. "Oh look. A goat."

. ♡ ♡ ♡

Jordyn dropped Spencer's hand and pinched her nose. "This is not pleasant. The smell, the sounds." She rubbed her eyes and took a deep breath. "Okay, let's do this."

Once Courtney threw the show back to them, Spencer was first to introduce his farm friend. "We're back at the Chemung

County fair. Jordyn and I are inside the Vitrix Building where they house the 4H animals. With me is Horseheads high's senior Chris Barrone." He turned to the teen. "Who did you bring with you?"

"This is Rex the goat. Do you guys want to pet him?"

Nope. But this is live television. Jordyn stepped forward.

"Just make sure you don't approach from behind." Chris warned.

"Why?" Jordyn asked.

Spencer gave the animal a pat on the back. "Goats kick."

The two bantered with other high-schoolers and their pet pig, chickens, and even a sheep. Jordyn extended her hand to Brady, the sheep bleating louder than her conversation with Spencer. Natalie gave a fifteen second call through the ear piece.

"Thank you, Dylan for bringing Brady for us to meet." Spencer swiped at his hands and faced Jordyn. "Next up, viewers favorite feature, we share our likes."

Jordyn chuckled. "And it will not be in this building."

Sam followed the duo outside where a crowd gathered. Jordyn thought her notes said they were to return to the tent, but Spencer stopped mid-way between the building and the tent.

"Before we do our likes, let's acknowledge the viewers who came out so early to join us."

Jordyn glanced to the crowd. *Wait. Is that Ray and Carson?* "I see some familiar faces." She shifted her gaze to the right. Dad, Shelly, Evan and Ryan were up front.

"I know this is a fair edition of what we like, but since it's your last day, Jordyn, I got permission to bend the rules a little." Spencer's voice wavered as he shifted his attention to the crowd.

What is he doing? Jordyn cocked her head, trying to see what Spencer was showing the crowd. "Hey, no fair, Collins. You need to let me in on what your like feature is." Jordyn protested, putting a hand on her hip.

"Okay, I can do that." Spencer faced her, palms open. A small box was in the middle of his shaky hands. He dropped to one knee.

Jordyn's jaw lowered as the crowd gasped. "Spencer?" She could barely squeak out the words.

"Jordyn Hart, I like working with you. It's been a blast. I'll miss not seeing you at the station every day." He opened the small box. "But I love you. I love your chocolate stash and your big, brown eyes. I love how caring you are and how much you adore your family. I don't want to lose you. Will you marry me?"

Jordyn covered her open mouth with her hands. A haze of activity surrounded them.

"Say yes, Jordy!" She heard Ryan's voice above the rest.

"Spencer." Jordyn ignored the crowd and focused on her best friend. She cleared her throat, but still only a volume not much louder than a whisper came out. "I love you so much. Yes. I definitely want to marry you." She didn't wait for him to place the ring on her finger before wrapping her arms around him and delivering a kiss that confirmed her love and their future.

This time Dad's voice came to the forefront. "Hey, looks like Jordy is moving out!"

If You Loved Anchored Hearts

It would mean a lot if you would leave a review on Amazon, BookBub, and Goodreads. The more reviews a book has, the more publicity it receives on Amazon.

A review can be as short as "I really liked it!" If you aren't sure what to write, you can share a couple things that stood out to you, as long as you don't give the plot away. Thank you for taking the time to share your thoughts.

A Note from Julie Arduini:

The Surrendering Hearts series is a huge undertaking, and one I started after watching the television show, *This is Us.* I was amazed at the writing and the ability to create such rich characters. Talking about it with my sister, she mentioned unique birth stories. Although her pitch was about donor babies, I didn't feel ready to tackle that. However, I wondered about multiples.

What if a family had a unique birth story but stayed in the spotlight because of tragedy?

That's how the series began. From there, I went to my passion to encourage readers to find freedom in Christ by surrendering the good, the bad, and---maybe one day---the chocolate. Everything I write or share with audiences contains surrender issues and a chocolate mention. Since Jordyn is the oldest Hart sextuplet, I thought it would be great to kick off the series with an issue I know well: Surrendering Control.

Writing *Anchored Hearts* took years. Once I started, an opportunity came up to participate in a Christmas anthology (*Restoring Christmas,*) and then the YA series I co-wrote with my daughter, Hannah, Surrendering Stinkin' Thinkin' (*You're Beautiful, You're Amazing, You're Brilliant.*) Then, my mom became ill and I spent a couple months away from home to care for her. We all thought she was recovered when she suddenly passed away. The shock and grief ruled 2021.

Mom's death and all that came with it was a harsh training ground for surrendering control. When I finally felt ready to write again, there was something improved about my work. God had taken me through the fire. I lived the theme.

Living to control the people you love and the situations around you isn't living at all. It's not healthy or peaceful. My prayer is Jordyn and Spencer's story encourage you to seek the freedom Christ gives. It comes from surrendering it all to Him.

May this verse encourage you as it continues to guide me:

I know, LORD, that our lives are not our own. We are not able to plan our own course. *Jeremiah 10:23, NLT*

Acknowledgements

Scribes 202, LoRee Peery, Emily Grey, and Julie Brown were instrumental in their critiques, edits, and proofreading. Thank you for your patience and skills.

Ruth, Kara, Tracie, Summer, Brenda, Rita, Noreen, Vickilee, and Amy, your prayers literally cover everything in my life. Thank you for lifting me up during one of the hardest times I've known.

Pastor Gary Gray for giving counsel regarding my anxiety and surrender issues that resulted in the arch object lesson.

Randy, Mandy, Oliver, Felix, Matt, Stephanie, James, and Grace, thank you for the support and prayers you gave, especially when I was in NY away from your dad and siblings.

Cheryl and Holly, thank you for all the Marco Polo videos where you prayed for me and were just what I needed. Your friendship means everything.

Heidi, thank you for checking in on my family when I could not, and especially for looking out for Hannah. Thanks for the daily Snapchats. It meant a lot that you asked about book progress when you admitted you don't love reading.

Brian and Brianna, thank you for picking up the slack when I was in NY. I will never have enough words to convey my thanks.

Hannah, you have the ability to discern when I'm ready to give up and you say the perfect thing. You also have mad plotting skills. Don't go too far, I have five more books in this series.

Tom, you have supported everything I've put a hand to. You were a lifesaver when Mom was sick and I left to care for her, and you kept me going through all the grief. Thank you for never critiquing the house or meals when I was deep in Jordyn's world. I promise I can mop the floors now.

Jesus, You are a true Promise Keeper. You took me through the fire, not around, and boy, I still smell the smoke. However, the last two years grew my faith and writing in ways I could not have experienced without the pain. I'm ready to advance Your Kingdom for Your honor, glory, and praise.

The Julie Arduini Newsletter

Surrender Issues and Chocolate

Delivered twice a month, The Julie Arduini Newsletter offers writing updates, character interviews, reading excerpts, personal updates, recipes, giveaways, and more.

New subscribers receive digital copies of the Surrendering Time contemporary, clean romances *Entrusted* and *Entangled*.

To subscribe, please visit http://linktr.ee/JulieArduini.